SHADOWS

BY THE SAME AUTHOR:

Siege

Hijacked

The Jesus Factor

SHADOWS

a novel by

EDWIN CORLEY

STARRING:

Tallulah Bankhead	William Randolph Hearst
John Barrymore	Vivien Leigh
Humphrey Bogart	Carole Lombard
Marion Davies	Dorothy Parker
Scott Fitzgerald	Louella Parsons
Errol Flynn	David O. Selznick
Clark Gable	Spencer Tracy
Judy Garland	Jack Warner

AND INTRODUCING:

Mitch Gardner

Charlie Gardner

STEIN AND DAY/*Publishers*/New York

Shadows is fiction, and all events and characters relating to the Gardner family are the product of the author's imagination. However, the general events concerning the history of the film industry, and the words and acts of its historical personages, are offered as being either factual or derived from accounts of their words and acts in similar situations. The occasional references in the development of the story to actual living persons, or actual entities, are not intended to be taken as factual, nor are the incidents relating to them intended to be other than fiction.

First published in 1975
Copyright © 1975 by Edwin Corley
All rights reserved
Designed by EKDM
Printed in the United States of America
Stein and Day/*Publishers*/Scarborough House,
Briarcliff Manor, N.Y. 10510

SECOND PRINTING, 1975

Library of Congress Cataloging in Publication Data

Corley, Edwin.
Shadows.
I. Title.
PZ4.C7995Sh   [PS3553.0648]   813'.5'4   75-11832
ISBN 0-8128-1741-9

For BOWN and VIRGINIA ADAMS

who were always there
when a young writer needed them

"What are motion pictures, really? Nothing but shadows on the wall, mummified memories of a performance someone gave long ago."
—Tallulah Bankhead,
in conversation with Mitch Gardner

PART ONE

The Party

"Do not look back, young man. There is nothing there. It ceases to exist the moment you pass it by."

—WILLIAM RANDOLPH HEARST,
to Mitch Gardner

1

Clark Gable crumpled the front page of the Los Angeles *Times* and threw it down on the table. One of the Brown Derby's fragile coffee cups tinkled, then crashed to the floor.

Gable's eyes brooded in his heavily tanned face, glittering above the neatly trimmed mustache. At thirty-nine, Gable looked much younger. The slimness of his body made his broad shoulders seem even broader; his voice was the deep baritone so well known to moviegoers the world wide.

"Cheer up," said Mitch Gardner. Just a year older than Gable, Mitch was even more deeply tanned. His face was lean and looked weathered by long hours beneath the sun and rain. Tiny crows's-feet radiated from his eyes like wagon spokes. His voice was deep and rumbled. Although Mitch was a screenwriter, not an actor, he had that same star personality—the ability to stop all conversation merely by starting to speak. A simple gesture, such as reaching down to pick up the broken coffee cup, became infused with drama. He examined the pieces carefully, squinting closely. Were they some dangerous explosive, hidden near this table by a sinister enemy? Then came a tilt of his head, a crinkling of his eyes, a sudden laugh, and the two halves of the cup—revealed as only a cup—were placed carefully on the saucer.

Mitch leaned forward and placed a hand on Gable's shoulder. Fast becoming one of Hollywood's most successful screenwriters, Mitch had won his initial entry to the film capital as the only son of famed Broadway actor Charles Gardner. Being constantly labeled as "Charlie's boy" did not sit well with Mitch. One night at Romanoff's he and his fellow writer John Huston had decided to form a "Sons of" club. The project foundered because of a disagreement over the rest of the club's name. "Bitch" was inappropriate, since both writers suffered under the handicap of having famous *fathers*. And "Son of a Bastard" lacked class.

He tapped the newspaper.

"This is only an advance copy," he told Gable. "Nobody at the ceremony will have seen it."

"In a pig's ass they won't."

Gable's wife, blond actress Carole Lombard, looked at her watch. It was 9 P.M. Gable and his party, which included Mitch's date, actress Veronica Lake, were already late for the 1940 Academy Award ceremonies at the Ambassador Hotel.

"Now, Paw," said Carole. "Don't be a poor sport."

She fluffed her short, curly hair. It was a gesture that would have identified her anywhere. A year ago, when she was thirty, Carole had been voted one of the five most beautiful women in the world.

"Poor sport, hell," said Gable. "I can live without another Oscar. But the hell with sitting there while they hand them out with everybody already knowing that I didn't get one! Newspaper bastards!"

He began tearing the *Times* into shreds, then held up one strip of newsprint.

"Look at this. *Gone with the Wind* grabbed eight awards. One for Vivien Leigh, one for best picture—hell, Maw, everybody connected with it won something, right down to a special award for the traffic guard at Selznick's fancy studio gate. Everybody, that is, except for the star, yours truly, yours dispensable, the hired man for Louis Bastard Mayer!"

Carole began to gather up her things.

"It's all true, Paw. But you're too big a man to let this slow you down." She looked around. "Is everybody ready?"

Gable stared at her, his mouth open.

"Careful," said Carole. "You're exposing your China clippers."

Veronica Lake peered from behind her long blond hair and asked, "His what?"

Gable threw back his head and laughed, a hearty, lusty bellow that broke the tension.

"My China clippers. That's what we call my false teeth, the real ones I use for eating as opposed to the fancy caps I wear for the camera."

His hand moved toward his mouth.

"You take them out," said Carole, "and I'll divorce you for every red cent you own."

"You wouldn't get much. My last divorce saw to that. All right, Maw. You're right—as usual. Come on, Mitch, let's go over to the Ambassador and let the vultures stare at my body."

"That's more like it," said Carole. "I knew you wouldn't let those no-good cocksuckers get you down."

Bob Hope, master of ceremonies for this twelfth presentation of the Academy Awards, looked around the crowded room. The young comedian had risen to prominence quickly. Only two years had passed since he had first come to Hollywood for his film debut in *The Big Broadcast of 1938*. Now he was firmly established as one of the hottest young comedy stars.

He waited until *Gone with the Wind* had received its eighth award before dropping his one-liner into a calm moment between applause.

"What a wonderful thing you've done," Bob Hope told the audience. "Throwing this benefit for David O. Selznick."

Clark Gable laughed and applauded as hard as anyone else in the room. He pounded Mitch Gardner on the shoulder. The lanky screenwriter winced.

"Watch it," he said. "You're putting bruises on my bruises."

"Some female claw you? Or did your buddy Errol Flynn finally slug you one?"

"Errol's on location for Warners," said Mitch. "No, a horse threw me."

"One of your own?" Gable shook his head in disbelief. "Were you drunk? I thought the horse didn't live that could dump Wild Mitch."

"This one did. He was one of that herd of broncos we caught up in Box Canyon."

"Riding a wild horse?" said Carole. "Are you crazy?"

"I guess I saw one too many Randolph Scott movies," said Mitch. "I thought all I had to do was keep my feet in the stirrups and hang on. He taught me different."

"I would have paid cash money to see that," Gable said.

Carole frowned. "And you would have tried to ride him yourself too, wouldn't you?"

"Probably."

"Well," said Mitch, "it's too late for you to ride him now. After he tossed me, that four-legged bastard came back and tried to walk on my head. I rolled away, but he bent over and took a big bite out of my leg. Well, he won't do that again."

"Did you sell him?" asked Veronica Lake.

"No," Mitch answered calmly. "I shot the son of a bitch."

"You're a nice man," Carole said. "No wonder you never got married."

"Carole!" warned Gable

She flushed.

"Oh," she said softly. "Mitch. I'm sorry. I forgot. Forgive me."

"Nothing to forgive," Mitch said, tossing off the rest of his drink. "Some of us live forever, some of us die young."

Carole leaned over and pressed her cheek against his arm. "I didn't mean to hurt you, Mitch," she said. "But for a second, I honestly forgot."

Gable said, "It's a little hard for me to believe that you could forget Jean Harlow, Carole."

Carole looked as though she had been slapped. By calling her Carole instead of Maw, Gable was demonstrating the most hostility he ever permitted himself in public.

"Both of you, be quiet!" said Mitch. "That was a long time ago. Let's drink up."

"Okay, we'll change the subject," said Gable, looking around for a waiter. "Are you going up to Hearst's Castle for the costume ball?"

Mitch laughed. "It's my birthday party, isn't it?"

"Are you joking, Mitch?" asked Carole. "Marion's throwing the ball to celebrate the Oscars."

"Maybe that's what *she* thinks. But once I get there, the whole festival's going to become one big fund-raising gala for Mitchel Gardner, boy director."

Gable groaned. "Are you still on that kick? Do you really think you're going to get some sucker to hand you half a million to direct your first film? Times are getting hard, boy."

"We'll see. Are you and Carole coming up?"

"Not me," said Gable, grabbing a waiter by the arm and holding up four fingers. "Not my style. San Simeon is for brown-nosers." He turned to Veronica Lake. "Excuse me. Anyway, I wasn't invited."

"Most of the people who'll be on Hearst's train weren't," said Mitch.

"Were *you*, Mitch?" asked Carole, fluttering her eyelashes.

"Could be." he answered. "Train time is 1 A.M."

"At 1 A.M.," Gable said, smiling broadly as he pinched his wife's thigh, "I intend to be in the sack giving Carole's kidneys a prod."

"Talk, talk," she said. "We both know you're lucky when you get it up once a week for old times' sake." To Mitch, she added, "How old are you, anyway?"

"Ten," he said, not smiling.

"Ten *years?*" said Veronica.

"Ten centuries is more like it," said Carole. "Look at his face. It's like six miles of bad road."

"Ten years old," Mitch repeated. "She may not know it, but Marion is throwing my tenth birthday party for me."

"Oh-ho," said Gable. "Now I get it."

"Well, I don't," said Carole, fluffing her hair. "Will you enlighten me, or do I have to phone Walter Winchell?"

"Leap year," Gable said.

Carole patted Mitch's cheek; he twisted his head and nibbled at her fingers.

"You were born on February 29th," she said.

"Turn of the century, nineteen hundred."

"Well, happy tenth birthday, darling." She bent over and gave him a wet, open-mouthed kiss. Veronica looked the other way. Gable yelped, "Hey, Gardner, that's private property there!"

"I'm sorry, Mitch," said Carole. "We'd like to go with you, but Paw's got this thing about San Simeon. We'll think of you."

"While I'm in the saddle," Gable said.

"All brag," Carole said. She looked at Veronica, who was frowning. "What's wrong, dear?"

"I was just trying to figure Mitch's horoscope. I think it would be very interesting."

"Baby," said Mitch, projecting a phony leer, "everything about me is interesting."

Veronica tossed back her hair and looked straight at Mitch.

"That's what everyone says."

"I hope not *every*one," said Carole.

Vivien Leigh arrived, forcing her way through the crowd. As she threw her arms around Gable, a huge opal ring on her left hand almost hit him in the nose. She wore a flowered satin gown. Her wrist sagged under a heavy gold bracelet. She was slim, dark, and vivacious. At twenty-seven, she was at the height of her classic beauty.

"Oh, Clark, Clark!" she said. "How sorry I am!"

"Not for me, Viv."

"Why, yes for you. Hello, Carole. Mitch, is this Miss Lake?"

"How do you do," said Veronica.

"My dear," Vivien said, "what fantastic energy you must have! I've heard all about the tests for *This Gun for Hire*. How ever do you get through those exhausting scenes, take after take after take?"

"I almost never have to do more than one take."

"Of course," said Vivien, "you must keep in very good shape. I hear that ugly old man L. B. Mayer chases you around the set twice a day."

"He's not old," said Veronica, "but only in his fifties. And ugly is as ugly does. I have never heard him say an unkind word about *you.*" She stood up. "Excuse me, I really must be going. My mother is expecting me."

Vivien laughed. "Your *mother?*"

"Yes," said Carole, "her mother. Veronica lives at home, and I think that's swell. So if you want to fight, Vivie dear, pick on someone your own size. I'm available."

Mitch stood up.

"I'll get the car."

"No, you stay. You don't have much time before your train leaves. But thank you for asking me to dinner. I enjoyed it."

She turned and vanished into the crowd.

"Even odds," said Vivien, "that she's headed straight for Mayer's table."

"With his wife there?" said Carole. "Oh, Viv, that's bitchy, even for you."

"Hey," said Gable. "What the hell is this, a cat fight?"

"Cease firing," said Mitch. "Viv, are you coming up to Marion's party?"

"You self-centered bastard," said the pert English actress. "I have just won the Academy Award for best actress of the year and you want to know if I'm attending another of Hearst's parties?"

"Rumor has it we will roast a whole ox on the train. However, on the other point, you're right. I admit to being a self-centered bastard."

"Maybe I'll come, love," she said. "I know Larry will be furious, but until he divorces that bitch, I intend to maintain at least some semblance of a personal life. But I have to take the next train back."

"Well played," said Carole. "That's called having your cake and throwing it in Larry's face too."

"Well, ta," said Vivien. "Good luck, Clark. Now that I've met your wife again, I can see you'll need it."

To her departing back, Carole called, "Watch out for falling debris!"

"Maw," said Gable, "why do you and Viv have to fight every time you get in the same room?"

"Because that little piece of Stilton cheese pisses me off."

"Sure, and 'tis it my daughter Katie Scarlett O'Hara you've been talking about?" said a new, richly Irish voice.

"Tom!" said Gable. "Sit down, have a drink. Jesus, it's good to see a friendly face. We've been fighting the Civil War all over again at this table."

Thomas Mitchell seated his stocky figure.

"Whatever you're having. The thieving bastards, Clark. They robbed you."

"I agree," said Carole, snapping her fingers for the waiter. "But at least you got one for *Stagecoach*, Tom. What's next for you?"

Thomas Mitchell shrugged. "Johnny Ford's mumbling about doing O'Neill's *Long Voyage Home.*" He turned to Mitch. "Mr. Gardner, we've not met, but I heard your name mentioned in connection with the O'Neill project. And, of course, I know your father very well. It's been a long time since I saw Charlie. How is he?"

"Still in the Lincoln play back East. The old fool signed a run-of-the-play contract and the damned thing turned out to be a hit, which surprised Dad as much as it did the backers. As for *Long Voyage,* yes, I talked with Ford. But I've got a project of my own on the fire, and if I get it moving there won't be time to write your film."

"Don't make it my film yet, boy. There's a little matter of money talking, and after tonight, my thought is it'll have to shout in my direction before I take notice."

"Yes," Mitch said. "The song of money is easy to ignore. I only wish I had the chance to try it."

Thomas Mitchell nodded agreement.

"Having a hard time getting up the pot of gold for your film, Mitch?"

"Ever stand on a street corner yelling, 'Apples! Apples!'? That's easy, compared to this. I feel like a whore."

"What do bankers know about making movies, Mitch? All they can do to copper their bets is go with a team that's already made a track record. And you've never directed a film."

"No, I haven't. But I've written two that were nominated, and I've directed on Broadway, and that's more than any of those bastards in the corner offices could have said when *they* did their first movies. Tom, believe me, they're going to have to get off their duff and listen. One of these days the Justice Department is going to come down on block booking with an antitrust suit. Then what? What the hell is Louis Mayer going to do when he has to sell each film on its own merit instead of forcing the theaters to take whatever he decides to dish out to them? He's going to need guys like me to come up with products the exhibitors will sign for. Except by then we'll all have starved to death."

Carole Lombard leaned forward, her eyes bright.

"So *that's* why you're going up to the Castle tonight. Paw, do you realize what our crazy friend is going to do? He's going to try to hustle William Randolph Hearst."

"It couldn't happen to a nicer billionaire," said Gable. "Take him for everything down to his long johns."

Mitchell quaffed deeply from his drink.

"Bitter, bitter. There's more to this business than money."

"That's easy for you to say," Mitch grumbled. "Sitting there with a brand-new Oscar jammed up your ass."

Mitchell let the comment pass.

"What would you be calling this film you want to make?" he asked.

"*Donner Pass,*" Carole supplied. "Ask me anythimg about it. I've had the entire semester."

"It's a Western, right?" asked Mitchell.

"Wrong!" said Mitch. "That shows how much you goddamned actors—"

"Hold on," said Mitchell. "*Donner* Pass. . The party of settlers who got trapped in the mountains and were nearly wiped out when winter set in." He frowned. "They turned to cannibalism, didn't they?"

"So?" Mitch said.

"Well," said Mitchell, "if you merely wanted to direct a film for the money and prestige involved, you'd certainly pick a safer subject than the Donner party. Instead, you've taken material that would frighten the best established directors, and you're trying to do something new and honest. I fail to see how that can make you feel like a whore."

"It's not the film," Mitch said. "It's the things I have to do. Sucking up to studio heads. Party-crawling, complimenting idiots on their latest insult to the art of film-making. Being *nice.*"

He tossed down the last swallow of his drink, then leaned forward toward Thomas.

"But I'll do it. I'll do whatever I have to, Tom. Because I *will* make this movie. You can take odds on that."

Mitchell smiled. "You know, I believe you." He patted his hip pocket. "Those rich offers haven't started coming in yet, so I'm not as flush as I hope to be, but if two or three thousand would help—"

"No, Tom," said Mitch. "I don't want to handle it that way."

"Good luck to you then, Mitch. And remember me to your father." Thomas Mitchell lifted the gold Academy Award statuette and kissed it on its shiny pate. "Ah, me boy-o, me precious lad, you've changed my world."

"Oscar can do that," Gable agreed. "I remember when Mayer told me he was loaning me out to Columbia to make *It Happened One Night* with some guy named Frank Capra directing. That was in 'thirty-three, and Columbia was shooting nothing but quickie program fillers. I knew L.B. was mad at me for something, and this was his way of punishing me. But when I read the script—well, I couldn't believe it was *that* terrific, and it won the award for me, and without Oscar, I never would have gotten *Mutiny on the Bounty*. We've joked about the bad luck he's brought some people. But there's a bright side to old Oscar, too, and I guess I've seen it."

"Oh, my," said Carole. "He's sloshed to the gills already, getting sentimental over a chunk of gold-plated tin. I might as well go along on your party train, Mitch. Paw won't be any good to me tonight."

Thomas Mitchell stood up.

"I'd better do some more circulating. I'm just a busy little bee, planting a little nectar in every producer's ear. Clark, my boy, it's harvest season."

Gable stood up and embraced him.

"And high time. You've earned it, Tom."

"What about you, my friend?" Carole asked Mitch. "Do you plan a minor harvest of your own tonight?"

"Could be. I'm going to give it the old college try."

"For what, Mitch?" She leaned forward. "What do you really want? Money? Women? Fame?"

Mitch took a Wings cigarette from its pack, put the long tube between his lips, produced a wooden kitchen match, and struck it with his thumbnail. He held the burning match for a moment, lit up, then put out the match by pinching it between his thumb and forefinger. His eyes were squinted, as if he were staring into a distant sunset.

"I want to succeed, not just *be* successful," he said finally. "Do you see the difference?"

"No."

"Well, I don't know if I've got a conscience. Enough people around this town are willing to swear that I don't. All I know is that if I knock out a script off the top of my head, and the producer loves it, and the picture grosses five milllion bucks, and everybody tells me what a hero I am, it tastes like soap in my mouth. *I* know I cheated."

Carole looked around. Gable had vanished into the crowd with Thomas Mitchell. She leaned forward.

"Cut the horse manure, Gardner. You're forty years old, never mind this cutesy leap-year birthday bit. You used to make a good buck on Broadway writing plays, and now you're making a better one cranking out good filmable scripts, which is more than a lot of 'literary' writers are able to do. What do you want next? The Pulitzer Prize?"

He shook his head.

"I don't care about awards, Carole. I care about me, about what I think of myself and my work. That's why I want to direct my own

20

film. That's the only way to control your work's direction. You know what a writer's standing is in this town. Slightly less than zero. The director turns to the producer and says, 'Send for the writer, we need some garbage for this scene.' Garbage!"

"I haven't noticed any lack of respect for Ben Hecht and Charlie MacArthur. Your great good friend Dorothy Parker isn't exactly sneered at. S. N. Behrman calls his own shots, and so does Sidney Howard."

"Of course they get respect," he said. "But what about Mitch Gardner, just two steps up from being a human typewriter? That's the way they see me, and they're wrong. But I'll never prove it until I've managed to do a film *my* way. That's the only way I'll stop being Charlie Gardner's son."

"That's really it, isn't it, Mitch? Your father. You can't stop competing."

"Listen, he never wrote a coherent line in his life. The old bastard—"

"Has been a success since before you were born! He's been on top, and he's stayed there. How do you always say it, Mitch? He's gone first class, all the way."

"And so have I!"

"Then why do you envy him so? He's one of our finest stage actors."

"*And* screen," Mitch added. "He didn't get thrown out of Hollywood, he turned his back on it."

"First you attack him, then you fly to his defense. You're impossible. I'd hate to have you direct me."

"You might like it," he said. "If I ever get the chance. Carole, I *see* film in my head. Not just spoken lines, not stage directions, not even actions, but complete images. They move, they're alive"—he touched his forehead—"ready to run through a projector. But here's where they'll stay, as long as Sam Wood can turn to David Selznick and say, 'Send for Gardner, we need some garbage for the scene.' Don't you get what I'm saying?"

"Of course I get it. Do you imagine I want to spend the rest of my career waving my heinie at the camera and letting the director sneak in at least one crotch shot in a wet dress? It's been a long wait for me too. Why don't you help me out, old chum? Write me a good story. I can get it produced. Paw and Selznick aren't hitting it off any too well just now, but David will send me across the street to another producer. He's good like that."

Mitch sipped at his drink. "That's not an answer, Carole. That'd mean settling for only half of what I want."

She stroked his cheek.

"Mitch, someone once told me something terribly profound. Someone said, 'Be very careful what you wish for?' "

"Why?"

"Because you might get it."

Mitch had once used the identical words to Jean Harlow.

"I want it all right now," she had said. "Mitch, tell me I'm going to get it."

Instead, he said, "Don't wish for too much."

"Why not?"

"You might get it. Then what do you have left to wish for?"

She tickled his skinny sides.

"Ouch," she said. "It's like running my knuckles along a washboard. Why don't you start eating regular?"

"I eat all I want," he said, smiling and staring at her lap.

She was still inexperienced enough to blush.

"Fresh," she said. "Oh, you kid."

The daughter of a Kansas City dentist, Harlean Carpentier had taken her stage name from her mother (Jean), and from her maternal grandfather (Harlow). In 1929, it was still new enough to her ears that she often failed to answer when called.

Mitch, who had been writing some silent "business" for the latest Warners "All talking, all singing, all dancing" musical, first saw her at the Hal Roach studios, where he had gone to trade jokes with comedian Stan Laurel.

Agent Arthur Landau, frantically scouting for a girl to replace the untalkative Greta Nissen in Howard Hughes' *Hell's Angels,* was complaining to Laurel.

"I sold Nissen to Hughes. Now that they're scrapping the silent version and going to sound, my tail's on the griddle."

"What about Garbo?" asked Mitch.

Landau groaned. "You could cut her accent with a knife. What are you doing over here, Mitch?"

"Stealing jokes from Stan. But I think I see some action a little more interesting." He nodded toward the coffee wagon. "What's her name?"

Stan Laurel peered into the darkness outside the lighted set.

"Jean something. We used her in *Double Whoopee*. Remember the girl who gets out of the cab and it slams on her skirt and strips it off, down to the black underwear?"

Mitch nodded. "A real boff."

"In more ways than one," said Laurel.

"Is she on the loose?"

The comedian shrugged.

"She isn't turning tricks behind the sets, if that's what you mean. I've never even seen anybody pick her up at the gate."

"See you later," said Mitch, doffing an imaginary derby. Laurel flicked his own tie in an imitation of his partner, Oliver Hardy, and turned back to his conversation with the agent.

Standing near the girl, Mitch said, "Is it hot?"

"Steaming," she said. Then, realizing he was staring at her braless chest, she tightened her lips. "I see. Another good-time Charlie. Well, you're buzzing around the wrong bush, buddy."

"I meant the coffee."

"Naturally." She held out her cup. "Okay, friend. Here."

"Thanks."

He took a sip and extended his hand.

"I'm Mitch Gardner."

She stared at it. "Is that supposed to make me fall down in a swoon?"

"What's yours?"

She hesitated. He sensed that she was examining him ... his carefully tailored tweed suit, the forty-dollar English boots ... even the scent of his cologne.

Apparently he passed muster.

"Jean Harlow. That's my stage name."

"Stan said you're going to make a real comedienne," he lied.

She colored. "Do you know Mr. Laurel?"

"I wrote a film for him once."

"Oh, you're a *writer?*"

The tone in her voice pleased him. Some women made the instant assumption that writers *had* to be interested in their minds rather than those points farther south. Obviously Jean Harlow was one of these.

They sipped coffee and by the time the cups were empty, he had arranged a date for that evening.

An assistant director came hurrying past. "Stage two, Jean. Everybody's waiting."

She gave Mitch a little wave and followed.

He watched after her. The sleazy blue dress clung in all the right places, glistening under the studio lights. Her breasts bounced as she walked, and so did her derriere. Her heels were too high, and her skirt too short. Everything about her, Mitch thought, spelled T-R-A-M-P.

Except she wasn't. He knew that. And as she brushed her silver-blond hair back, he knew something else about her: she was young, she was unformed, she was untrained. But she had that magic presence that might light up a movie screen.

Mitch went back over to the Laurel and Hardy set.

"Arthur," he asked the agent, "where's Howard shooting these days?"

The Academy Award party was thinning out. Bob Hope stopped at the table and shook Gable's hand.

"Tough break, Clark. But nothing like this will ever happen again."

Gable laughed. "You mean I'll get the little bastard next year?"

"Watch it," said Hope. "I get to say all the funny lines around here." He sobered. "No, I mean the way they released the names of the winners early. They should have known the papers couldn't be trusted to keep them secret. But next year, the Academy will have an independent accounting firm handle the ballots, and the winners will be in sealed envelopes. Until they're announced right here nobody will know who they are, and that includes me."

"Nice gimmick," said Mitch.

Hope turned to him. "Gimmick?"

"Sure. *All* the candidates will have to show up, won't they? To find out if they won? So it'll be an even bigger bash than ever."

"Who's your cynical friend?" Hope asked Gable.

"Bob Hope, meet Mitch Gardner."

"Charlie Gardner's boy? I—"

"—Knew him back in New York," said Mitch.
Hope examined him sympathetically.
"Hear that a lot?"
"Every day since I got here," said Mitch.

When Hope had gone, Mitch asked Gable, "Why are you mad at Selznick?"

"Why the hell not? I didn't ask to play Rhett Butler. MGM provided me, and half of the first budget of two million five. In exchange they got half ownership of the picture for seven years, and 25 per cent for eternity. But the kicker was that Loew's Incorporated would distribute, for 15 per cent of the total gross, right off the top. David swears that insisting on me for Rhett cost him around thirty million dollars."

"I still don't see where you have a complaint coming. The man went way out on a limb because he thought you were best for the part."

"That's not true either. Hell, at one time he had your buddy Errol Flynn penciled in. Not to mention that he was after Coop, too."

"Gary Cooper as *Rhett Butler?*"

"Hell, he would have done fine. Anyway, with all these million-dollar bills floating around, do you want to know how much my share of the prize was? Zero. A big fat nothing. They tied me up for twenty-two weeks of shooting, not to mention the publicity appearances, and everybody in sight is getting rich except for me. That goddamn Selznick has a genius for squeezing the last drop of publicity and energy out of his artists, then he waltzes off to the next project and leaves us hanging by our thumbs."

"I know what you mean," said Mitch.

"Sure you do. I know you wrote some of the dialogue for it. You creep! That gag you and Scott Fitzgerald pulled cost Scotty his job."

"No it didn't. Scott was already out. That's why we did it." He examined Gable carefully. "How did you know about it? I thought Dos hushed it up, under pain of death."

"David O. Selznick in league with God himself couldn't have hushed that one up. Shooting a phony scene that made Leslie Howard out to be a eunuch? Not a chance. Besides, Ernie got drunk up at hunting camp one night and told me about it."

"Hemingway's mouth is even bigger than his prick," said Mitch.

"He claimed he helped you write the scene."

Mitch shrugged. "He fed us some dialogue, but I think he was just quoting from memory. Straight out of *The Sun Also Rises.*"

Gable stared at him.

"Jesus, what an ego! Here a bunch of drunken writers collaborate on a gag to run Selznick up the wall, and you're quibbling over screen credit for it!"

Carole came back from the lounge. She stroked Gable's neck.

"Come on, Paw, while you can still walk. Let's see if you're all talk again tonight."

As they left, Gable spread his hands.

"You see the way she treats me?"

"I treat you like you deserve," said Carole Lombard. "I love you dearly, but not even your own mother would say you are anything but a lousy lay."

"Is Howard a good lay?" Jean Harlow had asked Mitch.

"Hughes? Nobody knows?"

"Don't be drudgy. Of course someone knows."

"If they do, they're not talking. Billie Dove thought she had him locked up, but even after it fell apart, she never gave that a mention."

Jean smiled. They were in Mitch's latest car, a 1929 Packard with wire wheels and a huge trunk.

"I thought you said he's a friend of yours."

"I said I *know* him. Now shut up and let me drive."

Jean Harlow smiled. She had long since learned her lesson on how to handle impatient Hollywood men.

Her platinum-blond hair had brought her many propositions so far, but no offers of stardom. Her wealthy husband, busy with other interests, did not mind when she took up extra work in the movies. Nor did he mind when Mitch Gardner, recently arrived from New York, became her public escort around Hollywood.

"Even if you get the part, you won't get much money," Mitch warned Jean as he turned the Packard into the airport gate. "Howard's sunk a fortune into *Hell's Angels* already. He shot it first as a silent with Greta Nissen. Then, when he was ready to release, sound came in."

"So talking's all he'll want from me?"

Mitch glanced down at her voluptuous figure.

"Maybe a little more. But you can handle it."

He parked the car. Nearby, a group of men were gathered around a tripod-mounted motion-picture camera focused on a World War I Spad biplane.

Mitch led Jean over to the group.

"Howard," he said to a tall, youthful man, "I want you to meet Jean Harlow."

Howard Hughes turned slowly. "Hello, Mitch. And Miss Harlow."

Jean, wearing a revealing satin gown, stood ankle-deep in the churned mud of the airstrip and smiled up at the young producer.

"Pleased to meet you," she said to Howard Hughes. "Tell me, bub. Nobody seems to know. Are you a good lay?"

Hughes laughed.

Two days later, he started reshooting *Hell's Angels* in sound. The new female star was Jean Harlow.

In Mitch's arms one night, she whispered, "Want to hear a secret?"

Sleepily, he murmured, "What?"

"Howard *is*."

2

Ordinarily, William Randolph Hearst's private train left Glendale station at 7:35 P.M., arriving at the coastal town of San Luis Obispo around midnight, to be met by a fleet of limousines for the drive north to the castle. Weekends at San Simeon were the cream in Hollywood's coffee. Special guests might be flown directly to the new airstrip at San Simeon village, down near the beach, leaving from Burbank aboard Hearst's new toy, a metal Fokker.

But this trip was special. In deference to the fact that many of the guests would first be at the Academy Award ceremonies, the train was to leave from Los Angeles' Union Station, and at 1 A.M. Since arrival at San Luis Obispo could not reasonably be expected before 5 A.M., Hearst had made certain arrangements a mile north of town: tents were to be put up so that a sunrise brunch could be served, complete with eye-openers for those who needed them. Then the caravan of limousines would proceed along the coastal road to the village of San Simeon, some forty miles north.

In 1940, the "ranch" occupied 265,000 acres of land along the coast and ranging up the sides of the Santa Lucia Mountains. The "Castle" itself had been under construction for more than twenty years, and was still not completed—nor would it ever be. Its 146 rooms sprawled over some 123 acres of mountaintop, called La Cuesta Encantada; the Enchanted Hill. Clearing the land had been difficult, thanks to Hearst's refusal to have a single tree cut down. It cost thousands of dollars and many hours to move each of the giant oaks that blocked construction.

When Mitchel Gardner mounted the Enchanted Hill on the morning of March 1, 1940, looking for half a million dollars, it could have been furnished to him out of household petty cash.

The train was teeming when Mitch boarded. By stopping at the Garden of Allah for his suitcase, he had come very close to being late. The tide and William Randolph Hearst's private train wait for no man.

Squeezing his way down the aisle, he collided with Robert Taylor. The young actor tried to step aside, but Mitch caught him by the arm.

"How's it going, Bob?"

Taylor stroked the thin mustache that he could not get used to.

"Hello, Mitch. What are you doing here? Louella said she didn't think you were coming."

Which means, thought Mitch, she's told Taylor and everyone else I'm not invited.

"That old dragon. Why doesn't she mind her own business?"

Taylor rubbed his hands over his high forehead.

"Lolly thinks everything in Hollywood *is* her business."

"Listen, Bob, speaking of business, have you had a chance to give *Donner Pass* some thought?"

Taylor looked down at his shoes.

"Well, they're keeping me very busy, you know. I was promised a rest after *Waterloo Bridge,* and they've already got me scheduled for *Eagle Squadron.* And *Billy the Kid* after that. I just don't know when there'd be time for a loan-out."

"What did you think of the treatment?" Mitch persisted.

"Well . . . it's different."

Mitch knew an evasive answer when he heard one.

"Hell, it probably wouldn't be right for you anyway. I just didn't want you showing up later pissed off because I didn't give you first crack at it."

"You did, and I appreciate it. It's just that with all they've got lined up for me . . ."

"Well, don't fall out of the saddle," said Mitch, and headed for the end of the car. He found a shelf for his suitcase, slid open the doors to get into the next coach. The din was ear-shattering. The car was packed wall to wall with guests, frantically filling up on cocktails before reaching Hearst's Magic Mountain, where the supply would be severely limited.

Mitch looked around for a friendly face. He had to find someone who would say he—or she—had brought him along. He thought he saw Spencer Tracy near the bar, but before he could start toward the actor a short, dark man blocked his way, a huge brown cigar jutting from his jaw. He looked up at Mitch.

"Hello, friend. I'm Mike Todd. Who are you?"

"Mitch Gardner. Todd? *Mike Todd's Peep Show?*"

"The one and only. Hey, are you any relation to—"

"Charlie Gardner? He's my old man."

"Real trouper," said Todd. "You in the film biz, Gardner?"

Mitch stared down at the arrogant little man.

"In a way," he said. "I suppose you've come out here to make a film of your *Peep Show.*"

Todd laughed. "With the Hays Office looking over my shoulder? That'll be the day. No, you might say I'm looking for investments."

Mitch forced a smile.

"This might be a lucky meeting for both of us. It so happens that I'm finalizing an independent production—"

Todd held up both hands.

"Whoa! Gardner, do I hear right? Are you trying to hustle *me?*"

"You did mention you were looking for investments—"

"Your investments, not mine. Believe me, Gardner, I'm overextended. I've got two shows running on Broadway and one at the World's Fair. They're cleaning up. But it takes all my cash flow to keep them open. In the long run, we'll take a pile out. But I can't bleed them right now without hurting their stage value. Do you understand?"

Mitch laughed. "Yes. It looks like we're both in the same business, Mr. Todd."

"Gypsy Rose Lee's got money in the next one with me," Todd said. "That's how much she thinks of it. It's a musical, *Up in Central Park*. All about Boss Tweed and Tammany Hall."

"I meant I'm in the money-raising racket too," Mitch said. "And, frankly, Mr. Todd, you're poaching on my territory."

"You posted no signs," Todd pointed out.

"Just stay away from Hearst. He's my pigeon."

"Or?"

"Or," Mitch said, leaning down, "I will take your little ass outside and kick it until it drops off."

Todd stood perfectly still for what seemed a long moment.

"All right," he said finally. "Hearst is out of bounds. He wouldn't be interested in my kind of action anyway. But with anyone else, I intend to take my best shot."

"Shoot away. And good luck."

"The same to you, pal," said Todd, moving away.

Mitch stared after him. Pushy little hustler! He turned and made his way to the bar, where a hand gripped over his wrist.

"Mitch, my boy! Glad you could make it."

It was John Barrymore. Mitch was safe.

"I'm crashing," he said, looking into Barrymore's eyes. "I wasn't invited."

Barrymore laughed. He had just turned fifty-eight, and looked every year of it. His face was thin and deeply lined, puffy from drink.

"Ah, but now you are," he said. "Charlie would never forgive me for letting his boy be turned away from the golden gates."

"I'll see that good old Charlie sends his thanks."

"I saw him last week," said Barrymore. "We hoisted our share of tankards at the Players. He spoke mostly of you."

"Next time you're hoisting, check and see if his writing hand's busted. I haven't had a letter since the *Titanic* went down."

Barrymore put his hand on Mitch's shoulder.

"You're his pride, Mitch. You must know that."

"Is that so? How well do you really know my father?"

"We've been friends—close friends—since the old silent days."

"But do you *know* him?"

Barrymore hesitated. Then he shrugged.

"I know that side of Charles Gardner that he chooses to reveal."

"Well," said Mitch, leading Barrymore toward the bar, "Let me tell you about another side."

Charlie had been drunk when he returned to the dressing room at the Kansas City Rialto Theater. Mitch looked at the double-bell alarm clock. It was four in the morning.

Charlie Gardner scowled at his fourteen-year-old son.

"What are you doing here? You were supposed to go to the hotel."

"I didn't have the key," said Mitch, rubbing his eyes.

"They would have given you one at the desk."

"And I wanted to talk with you!"

Charlie lifted his hand, then lowered it.

"Boy," he said, "Never raise your voice to me like that. I won't put up with it."

"I'm sorry," said Mitch. But his voice was still shrill. "It's only that...Dad...please don't send me away."

Charlie fumbled in his suitcase, looking for a bottle. Mitch knew he wouldn't find it.

"You've got to go to school," said Charlie.

"I'm up on my studies. I can pass any test they give me."

"That's not enough. You've got to get a diploma. What you know doesn't count these days, it's what they *say* you know."

"None of the other kids on the tour are worried about diplomas."

"And none of the other 'kids' is a Gardner. My brother Samuel is a very successful banker. I could have been the same. And so can you. Just because I got off on the wrong track doesn't mean you have to."

"You're a headliner. How is that the wrong track?"

Charlie waved his hand around the crowded, dingy room. With the other hand, he kept pawing around in the suitcase.

"Look at this place. It's the star dressing room, and you wouldn't stable a self-respecting jackass in it. What about our hotel? Hardly the peak of fashion, wouldn't you say? And what about the sign over the door? *'We cater to the trade.'* That means they'll accept thieves, drunks, rounders, tarts—*and* actors." He gave up the search. "You're almost fifteen. You'll be starting late, but Samuel will help. You can still amount to something."

"If you're looking for your whiskey," Mitch said, quietly, "it's in the costume trunk."

He stared at his father until the older man looked away.

"I hid it so you wouldn't get drunk tonight until I'd had a chance to talk to you."

Charlie opened the trunk and found the quart, pulled out the cork with his teeth, and held the bottle up in a toast.

"Thank you, son."

"Don't thank me. I only told you where it was so you'd go ahead and pass out."

Charlie lowered the bottle without drinking from it.

"Buzz," he said slowly, "if I didn't know better, I'd say those words came from someone who hates me, not my own son."

"You're right both times. If you send me away, I'll have to go, because you're bigger than me and you can force me to do what you want. But only when you're standing over me. You can't stand over me all the way to Chicago. And I'll run away. I mean it, Dad."

Charlie swore and gulped from the bottle.

"Fourteen years old and talking like a hard-assed theatre manager. See what this road life has done to you?"

"You're not worried about what the road has done to me," said his son. "You were glad enough to have me along with you these past three years since Mama died. You needed somebody to fetch and carry for you, somebody to boss around, somebody to take your shoes off when you passed out. And that was all right with me. That was a fair price to pay, to be on tour with you instead of being shut up in a home somewhere. But you don't need me anymore. You've got your whore now."

Charlie's hand jerked into a fist and just missed the boy. He sloshed whiskey all over Mitch's trousers.

"Shut your filthy little mouth!"

"She boils your coffee and shines your shoes and makes sure you eat. And she does something I can't do. She sleeps in your bed!"

"You're a Gardner all right," said Charlie. "Listen to you talk. Like a man full grown." He put the bottle down and reached for his son.

Mitch jumped back.

"Don't do that," said Charlie. "I wasn't going to hit you."

"I don't trust you."

"Son, you just don't know how things are when you're grown up. Man or woman, we all *need* someone. I loved your mother, but she's been gone these three years now." His voice rumbled deeper. "It isn't natural for a man to go through life alone. 'Go two by two,' said the Lord, 'Be fruitful and multiply.'"

"You put two pieces from the Bible together there," said Mitch, "and you got both of them wrong. Anyway, you and Lulu aren't interested in multiplying. I saw that tin of French letters—"

"You little sneak! You've been prying through all my stuff."

"I was only trying to find some money to buy breakfast."

"You little shit, you're catching the first train out in the morning."

"All right," said Mitch. "But you'd better make sure of one thing."

"What now?"

"I ride first class, or I don't go."

His father started laughing, grabbed the boy, and crushed him in a bear hug.

"You're sure as hell my son," he said. "That's telling the old man. Never settle for anything less, Buzz. Go first class all the way!"

John Barrymore stared down into his empty glass.

"Despite what you say, Charlie loves you, Mitch. Anyone can see that. Even you. But he's only a man. And men are weak."

"You're right. We've both been through enough to agree on that."

He shook Barrymore's hand.

"Thanks, Jack."

"Charlie wouldn't mind me telling you," said Barrymore.

"I mean about letting me share your room," said Mitch.

As the train meandered north, the liquor flowed, and so did the music, and a young trumpet player named Louis Armstrong stole the club car away from Raoul DuPre and his French Canadians and never gave it back. Within a few miles the amateur drinkers surrendered and departed to other coaches where they could doze through the predawn night. This left the club car to Armstrong and the serious boozers, who for two hours, shared a show that would have sold out for six-fifty any night on Broadway. With Louis Armstrong on trumpet, Maurice Chevalier chiming in on those choruses he knew in English and tripping a tipsy soft-shoe in between, with Nelson Eddy happily going solo without Jeanette MacDonald, with Rudy Vallee scuffling for equal time with an opera basso from the east named Ezio Pinza, it was all Mitch Gardner could do to move around trying to do a little business.

He found Vivien Leigh sitting alone near a window, filled her request for a scotch, no ice, and joined her.

"No Miss Lake?" she asked him.

"Miss Lake went home to Mama."

"Poor Mitch. That means you're alone for the night?"

He grinned. "I'm shacking up with Jack Barrymore."

"How gruesome." She sipped her drink. "Well?"

"Well what, Viv?"

"When are you going to proposition me for this dreary film of yours?"

He stood up. "Farthest thing from my mind."

"Oh, sit down you fool." She caught hold of his wrist. "Can't you take a tease? Actually, I want to hear about it. If you must know, I'm miffed that you *haven't* been pursuing me."

"What good would it do? You've just won an Oscar. You can write your own ticket now."

"Dear Mitch." She stroked the palm of his hand. "You are such a boy sometimes."

"Careful," he said. "What you're doing has a special meaning over here."

"It has the same meaning over there . . ."

He removed his hand from hers.

"Business first," he said.

"And then?"

"How do I know? I thought you and Larry—"

"Do you see him here, Mitch?"

"No."

"Then don't ask foolish questions. Tell me about this *Donner Pass* of yours."

"It's a simple story. A party of settlers is trapped by winter in what we now call Donner Pass, between Nevada and California. Some live, some die. It's a story of courage."

"And there's a role for little me?"

"There's a hell of a role. Tamsen Donner. She's the wife of the party's leader. She's the strongest personality in the story."

"I suppose she single-handedly leads the settlers to safety in sunny California?"

Mitch shook his head.

"She's killed and eaten by one of the survivors. You see, love, the Donner party is famous because they resorted to cannibalism."

Vivien Leigh finally looked away. After a moment, she said, "How disgusting."

"I told you it would be a waste of your time."

He started to get up. She stopped him again.

"I didn't say I wouldn't do it, Mitch. As a matter of fact, being eaten might be rather—jolly." Her tongue flicked out and touched her lips. "So, you see, perhaps you haven't wasted my time after all."

"What makes you think Selznick would release you for an outside picture?"

"We'll see. Stop by my room this afternoon and we'll discuss your . . . problems."

She turned away and began talking to a man Mitch did not recognize. He took his empty glass back to the bar, had it refilled, and looked around the club car.

A woman's voice nearby said, "Oh, Mitch, stop operating for a minute and s-s-sit down."

He turned. At a tiny table in the corner sat Marion Davies, winking at him as she drank down brandy from a huge snifter.

She patted the chair next to her own. He went over and sat.

"Party crasher," she said, smiling.

"Jack Barrymore—"

She waved her hand. Her slight stammer made her seem vulnerable, and yet Mitch sensed great strength.

"Jack would lie on a s-s-stack of B-B-Bibles to help a friend. That's why I l-l-like him." She sipped some more brandy. "He tells me today's your b-b-birthday."

"My tenth."

She raised her eyebrows, then nodded.

"Leap year. Well, ch-ch-cheer up. Life begins at forty, or so Will Rogers says." She sipped again. "it was small c-c-comfort to me when I hit that great divide."

"You?" Mitch said, forcing gallantry. "Hell, you're not even—"

"Beautiful liar. Well, w-w-welcome aboard. I'll t-t-tell Bill I invited you myself. He knows h-h-how unreliable Jack is."

"Thanks. Would you like some more brandy?"

"I'd better n-n-not. Mitch, you have the reputation of never d-d-doing anything without a reason. Why d-d-did you pick this particular party to c-c-crash?"

"The truth?" She nodded, and he went on: "I knew there would be a lot of big operators around—Oscar night and all. I'm looking for backing to do a film. My own. I suppose you think that's crazy."

"No," she said. "I think it's very commendable. *Donner Pass* could make a f-f-fine movie."

"How do you know?"

"I r-r-read your treatment."

"*How?*"

"This is a small t-t-town. Whenever anything comes along that I might be interested in, it always gets to me."

Mitch smiled. "I thought you were retired."

Marion Davies' relationship with William Randolph Hearst having begun when she was still in her teens, Hearst had attempted to win respectability for her by making her a movie star through his own company, Cosmopolitan, which worked with MGM. She achieved silent stardom, but had performed less and less often since the coming of sound. And, perhaps because he had never divorced Millicent, his wife, Hearst was frustrated in his primary reason for allowing Marion to act. She achieved a certain fame and respect as a performer without ever being fully accepted in Hearst's own circles.

"The reports of my retirement have been greatly exaggerated," she said, smiling.

He smiled back at her.

"Well. Do you really like the treatment?"

"Very much."

"Then do you think—"

She leaned forward and brushed his cheek with a kiss.

"Mitch, you weren't cut out to b-b-be a con-man. Yes. I'll make s-s-sure you get a chance to t-t-talk with Bill. He'll listen. But that's all I c-c-can promise."

Mitch squeezed her hand.

"That's all anyone could ask."

3

At seventy-seven, William Randolph Hearst was an imposing figure of a man. He was bulky and overweight, his white hair was still thick and shaggy. His ears were large, with pronounced lobes. His nose was slender and long, and beneath it the smile was casual and friendly. He favored four-in-hand striped ties which disappeared into a conservative vest on most occasions, although colorful costume parties were his favorite entertainment. Only his voice broke the image of hearty pioneer, self-made business giant. It was high and tended to crack with excitement.

Hearst met the special train, rising early and driving down the coast to reach San Luis Obispo a few minutes before it arrived. He waited in his car, stroking Helen, his dachshund. The dog, its rich brown coat shot through with gray, whimpered under his caress.

"There, there, Helen," said Hearst. "We are doing just swell."

Helen barked, and Hearst laughed.

"Oh, yes, Marion will be bringing Gandhi." This was Marion's own miniature dachshund, and Helen's favorite playmate.

"See?" cried Hearst in his high, cracking voice. "The train!"

Helen barked.

The caterer's men scurried around their steam tables beneath the large circus tent which had been erected near the road. An odor of scrambled eggs and crisping bacon filled the air. A dozen drivers polished the hoods of their limousines. Three school children, up early, stood near the edge of the field, wondering if the carnival had come to town. They were barefoot and the two boys wore faded blue overalls. The girl had on a dress sewn from rough cotton that had been a flour sack. Hearst saw them.

"Barkam?"

His butler turned away from the table design he was arranging.

"Yes, Mr. Hearst?"

"Those children?"

Barkam examined them as if they were a group of animals just delivered for the San Simeon zoo.

"They are not with our staff, sir. I'll ask them to leave."

"No, no," said Hearst. "Bring them over."

"As you wish, sir."

Barkam beckoned to the children. The older boy, perhaps ten, looked behind and, seeing no one else, pointed at himself.

"Yes, yes," said Barkam. "Come here. Be quick."

The children hesitated.

"Come here!"

They came forward, slowly. Hearst leaned out of the car window.

"Closer," he said. "No one will hurt you." He smiled as they approached. "Who are you, children? Do you live here?"

"Down the road a piece," said the oldest boy.

"What's your name?"

"Ronald. Ronald Tyson. And this is my brother Bobby, and this is Celia. We was just looking at the tent, mister. We wasn't going to steal nothing."

"Of course you weren't. Where were you going?"

"Down to the beach," said Ronald.

"Why?"

"Tide's out. We aimed to gather clams."

"To sell them?"

"Mama cooks them," said the girl, speaking for the first time.

"Does she indeed? For breakfast?"

"Sometimes. Or we fry them for supper. We like clams. I don't like artichokes, though."

Hearst laughed. "Neither do I. Are you hungry?"

The little girl started to say yes, and her oldest brother kicked her in the ankle.

"No, sir," he said. "We done had breakfast."

"Oh, of course," said Hearst. "But couldn't you put down a little snack before your clam digging? It would be a great favor to me, you see. We brought far too much food for this picnic and I am afraid we'll only have to throw it away."

"Well," said Ronald Tyson, "if it wouldn't put you out too much."

"Barkam," said Hearst, "show our guests to the large table."

"If you say so, sir."

"And be sure they get plenty of milk. Do you like milk, children?"

"When we get it, yes sir," said Ronald.

"Well, then, run along and enjoy yourselves. Oh, wait. What does your father do? Does he have a job?"

"Yes sir, he's got a good job. Only he doesn't make much money."

"Where does he work?"

The boy pointed north.

"In the fields for that millionaire up at San Simeon."

The butler Barkam returned, his stern face still set in disapproval.

"Barkam," said Hearst, "when we get home, locate the employment records of Mr. Tyson. See that he receives a promotion."

"But, sir, suppose he's only a field hand?"

"Then move him up to assistant gardener. See to it."

Barkam bowed.

"Yes, Mr. Hearst."

True to her promise, Marion Davies slipped Mitch through the crowd, introduced him to William Randolph Hearst, and set the old man laughing when she explained that today was Mitch's tenth birthday.

"Splendid!" cried Hearst. "We'll bake a cake! Ride with us, Mr. Gardner. You know, I once played a double with your father. I was in politics then, and he joined me in singing my campaign song." He sighed. "That was a long time ago. I hope he's well."

"He's tearing up Broadway," Mitch said as he climbed into the Rolls-Royce. He sat on one of the jump seats, facing Hearst and Marion Davies.

They talked idly of the theatre, of film, of mutual friends, until the car made a sharp right turn.

"The main ranch starts here," Hearst said as they drove through the gate. "Of course, we've still twenty miles or so of coastline before we start up to the Castle."

Mitch laughed nervously.

"For a guy who doesn't even own a corner lot in town, that's a lot of property for me to comprehend."

"I never think about it. That is, not in regard to size. It has always been here, and always will be. I am making plans with the state of California so that even after my death it will not be broken up. That is the nearest thing to immortality a man can achieve, don't you think?"

"I don't want to offend you," Mitch said, "but I would rather be remembered for what I did instead of what I owned."

"Well spoken, young man. But you see, Camp Hill is not merely something I own. I have, in essence, created a new world."

"Camp Hill?"

"That's the name my father gave the original part of the ranch when he purchased it in 1889. The acquisition was small, only forty thousand acres or so of the old Piedras Blancas ranch."

"Only forty thousand . . . Could I ask what it cost?"

"Seventy cents an acre. My father originally used it as a camp for my mother and me, when we lived in San Francisco. He was a United States senator, you know, and his home district was the Bay area. My mother, Phoebe Apperson Hearst, was probably behind the purchase. She always respected things historical and native. It was my mother, you may have heard, who saved Mount Vernon from being razed. She preserved all of the original furniture, and saw that Washington's old place was restored."

"She sounds like quite a lady."

"Yes," Hearst said. "She was always very kind to Marion. Well, my father added to the original property, and, of course, I have continued to do so. I began the construction of San Simeon on the Enchanted Hill the same year my mother died. That was in 1919. I was fifty-six years old, and felt that I had waited long enough to achieve my dream. Although I have always enjoyed good health, you must remember that in those days, fifty-six was getting on in years. Our biggest problem was in getting materials here. There was no train service and to construct a line privately would have been prohibitive, even considering my resources. It was my architect,

Miss Julia Morgan, who came up with the idea of building a pier and bringing in what we needed by boat. And so we did, at a considerable saving over land transportation, particularly since many of the hand-carved ceilings were already on board vessels from Europe."

"Is it true that you bought the roof of a church?"

Hearst laughed. "Actually, it was an abbey. You'll see it today. The rooms were often designed around the ceilings we were able to purchase. You must remember that Europe was devastated by the war. Money, in any hard currency was precious. I always paid the asking price, without a quibble, and yet today I still have occasional feelings of guilt."

The car turned right off the road, through a wide double gate.

"Now we are entering the drive to La Casa Grande," said Hearst. "We're only five miles away. See? Up on the escarpment?"

"Yes, I do," said Mitch. The morning sun had caught the twin towers in its rays and the colored tiles were blazing against the deep-blue sky.

The car passed a large sign: ALWAYS DRIVE SLOWLY. ANIMALS HAVE THE RIGHT OF WAY.

"No elephants, I hope," said Mitch.

The car slowed.

"No," said Hearst. "They do too much damage to the landscaping. But there's a water buffalo lying in the road."

Mitch started to roll down his window.

"Leave it up," said Hearst. "These animals are tame enough, but we don't care for accidents. No one, other than gardeners and gamekeepers, is allowed out of vehicles on this drive. A precaution."

The driver honked his horn; the reluctant buffalo snorted and strolled into the underbrush.

"You'll see giraffe and llamas anywhere along here," Hearst continued. "We have yak from Tibet and sacred fallow deer from India. From this continent, we've stocked mountain sheep, elk, and bison."

"And they all run loose?"

"Within reason. Natural enemies are kept separated by landscaping or hidden fences. Our goal is to give them the most natural habitat possible, and yet be able to refresh our senses by seeing them occasionally."

The Rolls moved suddenly into a cloud of foggy mist.

"We've climbed more than a thousand feet," said Hearst. "Often, on a morning, I can look down from my bedroom and see only the tops of clouds."

"This must make you very happy, Mr. Hearst."

Hearst thought for a moment.

"I am not sure, Mr. Gardner. Proud, yes. I have taken mountain wilderness and created a paradise. But as for happiness . . . no, I do not believe I can claim that without reservations. You see before you all that you think a man might want. Yet I wanted more, much more, and never got it. Nor will I ever, for I am nearing my eightieth year, and when a man reaches that plateau, there is far more behind than there can ever be ahead."

"Did you really want to be president?"

"Of course. Oh, I denied it many times over, yet in fact I felt I had much to bring that office. I still believe that I did. But . . . the world turns, and some are carried along with it, and some are left behind. I made one false step, turned to the right instead of the left, spoke when I should have been silent. Held silence when I should have spoken. Who can say where the original flaw began, when its insidious rust penetrated beneath the skin? One day the façade crumpled and fell away, never to be the same again."

The old man remained silent for a few minutes as the limousine wound its way up the foggy hillside. When he spoke again, his voice was deeper.

"Do not look back, young man. There is nothing there. It ceases to exist the moment you pass it by. Never look back."

Mitch was taken to his suite in La Casa del Sol—the House of the Sun, one of the guest "cottages" overlooking the Pacific Ocean far below. Entering, he stared at a copy of Donatello's *David*, then turned to the valet carrying his bag.

"Where's his fig leaf?"

"I'm sure I don't know, sir," said the man, unperturbed. In his years of service at San Simeon, he had seen and heard almost everything. He was wary of Mitchel Gardner, and hoped this would not turn into another of those riotous parties that disturbed Mr. Hearst so much.

His suspicions were confirmed when, unpacking Mitch's bag, he came upon two bottles of scotch and one of gin. Mr. Hearst's orders were strict in matters of liquor. Yet despite the prohibition issued by the master of the house, most of the servants could not lower themselves to the office of paid spy and so, more often than not, the malefactors guzzled away in their rooms, unaffected by rules. The handsome tips they left on departure ensured their future indulgence.

"What's the schedule?" Mitch asked, loosening his tie and eyeing the shower.

"Lunch is at one-thirty, sir. Both pools are heated, if you would like a swim."

"Forgot my suit," said Mitch, who despised swimming.

"You will find a selection in the middle drawer of your bureau," said the valet. He finished unpacking, leaving the liquor untouched in the suitcase. "Will there be anything else, sir?"

Mitch nodded toward the antique French telephone near the canopied bed.

"Can I call another room on this thing?"

"I am afraid not, sir. We do not have a hotel switchboard." The butler put a subtle emphasis on the word "hotel," which was as far as he would go in expressing disapproval.

"Good enough. Well, thanks. I'll take care of you later."

The valet winced. Gratuities were welcome although not actively sought—servants known to have placed guests in the position of paying for service were subject to instant dismissal.

"My name is Moore, sir. Should you need me, just use the call button near the bathroom door."

Only when Mitch heard the door close did he open the suitcase and check to see if his potables were still there.

"Round one," he said, smiling.

4

Mitch roused from his nap. Something had just been slipped under his door. He weaved over, sleep-dazed, and picked up a heavy sheet of paper.

Printed on it was a short message, surrounded by an ornate border of gold leaf.

SPECIAL BIRTHDAY CELEBRATION

Master Mitchel Gardner

(aged ten today)

Years are short, and Art is long;
So with our merriment go along.
The Masked Ball begins at ten
And will conclude when Mitch says when.

Happy birthday!

Below printed in conventional lettering, Mitch read:

MENU

La Cuesta Encantade • San Simeon, California

Dinner

March 1, 1940

FRIED JUMBO SHRIMP with SAUCE

ROAST VENISON with BROWN GRAVY and DUMPLINGS

ARTICHOKES HOLLANDAISE

WILD RICE	BABY CARROTS
CAKE	STRAWBERRY ICE CREAM

MOVIE

(Special prerelease screening 3 P.M.)

"Rebecca"

(Selznick-United Artists)

Joan Fontaine　　　　　　　　　　Laurence Olivier

George Sanders

Also

Pete Smith Specialty

Breakfast 9:00 to 12:00　　　Luncheon 1:30　　　Dinner 8:30

    Mitch smiled and looked at his watch. It was five after eleven. He could have a late breakfast, or hold off for an hour or so and take lunch. He decided on the latter, and headed for the shower.
    He had expected the gold-plated faucet handles and marble-walled bathroom. He did not expect the bearskin rug on the floor, nor the array of expensive oils in crystal urns. He scrubbed his lean

46

torso, crisscrossed with old wounds, whistling happily; toweled himself vigorously and dressed casually in dark slacks, a polo shirt, and comfortable tan loafers. Masked Ball ... Did that mean costumes? He had none. Or did he? Never underestimate the efficiency of the Hearst minions. Mitch opened the closet.

Yes, he did have a costume. He was willing to bet it had been chosen by Marion.

Hanging on a metal spreader, garish in the daylight, was a crimson Satan suit.

Like all well-appointed villas, San Simeon had a game room. On the first floor of La Casa Grande, it had originally been the breakfast room, but in the mid-thirties Hearst had converted it into a billiards room, with two huge Brunswick tables. One was for straight billiards, the other gave a grudging nod to the twentieth century with its eight leather pockets. As Mitch entered the room, his eye was immediately caught by the tapestry which covered the back wall. He went over to examine it. It depicted a hunt scene, and the colors were brilliant in the gloom of the setting. The huntsmen astride their doglike horses, and the pack of dogs—which looked rather like tiny goats—seemed both humorous and yet disturbing to Mitch's eye.

A man with one leg in a cast came over.

"Fourteenth-century Flanders," he said. "A perfect match to the minds of most of the producers who try to hustle me on these pool tables." He held out his hand. "Herman Mankiewicz."

"Mank! Of course. Hell, we got drunk together once." Mitch gripped the writer's hand. "When you were writing the Marx brothers movie at MGM."

"Did we? I don't remember," said Mankiewicz. "But, of course, I seldom do. What brings you to this chamber of horrors?"

"Marion sucked me into it before I could say no."

"I know the feeling. Why am *I* here, instead of sitting happily down on Tower Road, enjoying my liquor and thumbing my nose at Harry Cohn?"

"Is that story really true?" Mitch asked.

"Of course it is," said Mankiewicz. Then, "Which one? They're all true, of course, but I like to keep track of my lies."

"When Cohn, at a big Columbia screening, turned to all of you and said he had an infallible method for telling when an audience would hate a movie. Didn't he say that as soon as his rear end started itching, he knew the film was in trouble?"

Sadly, Mankiewicz nodded.

"That he did. I needed that job, too. But the devil entered into me, and I said what I was thinking before I could strangle myself, and the bastard heard me."

Knowing exactly what Mankiewicz had said, but wanting to hear it again anyway, Mitch prompted him.

"Yes?"

"I said," Mankiewicz continued mournfully, " 'Isn't it wonderful? The whole world wired to Harry Cohn's ass?' I was fired, of course." He sighed. "It was worth it. But lately I seem to be running out of studios."

"Ever think of doing an independent?"

Mankiewicz sniffed.

"Some quickie down on Poverty Row? What the hell for?"

"I'm putting one together, and it isn't a quickie. Maybe we could work together."

"How?" Mankiewicz demanded. "I'm a writer. So are you. Unless you're looking for a character actor with one leg in a cast."

"You've got contacts."

"So do you."

"Mine are a little sour."

"That's not surprising," said Mankiewicz. "You've spent a lot of time looking down your nose at the boys with the money. Now that you want their filthy lucre, does it surprise you that they aren't exactly lining up to shell out?"

"Okay, it was just a suggestion. Say, I heard you were doing something with Orson Welles."

Mankiewicz lowered himself into one of the high-backed heavily carved chairs.

"Oh, I'm writing something for RKO, and they're paying me. But it'll never reach the screen."

"Why not?"

Mankiewicz nodded his head around the room.

"Because it's about Hearst. I wanted to write it as a novel. Even W.R. can't stop a novel from being published. But I needed money fast, out in front, and RKO has been pressuring Welles, the mad genius, to come up with something for his first contract film. Do you know what old putty-nose wanted to shoot first?" He laughed. "Joseph Conrad's *Heart of Darkness*. Now there's a real crowd-pleaser for you. That one got deep-sixed, and then Welles wrote a screenplay he called *The Smiler with the Knife*. I never read it, but I think it was about a modern Jack the Ripper. And do you know who he wanted for the Rippee? In a serious dramatic role, mind you? That crazy redhead, Lucille Ball. The one with the wild laugh. Boy, they practically handed him his head after that."

"How did you get mixed up with Orson Welles?"

"Oh, I was languishing, Camillelike, after my auto accident, and he turned up on the doorstep. He knew I came up here a lot, and he'd heard of my idea about examining the life of a gigantic figure, a tycoon, through several viewpoints. It excited his interest, particularly when I let it drop that I'd be using San Simeon as a background. One thing led to another, as the fallen lady said, and here I am. Spying on my host."

"Hell, the old man would probably get a laugh out of it," said Mitch, not sure if he meant it.

"I hope so. The whole mess is getting pretty incestuous. You may have heard, Welles' ex-wife Virginia is going to marry Charlie Lederer. Poor soul, he writes, too. *And* he happens to be Marion Davies' nephew."

"I see what you mean," Mitch said. "So how's the project going?"

"Dryly," said Mankiewicz. "Those bastards don't seem to understand that I am unable to write a sensible line when sober. I have been forced to sneak my drinks. But, of course, I get plenty of practice doing that during my visits up here."

"I've got a sneakaroo in my room if you want."

"Don't we all?"

"What do you have for a title?"

"*American*," said Mankiewicz. "And, now that you mention it, why should I feel guilty? Everybody who comes here to Hearstvalhalla ends up writing about it. Aldous Huxley used San Simeon in *After Many a Summer Dies the Swan*. When you've constructed the Panama Canal, you shouldn't get mad if someone sends their boat through it, right?"

"Right. I'd like to see the script sometime."

Mankiewicz stared at him.

"Why?"

"Oh, just to read it."

"Blow a buck, go see the movie," Mankiewicz suggested. "I don't give free peeks at the merchandise."

"Listen, Mank, I only—"

"Don't you think everybody knows why you're up here? Sucking up to W.R. to raise money for your goddamned trash about the Donner party? Why should I give you a lever to use against me? I'll deny anything I've said in this room, but it would be hard to deny a page or two of screenplay if you took them to Hearst, wouldn't it?"

"Hold on!" said Mitch. "I never had any intention—"

"Face up to it, Gardner," said Mankiewicz. "Stop trying to hustle me. You're second-rate, too little talent too late. What the hell is it with you guys, suddenly you all want to direct? John Huston has the same wild hair up his ass. He wants to remake *The Maltese Falcon*, for God's sake, and it's been a flop twice already. Preston Sturges is hustling a script around town. Does Ben Hecht want to direct? He does not."

"That's all you know. Ben told me—"

Mankiewicz wagged his finger. "Name-dropper."

"Go sneak a drink," said Mitch. "You crap artist, you're lucky you're in a cast."

"Don't let a little plaster of Paris stop you," said Mankiewicz, rearing up to his full crippled height. "Come on, big mouth."

"Oh, shove it," said Mitch, turning away.

He left the game room and found himself in Hearst's private movie theatre. The seats were heavily cushioned, the floor was plush with carpeting, the screen was covered with velvet curtains. Mitch found a seat near the stage and stared at the plush drapes, as if he could see the silver screen behind them.

It had been a long time since he had entered a private theatre like this one. April 3 of 1937, to be exact. It was a date Mitch would never forget.

Jean Harlow, pale and thin, had sat there with him. Marion had invited her to a small party at the Santa Monica house, and she had brought Mitch—to the quiet displeasure of her hostess, who did not then know the tall writer. Marion took grim pleasure in billeting him as far away from Jean's room as possible.

That morning, they had sneaked away from the guests and headed for her room—only to find it occupied by two maids, busily cleaning. In desperation, they slipped into the darkened screening room.

"We can't go on meeting like this," Mitch said, stroking her neck.

"No, we can't. Bill would never permit it."

She twisted the 150-carat star sapphire "friendship" ring William Powell had given her around and around on her finger.

"He's too old for you," grumbled Mitch.

"What does that matter? In a hundred years, we'll all be the same age." Her voice softened. "Maybe sooner."

"What's the matter, baby?"

She leaned against his shoulder.

"Oh, too much work, I suppose. We shot *Personal Property* in nineteen days, you know. L.B. put the pressure on. I was drinking like a fish just to keep my energy. You know what the lights do to me. I've been going around in a daze. And now the pressure's on for *Saratoga*."

"Can you handle it?"

She stiffened.

"What the hell do you mean, *handle* it? When have I ever missed a makeup call?"

"I know, I know. But if you need a week or so, Clark would be glad to call in sick."

"It's tempting. But I couldn't ask him to get in trouble with L.B."

"Mr. Gable would like nothing better than to piss off Mr. Mayer. How about it, want me to talk to him?"

She was quiet for a moment. Then: "No. Thank you, darling. It's not that bad. And I'll take a long rest after. We won't be shooting so fast this time, either. Jack Conway's directing, and he scheduled thirty days."

"Thirty days, shit! That's still an express run. No wonder everything that comes from MGM looks like it was stamped out with a cookie cutter."

"Shhh," she said. "L.B. has ears everywhere."

"Fine," said Mitch. "Then he'll hear exactly what I think of him." He ripped off a string of the filthiest descriptions he could find to fit the studio head, as Jean sat in the darkness and laughed. By the time he had finished, she was in hysterical tears.

"That's enough to get you in my dressing room for a week straight," she promised. She had long held a rule that anyone wanting a drink there had first to recite a new dirty story or limerick.

"Just so Old Man Powell isn't there ahead of me." Mitch's voice lowered. "Honey, don't marry that guy."

"What do you want me to do, Mitch? Wait around for you to get old too, and ready to settle down?"

"Listen, stall him. I've got to go to New York for the rehearsals of *Stumblebum,* but once it's open, I'll haul ass back out here and—"

"Stop it, Mitch. You don't want to marry me." He began to protest, and she shut his mouth with her fingers. "I don't take it personally, my dear. You don't want to marry *anyone.* Fine. But I'm tired of sleeping alone, and Bill really is a nice person, and you lie, Gardner, he's not all that old. Cut, that's a print, wrap and let's go have a drink."

"Just stall until June. I'll see you then."

She hesitated. "All right," she said finally. "We weren't in any great rush anyway."

He kissed her.

"Terrific. I'll be back in June to sweep you off your feet, you wait and see."

When Mitch Gardner returned, by chartered plane, he was too late to see Jean Harlow alive.

Saturday morning, May 29, she had been playing a scene with Clark Gable in which he was to carry her to a sofa. Having picked her up, he realized that she had gone limp in his arms, that her body was soaked with cold sweat.

"Cut it," Gable said, lowering her to the sofa. "Jean's sick."

The camera stopped rolling.

She was helped from the set, protesting. Production was suspended for the weekend, thereby blowing L. B. Mayer's thirty-day schedule out the window.

Jean did not report on Monday. She was by then too ill even to speak on the telephone.

Her condition was kept secret. At last, Gable called Mitch in the midst of his play rehearsals and told him Jean was dangerously ill.

At 11:37 A.M. of June 7, 1937—while Mitch was dodging mountain peaks in Wyoming—the Platinum Blonde coughed a last breath into a Los Angeles Fire Department oxygen mask.

She was twenty-six years old.

Mitch realized that he was slowly pounding his hand against the soft arm rest of his seat.

He got up and left the screening room.

After lunch and a quick drink in his room, Mitch went down to the outdoor pool. The Neptune Pool, a hundred feet long, was filled with more than three hundred thousand gallons of heated water held between marble walls and green mosaic tiles. A statue of Venus rose from the water, surrounded by cherubs and mermaids.

Mitch, still smarting from his encounter with Herman Mankiewicz, hoped the writer would not be there. He was not. But the poolside complement included Dolores del Rio, a gardenia in her dark hair. He waved at her; obviously not recognizing him, she nodded back. Nearby, Western star Johnny Mack Brown sat with his young wife, Connie. Mitch had written one of Brown's films, so he went over to say hello, and they made small talk for a few moments while Mitch cased the rest of the crowd with a practiced eye. Dick Foran chatted with comedienne Patsy Kelly. James Stewart sat, hands clasped over his bony knees, and discussed the war in Europe with producer Hal Wallis. At a table apart, columnist Louella Parsons drank tea with her husband, Dr. Harry Martin. Robert Montgomery and David Niven were talking with Mary Astor and Paulette Goddard. Charles Chaplin was nowhere in sight, though Mitch had heard on the train that he was expected to be present. No one, however, had actully seen the comedian.

Groucho Marx, sans mustache, sat down near Mitch.

"Don't put that expression of yours in the pool," he said. "It would kill all the fish."

"Is it that obvious?"

"You look like an insurance adjuster at the San Francisco earthquake. Cheer up, kid. Life ain't that bad. Take it like I do. Cursing and cheating."

Mitch laughed. "No thanks. I've got a father who's been a comedian, remember? There are easier ways of making a living."

"Well, life's no bed of roses," Groucho said. "But on the other hand, who wants to sleep in a thorn bush?"

The comedian hurried away, as if he were embarrassed to have said a kind word.

"I wasn't aware you knew Groucho," said Johnny Mack Brown.

"I don't," said Mitch.

Mitch got up and wandered around the pool, down near the grape arbor, looking for Marion Davies and trying not to be too obvious about it. John Barrymore, still in the rumpled suit he had worn the night before, grabbed his arm.

"Ho, lost soul! Alight somewhere. Bird thou never wert."

"I'm bored out of my skull," said Mitch. "Let's go have a drink in the room."

"In a moment."

Mitch stared at him.

"I never heard of you turning down a drink before."

"A little respect, my lad. I bear glad tidings. A certain lady, her name need never be mentioned, sends you What Ho and bids you go thither."

"Damn it, Jack, speak English."

"Shall I draw you a map? Miss Leigh awaits your pleasure."

"Where?"

"Down at the zoo, near the lion cage."

"The *lion* cage?"

Barrymore shrugged.

"It was the lady's choice, not mine. Perhaps she likes lions. Maybe her tour at MGM gave her the habit. Hurry along, Mitch, and remember, I shall hold you to that offer of a drink if and when you return."

"My suitcase is unlocked," Mitch said, surprising himself. "After all, you're my roommate, go in and help yourself."

"Gladly," said Barrymore.

Mitch talked to guests for a half hour or so, then slipped away from the pool and strolled down the hill, toward the part of the

Hearst estate where some of the animals were kept caged because they were too dangerous to roam free.

As Barrymore had promised, Vivien Leigh was seated near the lion cage. She wore a light bush jacket and riding trousers with mirror-shined boots. Her dark hair was tied back with a yellow bandana.

"You took your time," she said. "Can you have misunderstood?"

"Oh, I understood all right. It's just that I like to do my own chasing."

"You were more humble when you were trying to lure me into lending my name to that disgusting film of yours."

"One is business. The other is supposed to be pleasure."

She stroked his cheek.

"Can't they somehow be combined? After all, love, I'm in a position to rather do you some good, wouldn't you say?"

"I know you are. Look, Viv, I've always wanted to lay you. That's it, out in the open. But not this way. Not because you're probably mad at Larry for something and want to bust his balls. I never screwed a friend's wife and I hope I never will."

"Ass. I'm married to someone you never met. And Larry's married to Jill Esmond."

"And so what? Listen, baby, I want you bad. In both ways. Sure, after *Gone with the Wind,* having you interested in *Donner Pass* might just get me off the ground. As for the other, you're the jerk-off dream of every horny guy between here and good old Blighty. But I won't screw you to help you spite Larry, and I won't screw you to tie you up for my movie."

She threw back her head and laughed.

"Why, you prude! Suppose you 'screw' me, as you so delightfully put it, simply because you want to?"

As she spoke she reached down and caressed him and, predictably, found him erect.

"That's a different story . . . ."

"Tonight," she said. "After the party."

"I've got a roommate," he reminded her.

"I don't," she said, leaning forward to kiss him.

Promptly at 7:30 P.M. William Randolph Hearst greeted his guests in the Assembly Room. Eighty-four feet long, twenty-two high, and thirty-two wide, the huge room was dominated by its handsome French Renaissance fireplace, which had come from the antique collection of the famous architect Stanford White. The fireplace, of the style called "mantel over mantel," had been constructed in the sixteenth century. Marble busts extended over it for several feet, carved by a sculptor named Duquesnoy. None of this would have been known to Mitch Gardner, except for the running commentary given to him by Arthur Lake, the comedian who played Dagwood Bumstead in the *Blondie* movies. Lake, a frequent visitor to San Simeon, knew every room intimately.

As Hearst entered, bright lights flared.

"Everybody, act natural," said Ken Murray, who was filming the occasion. Murray, who had been coming to San Simeon since the twenties, had gradually assumed the mantle of court recorder with his sixteen-millimeter movie camera. His collection of movie and world greats at the Castle was, by now, priceless.

Mitch posed, self-consciously, against one of the four Giulio Romano tapestries, each of which, Arthur Lake said, was reputed to be worth more than half a million dollars.

"That's a lot of loot for needlepoint," said Mitch. "Maybe we're in the wrong business."

He sat down in an ancient choir stall which had once occupied an Italian monastery.

"I'm ready for a drink," he said.

"Enjoy it," said Lake. "You get one. One only."

"How well I know," Mitch said mournfully.

He caught John Barrymore's eye. The actor was freshly brushed and his hair was slicked back. Mitch supposed that Moore, the valet, had taken him in hand.

Lake noticed his glance.

"Isn't that John Barrymore?" he asked. "I thought he was dead."

Mitch cracked his knuckles and stared at his fingernails.

"No," he said softly. "But it isn't through lack of effort."

Hearst entered from his private elevator, having descended from his Gothic Suite in solitary splendor. As cocktails were served, he moved gracefully from guest to guest, greeting them, commenting on private matters.

"Mr. Mankiewicz. I hope your injuries are healing."

"Thank you, W.R. I should be on skis by the end of the year."

"Good. And say hello to your wife, Sara, for me."

"She'll appreciate it. She's sorry she couldn't come."

Hearst moved on to James Stewart.

"The industry is buzzing about your new film with Frank Capra," he said. "You seem to be setting us old fuddy-duddys on our ears."

Stewart laughed. "Fuddy-duddys? Come on now, Mr. Hearst. Your energy leaves us all behind."

"A word of warning, though," said Hearst, ignoring the compliment.

"Sure."

"There are influences gathering momentum in Hollywood which it would be wise to avoid. I know that you are not political, no more so than any good citizen. But unless you are in complete accord with their leftist views, you would be wise to shun the society of such individuals as Mr. John Garfield and Mr. Robert Rossen, to name just two."

"Well, now, sir, I thank you for that advice," said Stewart. "But, as you said, I am no more political than any other good citizen. And to me, being a good citizen also means minding my own business. I leave my friends' politics to them."

Hearst nodded—"As you wish"—and moved on.

He missed no one. He spoke for a few moments with Robert Montgomery, and then spent a fervent five minutes instructing Henry Fonda on some matter no one managed to overhear. When he reached Groucho Marx, the two apparently threw one-line jokes at each other, and separated wilted with laughter.

Mitch waited patiently for his turn.

"Ah, Mr. Gardner," Hearst began. "Is your room comfortable?"

"Actually, it isn't," said Mitch. Hearst's head snapped up. "I thought I'd be in the main house," Mitch continued. "What am I, some poor relation?"

Hearst stared at Mitch for a moment, then threw back his head and laughed.

"Well done!" he said. "A good attack is the best defense. You are perfectly correct, Mr. Gardner. Put the old bastard in his place, quickly, and get it out of the way. Shall I have you moved?"

"No. I'm settled in now. But next time . . ."

"If there *is* a next time," said Hearst.

"There will be, Mr. Hearst."

"Then you will occupy the Celestial Suite and sleep beneath the protective statue of St. Anthony of Padua. Or would you prefer Winston Churchill's favorite, one of the tower suites beneath the carillon bells?"

"Just so I go first class."

"That is an obsession with you, isn't it?" Hearst asked.

"I guess so," Mitch admitted. "Isn't it with you?"

"Point and game. Shall we go in? I hope you don't mind, I prefer to take Marion's arm."

"A delightful choice," said Mitch.

Hearst's dining hall, the Refectory, was his pride of the Castle. The floor was of Italian travertine. The choir stalls which lined the walls were five hudred years old; the thirty-foot ceiling was carved wood filled with life-sized images of the saints.

Along a sideboard were serving pieces, including Sheffield trays, Irish platters, and a wine cistern created by David Williams of London in 1710.

On the long dining table itself, piled neatly between the heavy silver and delicate china, were jars of Heinz catsup, Lea & Perrins Worcestershire sauce, Morton's salt, and French's mustard. All were in their store-bought bottles.

The napkins were paper.

Hearst, seated at the head of the table with Marion on his left, noticed Mitch's expression.

"An old man's affectation," he explained. "In the old days, when we camped up here on the Hill, as we called it, we used tents. There was one huge one, for dining and recreation, and three others, divided into four bedrooms and a bath each. Well, at that time, because storage facilities were so primitive, we used store-shelf condiments and paper napkins. I am afraid the practice has descended to this very day, and it is one thing I have never tried to improve."

"No reason why you should," Mitch said, dousing his venison roast with Heinz 57 sauce. "I'd rather know what I'm eating anyway."

Hearst turned to Marion.

"Your Mr. Gardner is a firebrand, my dear. Are we sure we can depend on him not to burn our castle down?"

"I think so," she said. "He is too w-w-wise to throw stones in a glass house."

Mitch grinned. "As long as we're slinging clichés around, let me add that I'm also well aware on which side my bread is buttered."

Groucho Marx, attacking his nonkosher shrimp with delight, asked, "Is this a private war, or can anybody play?"

"Armistice, Groucho," Marion said quickly.

"Darn." Marx nibbled a shrimp. "Tiny venisons you grow here."

The discussion bent its way toward the movie that had been shown that afternoon; Mitch, not having attended, stayed out of it. The consensus was that Selznick had done it again, and had a winner with Alfred Hitchcock's first American directorial assignment. The votes were evenly split between Joan Fontaine and Laurence Olivier's talents, and there were the usual snippy professional quibbles.

"She's just too pretty-pretty," said Paulette Goddard. "I know the heroines of Gothics are supposed to be standardized. Poor young thing arrives at terrible castle, inhabited by attractive man and assorted weirds, love springs forth, followed by terror. But Joan never had a hair out of place."

"You can blame that on Mr. Selznick," said John Barrymore from his post below the salt. "He has a mania for perfect photography. He will call an entire unit back because an actress has a mascara smudge on her cheek."

"How stupid," said Bette Davis. "It's the performance that counts. If the audience is noticing mascara, we haven't done our jobs."

"I agree," said Henry Fonda. "But you have to admit, Selznick films have a 'look.' You can tell who made them by watching a single moment on the screen."

"But movies aren't paintings," said Bette. "They're life! If we don't excite our audiences and sweep them away to a more exciting world than the one they know, why should they pay to see us?"

"All very well," said David Niven. "Yet there are good things to be said for Mr. Selznick's ways of working. When I did *Wuthering Heights* with Sam Goldwyn, I could not help noticing the short cuts Mr. Wyler took—short cuts that, while not visible to the audience, had to influence their viewing of the film."

"Oh, crap," said Mitch, watching for Hearst's reaction. "That was a fine movie."

"Speak for yourself," Niven smiled. "I played fifth fiddle to Larry and Merle and those everloving moors. Even the music upstaged me. But this is what I meant: despite the care Wyler took, we never went for that one extra take Selznick always makes. If we had a good one in the can, we moved on. As a result, in one sequence, you see Larry rushing up to Pillistone Crag with Merle following him . . . and, *behind* her, Larry again, chasing *her*. It's a bad cut and only carelessness let it happen."

"It was a *beautiful* film," said Louella Parsons. "I cried. Didn't I, Docky?"

"Buckets," said her husband.

"So sad," she said. "So lovely."

"Louella cries during the refreshment intermission," said Docky. "I think she feels sorry for the popcorn."

"No more business," said Hearst. "All everyone ever talks about is film."

Softly, Marion Davies said, "And don't you love it?"

Having begun outside on the main terrace, the Masked Ball ended up being held in the Assembly Room. There was no formal move inside. It began as a wandering of one or two shivering souls, but soon became a mass retreat. Hearst was one of the last to leave. His costume as a cloaked Napoleon, complete with cocked hat, protected him more effectively from the elements than did Bette Davis' thin gown in her role as the Bearded Lady.

Even Marion Davies, disguised as Pocahontas, was shivering under her deerskin robe when Hearst finally accepted the inevitable and followed his guests into the Assembly Room.

Charles Chaplin had not arrived, but Paulette Goddard was beautiful as "Little Mary," imitating Pickford right down to the last golden ringlet. Patsy Kelly was costumed as a female lion tamer, and her tame lion was Bert Lahr in his *Wizard of Oz* outfit. Louella Parsons wore a costume, borrowed from Paramount, which made her into a passable representation of a bejeweled Russian princess.

John Barrymore, incongruous as a police chief, carried a rubber billy club which he applied with vigor against the nether anatomies of any young woman he could get near. It was soon taken away from him.

Hearst had relaxed his no-drinking-after-dinner rule enough to permit a few magnums of champagne to be shared out, miser fashion, to the revelers. The bubbly was soon gone, and a steady trickle of guests slipping off to their rooms for a quick one could be noticed by the careful observer. And Mr. Hearst was nothing if not a careful observer. But he kept silent. He had learned that what he did not see, he did not have to fight over with Marion. She slipped away on several occasions, too, and returned with her laughter a little brighter, her step a little more unsteady, and her voice a little too loud.

Mitch, despite his Satan costume, was on his best behavior. He went from group to group, dropping references to *Donner Pass* whenever he found the chance. When he came to rest, briefly, near Michael Todd, the showman lifted his glass in a toast.

"I've seen hustlers come and go," Todd said, sloshing champagne over his blue serge suit, "but none ever worked harder than you do."

Mitch grinned. "What are you supposed to be? Where's your costume?"

"This *is* my costume. I'm a Wall Street Banker, grinding my feet in the faces of the poor." He twisted his foot against the tiled floor. "See? Grind, grind."

Mitch laughed.

"How's your fund-raising going?"

"*Up in Central Park*? It's going to make a million. Are you sure you ain't interested? I've got a couple of points out of the producer's share, going cheap."

"Wish I could. But I'll be lucky to get my own show off the ground."

Todd moved in close.

"You're going to make a movie, right? Well, that's what I want to do, one day. Only when I do it's got to be what you'd call a spectacular, you know what I mean? No plain old black-and-white mystery story is big enough for Mike Todd. I got some ideas. Maybe I'll drop around and tell them to you sometime."

"Why not?" said Mitch, moving away. He had seen enough Mike Todds during his years in Hollywood to recognize the breed. In the remote chance that Todd ever produced a film, it would be some cheap B-movie lucky to get on the bottom half of a Wild Bill Elliott Western.

"I'll take you up on that," Todd called, plunging back into the crowd, his shiny blue serge suit clashing with the expensive decor and fancy costumes.

"Who was that?" Marion Davies asked.

"Some Broadway hustler," said Mitch. "What the hell did you invite him for?"

Marion threw back her head and laughed.

"I didn't invite him. He told me *you* did."

"I'll be a son of a bitch," said Mitch. "That little shrimp has balls. Maybe he *will* make a movie someday."

"Don't bet on it," said Marion. "Are you having a good time?"

"Good enough."

"When are you going to ask me to b-b-be in your picture?" she asked softly.

"When am I—what?"

"Isn't that why you really came up here? To proposition me and to t-t-try to get Bill to back your play?"

"You know," he said carefully, "I never actually figured it out that way, but now that you mention it, you don't have such a bad idea."

"I thought it was a marvelous idea. You already know I like your story treatment. Do you have a script yet?"

"No. So much depends on the casting."

"Suppose I were to play your Tamsen Donner. D-d-does that alter the story much?"

He thought for a moment.

"Actually, it places it closer to real history. I mean, Tamsen wasn't exactly your everyday ingénue."

She gave him a sad smile.

"And, anymore, neither am I?"

"You know what I mean. She was a mature woman. Strong. Determined." He softened his voice. "Beautiful."

"Bull," said Marion. "What frontier woman was ever b-b-beautiful? Are you going to do this with soft focus and lots of makeup and celestial music, or are you going to do it right?"

After a pause, he said, "Marion, I would sure in hell hope that I'm going to do it right."

"All right," she said. "Try to stay sober. I'll talk to Bill, and see if he's at all interested."

"What if he is?"

"Then," she said, still smiling, "you're going to have to do the best goddamned selling job of your l-l-life."

5

Shortly after midnight, William Randolph Hearst drew Mitch aside and said, "Do you mind if we go upstairs and talk for a few minutes? Marion has suggested that you have a proposition which might be of interest to me."

"Lead on," said Mitch. He had been drinking less than usual, but his head was a little woozy. "I'd like to see where I'm staying next visit anyway."

Hearst's lips tightened. He made no comment, but Mitch knew instantly that he had made a mistake. He hastened to correct it.

"Listen, Mr. Hearst," he said as soon as the iron bars of Hearst's private elevator closed behind them. "I have to confess something that I'm not too proud of."

"Really, Mr. Gardner," said Hearst, activiating the mechanism. "Your private affairs are of no concern to me—"

"Yes they are. I just now shot off my mouth and I could see that you didn't like it. Well, I'm sorry. It was stupid. And I'd like to explain it, if you'll let me."

Hearst did something to the elevator controls, and it stopped between the floors.

"We're quite private here," he said.

"Fine," said Mitch. "Listen, sir, I know I've been coming on strong all day. Well, I'm scared. I want to impress you, I also want to hold on to my independence."

"I'm not sure I understand."

"I'm an upstart. I came barging in here with no credentials

except for my big mouth and the recommendations of my friends. And I—"

"Your big mouth, as you put it, doesn't offend me. I know what it's like to approach the throne of the great with nothing in my pocket but the knowledge that I am right. Mr. Gardner, I have lived a long time, and made a great deal of money. Both taught me lessons. So if you are asking, would I appreciate it if you would settle down and stop pushing so hard, the answer is yes. We may possibly be working together. It will be easier if we can be frank, yet not offensive, with each other. As for the rest, the recommendations of your friends, while I trust their judgments, I never commit money on the basis of anybody else's word. I took some time this afternoon to make my own investigations, Mr. Gardner. You met my requirements. Is there anything else you'd like to say?"

"Well, yes," Mitch mumbled. "Since we're being so frank with each other, where the hell do I go to the bathroom?"

"This is my hideout," Hearst said. "Since everything in the Castle must have a name, someone attached the title 'Gothic Suite' to this apartment. I don't mind. As you must have noticed, I am particularly fascinated by ceilings. This one, which is paint on pine, comes from the Spanish castle Marchino."

Mitch looked around the room. It was not very large. In fact, compared to the ones he'd been in all day, it was tiny. Less than twenty feet by twenty. It was dominated by a canopied bed, flanked by two antique lamps with parchment shades enscribed in Latin.

Hearst smiled. "The bed is fifteenth-century, French baldachin style. It's oak, and if you notice, each post is carved with a different design. The painting on the chest of drawers is Renaissance, Segna, and some say it is the single most valuable objet d'art on the Hill."

"Why?" Mitch asked. "Why do you buy all this stuff?"

Hearst shrugged and sat down in an incongruously modern easy chair, covered in a cheap floral print.

"Why not?" he asked. "I can afford to indulge myself. These things please me. No one suffers by my extravagances."

"But you could do so much with your money."

Hearst merely smiled.

"Mr. Gardner, the bathroom is just past those drapes. Why don't you avail yourself of its facilities, and then you may be able to settle down long enough for us to talk."

"Well, if you don't mind," Mitch said, edging toward the door. Hearst laughed and turned to a side table, where he picked up a folded copy of a Hearst newspaper.

The bathroom was in two sections, done completely in pink marble. All the exposed metal was gold-plated, even the drainpipes. The tub was oversized, to fit the height of the castle's master. Mitch lifted the seat of the toilet and relieved himself. When he flushed, he resisted an urge to take some toilet paper and wipe his fingerprints off the gold handle.

"Some john," he said, returning to the bedroom.

Hearst laughed. "Yes, it is. Now, Mr. Gardner, if we can devote ourselves to a few moments of business?"

"It's your nickel."

"Marion has told me a little about this film project of yours. I am sufficiently familiar with the incident at Donner Pass to applaud your choice of subject. It could make a very exciting and profitable film."

"Thanks," said Mitch. "Of course, I'm just getting the story started."

"Let's not have any false modesty, Mr. Gardner. I know you are just developing your story line. I am also aware that what you have developed is very good."

"How do you know that?"

"Marion somehow obtained a copy of your treatment. It shows a sound grasp of drama and of the screen medium. It's very good, and I assume your further work will also be good. So I am not concerned with a scene-by-scene discussion of the film. What I want to hear from you is your overall concept of the story's effect on an audience. What will it achieve? As a film, and—if she is so inclined—for Marion's career?"

The key words did not go unnoticed by Mitch. He bit his lip. There were at least two ways to play this. He could praise Marion as an actress and point out what a great asset she would be to the film. Or . . .

"Mr. Hearst," he said, deciding, "I don't want to offend you. Can I talk straight?"

"I want it no other way."

"All right. Marion Davies could have been one of the finest actresses of the generation. She is beautiful, she is talented, she has audience appeal, she is easy to work with and loved by every crew of every film she's shot. But she's never really hit it big, because she has one terrible handicap."

Hearst blinked his eyes.

"What handicap? She never stammers on camera."

"You're her handicap, Mr. Hearst." Mitch paused. The old man stared at him, but said nothing. Finally, Mitch continued.

"You have presented her to the world as you see her. As a fairy princess, a beautiful, shimmering vision. But always *your* vision. It has been a successful vision, yes, for she is all that you see in her. But—and this is what you must understand, sir—she is far more than that. You have only seen, only presented, one of her many faces. Mr. Hearst, Marion is an actress, a fine actress. And in a role like Tamsen Donner, she will prove it. She'll win next year's Academy Award for Best Actress, or I'll—I'll eat your goddamned fifteenth-century French baldachin bed!"

Hearst sat silent, stroking his chin. When he spoke, his voice was soft, almost inaudible.

"What you say, Mr. Gardner, is not completely foreign to me. I have entertained such thoughts myself. For the moment, let us assume that you're right. Perhaps I have been too tight on the rein. So tell me, what is it that you really hope to achieve with *Donner Pass?*"

Mitch bit his lip.

"That's hard. What I mostly want it to do is make ten million dollars."

Hearst laughed. "Well said. But beyond that?"

"Let me ask you a question. Do you still believe in heroes and heroines?"

"Oh, yes, Mr. Gardner, very much."

"Well, so do I. So let's examine this little piece of history we hope to get on film. It's 1846. We meet George Donner. He's a handsome man, a vigorous man, but he's also sixty-two years old. He lives in Illinois, on a profitable farm. Suddenly, he throws everything over and starts for California. Why? Because he's tired of the cold winters? Or because he has gold fever? I don't think so, Mr. Hearst. I think it happens simply because it is *time* for it to happen. He's an adventurer, a hero if you will. He departs from Illinois with twelve yoke of oxen, five saddle horses, five children, and his third wife, Tamsen."

"Marion," Hearst said softly.

"Yes. Massachusetts-born, forty-five years old—"

"Thirty," Hearst said. "Artistic license."

"Thirty-five, then," said Mitch. "Look, I'm going to try and get Judy Garland as the oldest daughter. Now. Her mother, Tamsen, has been a schoolmistress. She has strong will. And she weighs in at less than a hundred pounds."

"Yet for all that, it is her spirit that will sustain the Donner party," Hearst said.

Mitch hesitated.

"Yes, you might say that. Well, you know how the wagon trains were made up back then. People proceeded on their own as far as they could, at their own speed. Then they had to join up with others for the ordeal of crossing the continental divide. So it is with George and Tamsen Donner. The month is July. They stagger across the great desert, following a new route which was published in the newspapers—based on a description, it later turns out, by a scout who never actually traveled it. The thirst will kill half of their oxen and drive the Donners themselves near mad from its constant pain. But they will press on, toward the sheer barrier of the Sierra Nevada. The mountains form a wall a hundred miles wide, and they must climb that wall to reach the green grasses of California. The first sign of civilization west of the Sierra Nevada is Sutter's Fort. But to reach it, the settlers must cross the Humboldt River, climb up through the mountains along the Truckee, past the deep blue of the big Truckee Lake—"

"Lake Tahoe now," Hearst supplied.

Mitch nodded. "And by muscle power, if need be, drag their wagons over the mountain crest. Their way is hard, the trail is long. But their principal enemy is time. If they reach the crest of the Sierra by August, or even September, all will be well. Heavy snows will not be falling. But later than that, when the passes are blocked by snowfalls, it's a different story. And that is the one we will tell."

"The settlers will arrive late," Hearst said.

"Right. They leave the Little Sandy river in July, work their way to Fort Bridger. George Donner, as you know, has been elected leader of the newly formed wagon train. They are following the 'new' route described in the newspapers. According to the scout who wrote about it, this way will save three hundred and fifty miles between Fort Bridger and the Sacramento River. So the Donner party leaves the well-traveled Oregon Trail and sets off into untracked country. Well, you read my story treatment. They have all kinds of troubles. A shoot-out between two members of the party. They get lost. Indians kill their cattle and steal their horses. But they press on."

"And all through this," Hearst said, "Marion's character is dominant. She lends courage and spirit to her husband."

"All the way," Mitch said, clearing his throat. "So finally they reach the flats of Truckee Meadows. Above is Truckee Pass and, once through it, the downhill run to Sacramento. But they have been on the trail too long. It's the end of October. Snow is falling. The trap has already closed behind them. And, as they stagger toward the pass, the weather is working. They reach it on November 4, and it's too late. The pass is blocked. They can go neither forward nor backward. The Donner party is trapped."

"Where does Marion fit into all this?"

Mitch improvised.

"She's the inspiration of the party. When a child dies, it is Tamsen Donner who comforts the mother, and arranges the simple yet deeply moving funeral services."

"Yes," Hearst breathed. "I can see her doing that."

"Now we enter on winter," Mitch said. "It is a day-to-day struggle just to remain alive."

"But Marion never surrenders!"

"Never. She takes care of her husband, who has injured his hand, and, as time passes, watches it become infected. Tamsen manages to get some of the men who are pressing forward on foot to take her children, but she stays behind with George."

"Nursing him," Hearst said softly.

"To the end. She never leaves him. She has the courage of a lioness."

"Yes," Hearst said.

Mitch stood up. "Well, eventually the rescue party gets through.

The children are saved. And Marion—Tamsen—goes on to a new life in California."

"Beautiful," said Hearst. He rubbed his blotched hand across his face. "Yes, it's about time someone made films that celebrate the human spirit. And Marion could be superb."

"Then you're interested, Mr. Hearst?"

"Perhaps. It depends on many factors. We'll talk again. Now, if you'll excuse me . . . you can work the elevator?"

"Sure," said Mitch. Slowly, he left. Behind him, he thought he heard Hearst sobbing. Or possibly the old man was only coughing.

John Barrymore lifted his glass.

"Where, O smiling cat," he intoned, "hast thou concealed the canary?"

Mitch had gone directly to his room instead of rejoining the party and, there, found the actor drinking in solitude.

"Believe it or not," Mitch said, "I may just have talked Hearst into backing my film."

"I suspected as much from your Cheshire smile. Yet, old cock, you seem down. What troubles you?"

"I don't know." Mitch accepted the drink Barrymore offered. "I guess I just didn't think it would be so easy, playing on the old man."

"How, playing?"

"I told him everything he wanted to hear. That I could drag a great dramatic performance out of Marion—"

"Can you?"

"Who knows? She's spent more time in the gin bottle recently than she has in the studio."

Barrymore wagged his finger. "Ah, lad, if that were grounds for dismissal, the cameras would see nothing but empty sets."

Mitch started stripping off his red Satan costume.

"Well," he said, "if anyone can make her *act,* I can. Because I won't knuckle under the way all the others did. I don't give a shit if she's Daddy Hearst's little girl. If he shows up on my set. I'll tell him to shove it."

"You like him, don't you?" Barrymore said quietly.

Mitch studied the horns attached to the headpiece of his costume.

"Yes. I didn't think I would. But he's straight. That's why I feel so lousy, lying to him just to get his money."

"How did you lie?"

"I gave the film a happy ending. I sensed that was what he wanted. He'd go along with everything else that I plan to do, but if I had even suggested that his beloved Marion is supposed to be cooked and eaten . . . well, there was no way. He would have closed his ears."

"But he'll have to know, won't he? If he comes in, he'll be reading the script."

Naked, Mitch stepped into the shower.

"Scripts can have more than one version," he shouted over its hiss.

"I see," Barrymore called back. "The old Screw-ola."

"So?" Mitch bellowed. "Don't tell me you've never—"

"Gently, gently. I'm not attacking you, Mitch. Who am I to point the finger? No, if there is anything that I regret, it is perhaps that I sense a certain loss of innocence in you. No matter how profuse your other faults, I have never before heard you confess to a lie."

"Hah," Mitch said. A few minutes later, he stepped out of the shower.

"Have you ever made a movie in a primitive culture?" asked Barrymore. "It's amazing—no matter where in the world you go, there is a certain reaction universal to the taking of photographs. Eskimos, pygmies, South Sea islanders, nomadic desert tribes—they all have the same belief. They are convinced that being photographed steals one's soul. Isn't that interesting?"

"Who cares?"

"But what if they're right? Think about what we've seen in this lousy business. Think about Fatty Arbuckle, destroyed because of carnal appetite. Or poor Wallie Reid, killed by dope. Are you listening, Mitch?"

"I'm listening. But so what? They screwed up their own lives, that's all."

"Mitch, what if the savages are right? What if a camera *does* steal your soul through its lens? Suppose that once you've been captured on film, the body has no restraint on its animal appetites because it's only a godless, soulless beast?"

"Jack," Mitch said, buttoning his clean shirt, "if you're going to talk philosophy, I'll send in Groucho Marx. He'll fix your wagon."

Barrymore looked up at him.

"Where are you going?"

"I have a date with a lady."

"Ah. She of the lion cage?"

"You figure it out."

"But I thought you felt nearly certain you've got a deal with Hearst and Marion Davies."

"Maybe this is just a pleasure trip."

Sadly, Barrymore shook his head.

"Not you, Mitch. Well, why not? Go ahead, my friend, copper your bet. If anyone asks for you, I'll swear you're locked in the bathroom."

"Good night, Jack."

"Good night, Mitch," said Barrymore. And, as Mitch closed the door, he added, "Happy birthday."

PART TWO

Above the Line

"Where but in Hollywood have you seen so many unhappy people earning two thousand dollars a week?"

—JOHN BARRYMORE,
to Mitch Gardner

6

Prince Michael Romanoff was no prince. Nor was his name Michael. He had, nonetheless, become a highly successful restaurateur in Beverly Hills, catering to the film trade and enjoying every minute of it.

Mitch Gardner sat at his regular table. He was waiting for Marion Davies. It had been more than three weeks since the party at the Castle, and he still did not have a firm commitment from Hearst. Mitch was running out of time. If winter set in at his location site high in the mountains, the project would be dead for an entire year.

Romanoff came over.

"Stop suffering, Mitch. Have a drink on me."

"Only if you join me."

Romanoff looked around. The restaurant was almost empty. Still, he hesitated. His Imperial Highness, the Prince Michael Alexandrovitch Dmitri Obolensky Romanoff, rarely sat down with a customer.

"Come on," said Mitch. "Plant your ass."

Romanoff sighed and lowered himself into a chair. A waiter rushed over.

"Brandy," said Romanoff. "The *good* brandy, not the swill we serve these commoners." He smiled at Mitch. "Cheer up, my friend. You will find your front money."

"I'm starting to wonder. Maybe I've got bad breath."

"Mitch," said Romanoff, "you know I am your friend."

"I know you are, Mike. And you're getting ready to tell me something even my best friend won't tell me, right?"

Romanoff sighed. His face was serious. His heavy nose and shaggy brows projected an image of classic tragedy.

"The word has gone out, Mitch. You are playing both ends against the middle. You cannot give Marion Davies and Vivien Leigh the same role."

"I haven't given it to either one of them. Viv's a bankable box-office name. Marion's got Hearst. The one who shows up first with half a million bucks gets to climb a mountain with me."

"But, please, Mitch, be discreet! You cannot afford to make more enemies. Nor can you afford to laugh behind the backs of those who help you. George S. Kaufman and Dorothy Parker can get away with it because they were very successful before coming out here. But what is your record? Two Broadway plays that didn't run. Film credits—good ones, but now you seem to disown them. What else? Your father's name. It has protected you more often than you know."

"Leave my father out of this."

Romanoff got up.

"Customers are coming in," he said. Then, "Mitch—please be careful."

Mitch stared down at his brandy. The mention of his father had conjured up his anger and frustration at the last meeting with Hearst, the previous week.

"Mr. Gardner," Hearst had said, "I have by no means lost interest in your project. But these things take time. Were I to become involved, would you mind working through Warner Bros.?"

"Not at all," Mitch said. "Do you mean you'd be putting up the financing and renting Warner's facilities?"

"No," said Hearst. "I intend, if we go through with this, merely to guarantee Jack Warner negative costs. I will not put up a single dollar. I will, however, be in the position of indemnifying Warners. Do you see the difference?"

"Certainly. You'll be operating on Warner's money, yet you bond the studio against out-of-pocket expenses. Neither one of you loses."

"*Unless,*" Hearst said, "your picture is a failure."

"There's always that chance," said Mitch.

"A larger chance than usual, wouldn't you say? Since this is your maiden effort as a director, and since you have no completed shooting script?"

"I've written most of the script," Mitch said. "And we both agree Miss Davies' name on the credits will automatically give *Donner Pass* 'A' picture prestige even though nobody's ever heard of me."

"To be candid, Marion's last few pictures did not do well at the box office. One of her largest followings has always been in Europe, and the troubled conditions there are closing that market to American films."

"Well, if we work with Warners, we'll be able to get Errol Flynn. He's box office right now."

"No!" Hearst almost shouted. "I will not have that man on the same screen with my Marion."

"Why?"

"Don't press me. To be frank, there's only one actor I would accept in the role of George Donner."

"Who?"

"Your father. Charles Gardner."

Mitch choked.

"My *father?*"

"Your father. Sign him, and I think I can promise you we have a deal."

"Dad's over sixty, you know."

"So was George Donner."

"But audiences want a younger leading man. They won't accept a grandfather as the husband of—"

He stopped. Hearst smiled.

"Yes, Mitch," he said, using Mitch's given name for the first time. "Charlie Gardner is a fine actor. He'll be able to play younger than his actual age. But no matter how young he plays—"

"Marion will always look younger."

"I think we understand each other perfectly," Hearst said.

"It might work," Mitch said slowly. "Only thing, Dad's tied up in a run-of-the-play contract back East."

"We'll buy out the contract. Or, rather, Jack Warner will."

"I don't know if Dad will consent to doing films again."

"That's your problem, Mitch. Solve it."

"Miss Davies." Mike Romanoff's voice brought Mitch out of his reverie. He looked up and saw Marion at the rope; Mike opened it and brought her over. Mitch rose.

As she kissed his cheek, Marion said, 'Sorry to be l-l-late, darling."

"I just got here," he lied.

"Will you be having lunch, Miss Davies?" asked Romanoff.

"Just a martini," she said. When he had gone, she turned to Mitch. "I almost didn't c-c-come at all." By now, her stammer was so much a part of her that Mitch did not even notice it.

"Why not?"

"Hedda called me. What are you and V-v-v—that *Leigh* person —up to?"

Mitch controlled an impulse to gag and forced a smile instead.

"Same old hanky-panky," he said. "You know, boy-girl."

"With Larry in town? I d-d-don't believe you."

Mitch managed to turn his smile into a smirk.

"Goldwyn's keeping him pretty busy." He squeezed her hand. "Jealous?"

"As a matter of f-f-fact, yes!"

He stared at her.

"Marion, believe me, I—"

"—Never dreamed the f-f-fairy princess slept around?" She laughed harshly. "Maybe yes, maybe no."

"I'll be damned," he said.

She dug her fingernails into his wrist.

"Mitch, don't lie to me. Do you *really* want me to play Tamsen Donner?"

"Where the hell did that come from? Of course I do! What makes you think otherwise?"

She tossed her tightly curled blond hair, crisp with some preparation that smelled of banana oil.

"Look at me," she commanded.

"I'm looking," he said. "And I like what I see."

"Mitch, I'm f-f-forty years old." (He repressed a smile—she had shaved four years off!) "I'm starting to sag. My v-v-voice sounds like a crow. Who are we k-k-kidding?" She gave him a wan smile that had been practiced before a thousand makeup mirrors. "Maybe you'd be b-b-better off with your l-l-little English muffin."

"Now you be quiet and listen to me," Mitch said, knowing that he had to talk fast and very convincingly. "It doesn't matter what *age* Tamsen Donner is. In a sense, her courage and inner beauty is ageless. Add to that the outer beauty and, more important, dramatic artistry only you can bring to the role, and we're talking Oscar time, Marion. It's *you* I need, not some snip of a girl who's never lived, never suffered, never learned compassion. We've got to show this Midwestern schoolmarm turning into a tough, self-reliant pioneer woman, right before our eyes. You think Claire Trevor was tough in *Stagecoach*? Wait until they see your Tamsen! Marion, they'll knock down your door with script offers."

She stared down into her martini.

"Then it's really *me* you want. Not just Bill's m-m-money."

The gagging sensation rose in Mitch's throat again.

"Of course, it's you I want."

"That's good," she said. "Because Bill is b-b-broke."

Mitch forced a laugh.

"Hearst, broke? With a private train? A forty-million-dollar castle perched on fifty straight miles of the most valuable coastline in the world? Art treasures that—"

"Yes. All that is *why* he's broke. Bill's a compulsive c-c-collector. That's his problem."

She held up her empty glass and the waiter nodded. To Mitch, she whispered, "And t-t-this is mine." She rubbed her finger around the lip of the glass. "Bill's after me all the time to t-t-take the cure. But what good would that do? You can't cure a disease by putting a b-b-bandage on its sores. Liquor is merely my s-s-sore. The d-d-disease is something else. Call me courtesan, mistress, w-w-whore—call me anything you want, but never call me w-w-wife."

Mitch looked down at the table.

"You could force him to marry you, Marion."

"How? Mitch, he's almost eighty y-y-years old. For him, the world has s-s-stopped. Some young actor from RKO was up last w-w-week, and he told me, 'It seems as if Mr. Hearst does not like the world he is in, so he has created his own.' And he *has,* Mitch. San Simeon is like no other p-p-place on earth."

Impressed, Mitch asked, "Who was the actor?"

"The boy who did that Men from Mars scare show on radio, Orson Welles."

"Still, you ought to have some financial protection, Marion. No man is immortal."

She spread her slender hands.

"I'm protected. I own real estate. The Santa Monica beach place is in my name."

Mitch whistled. The "beach place" in question had ninety-six rooms and was reportedly worth more than seven million dollars.

"Back to Hearst, then. I guess what you mean is that he's land poor. His holdings are enormous, but there's a shortage of ready cash."

"Yes. You know, the b-b-banks made him put some of his art objects up for s-s-sale." She giggled. "He was furious. Things were so bad, I even had to l-l-lend him some money."

"How much?"

"A million dollars," she said, without a trace of stammer.

"I didn't know things were ever that tight for Hearst," Mitch said.

"Our l-l-luck started sliding in 1936," she said. "That was the year Bernard Shaw, who had absolutely p-p-promised me the film version of *Pygmalion,* gave it to Wendy Hiller. And Bill's c-c-creditors started closing in. The Canadians began the run, threatening to foreclose on notes Bill had signed for newsprint. Then they c-c-came from all sides, waving their obscene little writs. Bill came to me and said, 'They won't give me time to liquidate. I guess I'm through.' I offered to lend him some money, which was more than his legal w-w-wife Millicent ever did. I sold property, and I b-b-borrowed, and I came up with a m-m-million dollars. When I gave the check to Bill, he told me, 'I won't take it! And he was c-c-crying. So I gave it to Thomas Justin White, who was Bill's general manager then. Tom was g-g-grateful, but the other Hearst executives looked daggers through me. I knew then that they were wolves, gathered for the k-k-kill and the feast." She sipped her new martini. "It was a revelation, who came to k-k-kill, and who came to help. Cissy Patterson, a business enemy in direct competition—she owned the New York *Daily News* and the Chicago *Tribune*—lent Bill another million and didn't even w-w-want to take any interest. And there were others, unexpected friends. I don't know how we did it, but somehow we s-s-saved him."

"Yet he's still broke?"

"Poor Mitch. Does that change your plans about me?"

"Of course not," he said, his mind racing. "I'll just have to find the money somewhere else."

"Maybe I could throw a p-p-party. Invite the ones who have money to invest."

"It's an idea." Mitch studied the napkin, where his glass had left dark rings. "I just can't understand Hearst promising me—well, nearly promising me—that if I got my father to play George Donner we'd have a deal."

"Promise?" she said sharply. "When did he do that?"

He related his last conversation with Hearst. She listened without speaking. When he was finished, she said slowly, "Mitch, Bill does not l-l-lie. I don't know where he plans to get the m-m-money, but if that's what he told you, he would never go back on his w-w-word. I think if you sign your f-f-father, he'll get the m-m-money somewhere. Maybe he'll s-s-sell another radio station. He hates them anyway. There's nothing on them now but news of that awful w-w-war in Europe."

The pressure in Mitch's chest lessened.

"Well, I'm glad to hear that. It's a good thing we had this talk."

"Isn't it? Now all you have to do is c-c-convince Charlie Gardner to come back to Hollywood."

"That's all," Mitch said, waving for another drink.

Mitch sat drinking alone for more than an hour after Marion had left.

Hearst broke! Now all he had to go on was Marion's conviction that the old man wouldn't have strung him along with his condition about signing Charles Gardner unless he had some possibility of raising the backing.

He looked up, caught Romanoff's eye, and signaled for another drink. Slowly, Mike shook his head. No.

Indignantly, Mitch shouted, "Waiter! Check!"

The waiter came over, bowed.

"You're the guest of the Prince, Mr. Gardner."

Mitch stood, weaving slightly, and threw a twenty-dollar bill on the table.

"Buy yourself a starlet," he said, heading toward the front door.

The parking attendant was not at his post. Mitch looked around.

"Hey!" he yelled. "I want my car."

From the parking lot, he heard a voice shout an answer: "So do I, and this wop bastard won't give it to me!"

Mitch went over

"Spence? Is that you?"

"No," growled Spencer Tracy, "I'm George M. Cohan. Who the hell do you think it is? Listen, Mitch, talk to this cretin, will you? Make him give me my car."

"Mr. Gardner," said the attendant, "he's in no condition to drive. I tried to call a cab, but he won't hear of it."

"Did you hear the man?" said Mitch. "He says you're sloshed, Spence."

"He's right.But what does that have to do with it?"

"Well, I think Sam's right. Take a cab home and pick up your car tomorrow."

Tracy bristled. "Listen, I'm on my way to a very important poker game. I can't drive up in a goddamned *cab*. They'd think I was intoxishated."

Mitch took Tracy's arm.

"Well?"

Tracy relaxed and laughed.

"By God, I suppose I am." He pulled out a wad of money and shoved it toward the parking attendant. "All right, Sam. You saved my life again. Take this."

The attendant drew back.

"It's all right, Mr. Tracy. That's not necessary."

"Mitch, make him take some money. Hell, it's all we've got."

The parking attendant spread his hands in a helpless gesture. Mitch took the wad of money from Tracy, separated a five-dollar bill from the rest, and gave it to the attendant. He shoved the remaining money back in Tracy's jacket pocket.

"Come on," he said. "I'll take you to your game. Where is it?"

Tracy shook his head.

"You don't want to go there, believe me. I'll take a cab."

"The address?" said Mitch, opening the door of his old 1931 Cord and helping Tracy in.

"All right," said the actor. "Selznick's place. Listen, pal, I know you two are on the outs. You'd better let me—"

Mitch got behind the wheel.

"It's okay, Spence. This horseshit has gone on long enough. I'm not mad at David."

Tracy laughed, snorting happily. "That may be, kid, but he's sure as hell mad at *you!*"

"So I'll grovel," said Mitch, starting the Cord.

"I believe you know Ben Hecht," said David O. Selznick, introducing Mitch to the players around the green card table in the game room of his Beverly Hills home.

"Hell, yes," said Mitch.

"You know Jack Barrymore," said Selznick. "And, of course, you and Scott are old friends."

Mitch shook John Barrymore's hand and grinned down at F. Scott Fitzgerald.

"Hi, Scotty. I didn't expect to find you here."

Fitzgerald stared into the glass of Coke before him.

"David and I were ... ah ... talking about a new film project."

"Great." Mitch turned to his host. "Jesus, David, I've been trying to get you over into a corner to apologize for being such a horse's ass, but you wouldn't catch on. So here's my public apology. I am a shit, and deserve every lump you ever gave me. Only don't take it out on Scott, because he really didn't think I'd go as far as I did. Trot out the guy with the black mask and the cat-o'-nine-tails. I've got it coming."

David Selznick stood transfixed for a moment, then collapsed into the nearest chair, choking with laughter.

"David," said Mitch, alarmed. "Are you all right?"

"You bastard! Don't you ever do anything in a low key? Couldn't you just have sent a note around?"

"Hell, no. When I sin in public, I repent in public too."

"Repentance accepted," said Selznick. "It's good to see you."

John Barrymore had been staring at them, fascinated.

"I confess to confusion," he said. "What heinous crime precipitated this love fest?"

"Jack!" said Selznick. "Are you the only person on the West Coast who doesn't know what Gardner and Fitzgerald did to me?"

"Whatever it was," said Barrymore, "I pray it was painful."

"There was pain enough," said Selznick. "We were right in the middle of shooting *Gone with the Wind*. My director, Victor Fleming, had a nervous breakdown on me, and I had to bring Sam Wood in to cover. The banks didn't want to advance any more money, and the flood waters were rising. Cut to the comedians, these two bastards! I don't know how they did it, but somehow they managed to get a substitute page inserted into the master script I'd given Wood, and they got Vivien Leigh and Leslie Howard to go along with the gag. So Sam shot the goddamned scene!"

Barrymore sipped his own drink, which was obviously not Coke.

"*What* scene, O Mighty One?"

"The one in which Ashley, just back from the Civil War, confesses to Scarlett that he's been, well, emasculated."

"You mean . . ."

Selznick nodded. "They even used dialogue right out of *The Sun Also Rises*. I've never been convinced," he added, thoughtfully, "that Hemingway wasn't mixed up in it too."

Mitch crossed his arms over his chest.

"My lips are sealed."

Selznick shook his head.

"How the hell did Wood fall for it? Why didn't he check with me? My God, I can still remember the scene word for word. Scarlett says, 'Ashley, when I think of the hell I've put chaps through. But I'm paying for it all now.' " Selznick laughed bitterly. " 'Chaps!' I don't know how she could say it, in that sweet Southern accent, without breaking up. And Ashley comes back with, 'Well, it was a rotten way to be wounded.' And all the time, Vivien's groping Leslie off camera and whispering, 'There's something *missing* between us!' And some no-good bastard cut it into the rough sequence, and nobody warned me, and I nearly had my coronary right there in the screening room." He glared at Mitch Gardner. "The hell with you, Gardner! Now that I think of it, I *don't* forgive you! It was too rotten a trick. Besides which, it cost money."

"Raw stock and work print is all," said Mitch, taking out his wallet. "Sam wasn't ready to shoot anything else that day anyway. I figure it comes out to around three hundred bucks. Here."

Selznick picked up the money.

"Maybe you thought I wouldn't take this, but if so, you were wrong."

Mitch shook his head.

"I never doubted for a moment that you'd take it, David. Are we square?"

"Square," said the producer.

Mitch looked around.

"Where the hell is Spence?"

"Out in the kitchen, drinking black coffee. Do you want some?"

"I want a drink—scotch, if you've got it."

Selznick nodded to the waiting butler, who began mixing Mitch a drink.

"Film is the last refuge of the practical joker," said John Barrymore. He finished his own drink and handed it to the butler. Then he struck a wooden kitchen match, blew it out, and put the smoking end into his mouth.

Ben Hecht said, "What the hell did you do that for?"

"It kills the odor of the spirits," said Barrymore. "That can be important when you intend to speak to an abstemious producer later in the day."

"May be," said Hecht, "but it makes you smell like a charcoal grill."

"In this inferno," said Barrymore, "perhaps that is merely protective coloration." He leaned back. "Speaking of film jokes—"

"Let's not," said Selznick. "You geniuses don't care how much time and money you waste for a producer. Let's play cards."

He nodded at the butler. "Tell Mr. Tracy we're ready."

"David," said Fitzgerald, "Could I have another Coke?"

"Right away." Selznick nodded at the butler. "How can you drink those God-awful things, Scott? I'm surprised you don't have diabetes." He looked around at the other men. "When Scott comes to the office, he's got a whole briefcaseful of them."

"They help me think." Fitzgerald coughed. "Besides, I can use the energy. I'm afraid my T.B. might be acting up again."

"Well, cough on someone else," Hecht said, moving his chair away. "Who the hell do you think you are, Edgar Allan Poe?"

"I think," Fitzgerald said softly, "that in a previous incarnation I might have been Sotto Voce."

"So that's your private image of yourself," said Hecht. "The small, still voice under the breath who describes what's happening on the other side of the wall?"

"It's not such a bad role," said Mitch. "Where do you place yourself, Ben?"

"I'm the annoying gadfly, buzzing in your ear and biting you on the ass when you become too self-satisfied," said Hecht.

"Try biting me on the ass," said Spencer Tracy, entering from the kitchen with a steaming cup of coffee in one hand, "and you'll get gangrene of the tooth. Hello, Scotty. Jack. What the hell is this,

David, old retainers' night? Everybody here except me has been fired at least twice by Selznick International."

"I've got a short memory," said Selznick. "I'm trying to hire them all over again. But first I've got to win back some of my money."

Tracy sat down between Ben Hecht and Scott Fitzgerald.

"How much dough can you afford to lose, Scotty?"

Fitzgerald shifted uneasily in his chair.

"Well," he said, "I just got a five-hundred-dollar check from *Esquire.*"

"Two hundred bucks," said Tracy. "That's the table stakes, boys."

"Wait a minute," said Selznick. "Nobody's trying to buy pots from Scotty, but—"

"Let's not let ourselves be tempted," said Tracy. "Poker is a lousy business. My old grandpappy told me that thousand-dollar-a-week screenwriters should never play pot limit with ten-thousand-dollar-a-week producers unless they want a fast ticket to the poorhouse. What the hell, boys, we don't play just to win money, do we? So let's each put two hundred bucks on the table and keep the pots down to where nobody gets short of breath."

Selznick studied Spencer Tracy. The actor was not smiling. Selznick shrugged.

"Two hundred bucks' table stakes it is," he said, taking out two of the three bills Mitch Gardner had just given him.

Spencer Tracy shuffled the cards.

"Gentlemen," he said, "The name of this game is five-card stud."

7

"That no-good bastard!" said Mitch.

Fitzgerald, who had come out to the Selznick parking lot with him, asked, "Who?"

"That fucking Spencer Tracy, that's who! He stole my car!"

Fitzgerald laughed. "I wondered why he sneaked out early. I thought it was because he was winning. Where's *his* car?"

"The attendant at Romanoff's wouldn't let him have it. Spence was snockered."

"Let me give you a lift," said Fitzgerald. "I've got the old Ford here."

"Aren't you driving out toward Malibu?"

"Not anymore. We're over in the valley now. Are you still staying at the Garden of Allah?"

"Where else? The rent's high, but you get it back in free drinks with Bob Benchley and his buddies from New York."

They got into Fitzgerald's ancient Ford and started toward Hollywood. At no time did Scott drive more than twenty miles an hour. He noticed Mitch's impatience.

"I'm sorry, Mitch," he said plaintively. "I'm actually scared to drive any faster. It's in my head, I know. When Sheilo's driving, I give her hell if she gets over thirty. It's the old hypochondria, I guess. The cabinet's overflowing with pills again. I'm Schwab's best customer."

"You don't really have T.B., do you, Scott?"

"No," said Fitzgerald, after a long pause. "Sheilah and Scottie think I'm on the wagon, and most of the time I am, but when I go off,

I go off like a rocket to the moon, and it's easier to get out the old temperature chart and the X-ray reports and let T.B. take the blame instead of the sauce."

"Beautiful. Here we are, two old lushes . . ."

"You're not that old," said Fitzgerald.

"And you're ancient? You've got three whole years on me. I suppose that makes you one of the village elders. Scotty, what the hell is it? I'm fairly successful. You're one of the great writers of our time. Why do we deliberately poison ourselves?"

"I peaked early. What I'm doing now is the last effort of a man who once did something finer and better."

"Bull," said Mitch. "You've got a lot of mileage left. You're just beginning."

"Thanks, but no thanks," said Fitzgerald. "But *you're* just beginning, Mitch. You didn't peak too soon. You're one of the new renaissance men. You aren't simply a writer, or an actor, or a director, or, God curse them, a producer. You can achieve the whole thing. I can't. Ben can't. Neither can Spencer, nor, despite his high opinion of himself, can David. But men like you, and that kid from New York, Orson Welles, and wild guys like John Huston, you young Turks can bring films to their ultimate promise. I just hope I'm around to bum a job from you."

"You're depressing me," said Mitch. "The last thing I want is to be compared to a pile of ego like Orson Welles."

"One day you may eat those words," said Fitzgerald.

"Hey," said Mitch. "Why don't we do it? You and me, cut loose from this rotten town and its army of *nephews,* and go out on our own. We're two of a kind, we could cut it together! Where's the law that says films have to be made by the Pacific? We can shoot in New York, or Miami—London, for Christ's sake."

"Small matter of a war in London."

"Details!" Mitch shouted. "What do you say?"

"You're five years too late," Fitzgerald said. "The saps's all run out. I'm distilling down what's left, hoping to get one more serving, but there's nothing after that."

"God damn it, Scotty, if this is what drinking Cokes does to you, maybe you *ought* to get drunk! Better still, let's go get laid."

Fitzgerald laughed softly.

"Even that's vanishing," he said.

"Watch out!" yelled Mitch.

Fitzgerald hit the brakes. A man was walking down the shadowy middle of Sunset Boulevard.

"Jack!" called Mitch. "What the hell are you doing in the road?"

John Barrymore came over and put his foot on the running board.

"Your writing compatriot, Mr. Ben Hecht, turned me out like a cur when he learned that I intended to visit a local sporting house before returning to the sanctuary of Beverly Hills."

"That doesn't sound like Ben," said Mitch. "I thought he had a warm spot in his heart for such establishments."

"Not," said Barrymore "when he learned that I expected him to pick up the check."

"But Ben just dumped you on a street corner? I find that hard to believe."

Barrymore got into the car, tapping his breast pocket. "He was kind enough to present me with five dollars for a taxi."

"You shouldn't walk in the road," Fitzgerald said nervously. "You could get killed that way."

"Young man," Barrymore said seriously, "I was not born to be struck down by one of man's insolent chariots. It is written in my palm that my downfall will be due to toddy."

"Due to *what?*" asked Mitch.

"Halt!" cried Barrymore. "Observe, there! A watering place in the neon wilderness. Let us quaff deeply and wash the stench from our souls."

"That sounds like a good idea," said Fitzgerald. He pulled into the Hotel Roosevelt's parking lot. "I'm buying. I won tonight."

They found a table behind a huge potted rubber plant and when the waitress came over, Barrymore declaimed, "The fair Helen! Is this the face that launched a thousand launches? This vision of delight in blue cotton and frilly apron?" He put his hand on her waist. "Your place or mine?"

"Your order, gentlemen?" she said unperturbed.

"We crave the nectar of love's sweet potion," said Barrymore. "A loaf of bread, a jug of wine, and thou beside me fucking in the wilderness."

"Not so loud, honey," she said. "You know what the boss said about that kind of talk last time."

"We'll have martinis," declared Fitzgerald. "Cold and frosty in frozen glasses, with an olive *and* an onion."

"Listen, Scott," said Mitch. "Maybe this isn't such a good idea."

"It's the best idea I've have all day," said the writer. "It's a much better idea than the one I was trying to peddle to David, who, incidentally, wasn't buying. What the hell, where's the point? I get in trouble if I'm good, and I get in trouble if I'm bad, so I might as well have the fun of being bad."

"You said it, buster." The waitress plucked Barrymore's hand from her waist, like an unwanted appendage that had somehow grown there, and dropped it onto the table.

"I have a theory about martinis with both an olive and an onion," said Fitzgerald, his eyes glittering. "The liquid and the gin-soaked olive, they're illusion. The onion is reality."

"In toddy there is truth," agreed Barrymore. "*In vino veritas.* Did I ever tell you, old sport, how I opened my London *Hamlet* whilst soused to the eyeballs?"

"Were you really?" asked Fitzgerald, fascinated.

"I was completely shitfaced," said Barrymore. "It was the conclusion of a long, full day of whoopee and toddy. The curtain was run up half an hour late, and I don't even remember going on. But, during the 'rogue and peasant slave' soliloquy, I found myself unable to remain perpendicular. I lowered myself onto a prop wall and sat there, my head exploding in my cupped hands, and dangled my legs in an attempt to get the blood back into them. Otherwise, I feared, I would inundate the first three rows of spectators in a sea of puke. As a matter of fact, later in the evening, I *was* forced to scuttle offstage to barf in the wings."

"The critics must have crucified you," said Mitch.

"On the contrary," said Barrymore, "they wrote at length of my unusual 'leg-dangling' as if it somehow transformed the dreary scene. One even commended my sudden dash offstage, 'returning with ashen face,' as a great underscoring of Hamlet's inner torture. Do you wonder, old friends, why I laugh at acting as a profession when I can puke my way through a performance and have the critics dancing in the streets? To be an actor is to be the garbage man of the arts. Where but in Hollywood have you seen so many unhappy people earning two thousand dollars a week?"

"Crap," said Mitch Gardner. "I saw your *Hamlet* in New York.

Even if you weren't at your best in London, you already had a hundred Stateside performances under your belt. You must have carried on from instinct. If it were as easy as you say, everybody would be doing it."

"But they are, my dear boy," said Barrymore. "They *are.*"

A second round of drinks materialized. Fitzgerald lifted his.

"To Dos and may his bedpan overflow with those eternal memos he writes."

"Hear, hear," said Barrymore, sipping.

"What does the 'O' stand for?" asked Mitch.

Fitzgerald giggled. "You must be kidding."

"Am I supposed to know something I don't?"

Fitzgerald smiled, placing one finger along his nose. "Nize baby, et up all the 'O's'."

"Come on, Scotty. I'm serious. I honestly don't know the man's middle name."

Fitzgerald put down this drink.

"All right," he said, "but it's obvious your education has been neglected. I shall correct that. Imagine a doting father who provides his seventeen-year-old son with an allowance of seven hundred and fifty dollars a week and advises him, 'Spend it all. Throw it away, give it away, but get rid of it. Never try to save money, or you'll have two things to worry about—making and keeping it. Just worry about making it. The rest will take care of itself.' "

"Lewis Selznick?" said Mitch.

Fitzgerald nodded. "Lewis *J.* Selznick. One of the giants, along with Louis *B.* Mayer, Nicholas *M.* Schenck, Cecil *B.* de Mille."

Mitch laughed. "I get it. The old bastard didn't give David a middle name!"

"Not a trace. And that bone has always choked David. Even as a boy, he knew he was going to be a great movie producer. And every great producer he'd heard of had a middle initial. So, as he does with every major problem, David sat down to a sheet of memo paper and began writing out signatures. 'David A. Selznick . . . David B. Selznick . . . David C. Selznick . . .' "

"All the way to 'O'?" said Mitch. "I don't believe it."

"Ask him. He's proud of it. He liked the sound the 'O' made between David and Selznick. And that lucky fool, don't you realize what he got as an extra bonus? Half the movie-going population of the world thinks he's David O'Selznick, that great Irish film-maker!"

Barrymore finished his drink.

"Life is earnest, life is real, and O'Selznick is not the goal. Children, my dear children." He laughed and stood up, weaving. "Do not allow me to deter you from your revels. But I am off to see the fair Miss Polly and get me ashes hauled."

He lurched toward the door, almost colliding with the waitress, who was returning with another round of drinks. She looked after him, a sad smile twitching at her lips.

"He's all talk," she said, trying to explain something as much to herself as to Scott and Mitch. "He plays around with all the girls like he's Casanova, and then one night I went out with him and he drove me to Griffith Park and we drank wine and he quoted poetry to me most of the night. Poetry. Geez!" She put the drinks down. "These are on the boss. He's a real fan of Mr. Barrymore's."

"Thank the boss," said Mitch, "and ask him if he's ever heard of that great Irish producer David O'Selznick."

She laughed nervously and went back to her station. Fitzgerald sipped at his second drink.

"Don't let it slip away, Mitch," he said softly. "I had it all, and somehow it got away from me. What the hell am I doing here, scrambling for pickup jobs? Mitch, I'm *good*. So why do I have to kowtow to these instant geniuses who have never even read a book, except in a two-page outline written by their secretaries?"

"Take the money, Scott. Laugh all the way to the bank."

Fitzgerald reached across the table and caught him by both lapels.

"Mitch, get out of this town! Right now! To hell with the money. You've got a real talent, but you'll kill it here!"

"Come on, Scotty," said Mitch, pulling away. "I'm not being held in bondage. I went into this business with my eyes open."

"But you've been drugged, don't you see that? Your senses are being destroyed with big money and easy living. They don't care anything about letting you do your *best!* They're out to force you into doing your *worst.*"

"People are looking," said Mitch, embarrassed.

Fitzgerald leaped up.

"Go ahead, look!" he shouted. "My name is Scott Fitzgerald! I have been called the spokesman of my generation. I gave Ernest Hemingway his start. So how dare you treat my talent like an unwanted scrap of paper? It's not enough to dictate memos. It's not enough to move armies of extras back and forth like toy soldiers. You've got to *feel*, you've got to have *respect* for what has gone before."

"Please, Scott," said Mitch. "Sit down."

His friend's hand on his arm, Fitzgerald slumped back into his chair. The waitress came over and whispered. "Mister, you can't yell like that in here. The boss, he got real upset. I told him you were a friend of Mr. Barrymore's and he said okay, but you can't do it no more."

Wanly, Fitzgerald smiled up at her.

"I'm sorry. Tell your boss I won't cause any more trouble."

"I already did. But I don't think you ought to have any more of these things, you know what I mean?"

"Nize baby," whispered Fitzgerald. "Et up all the martinis."

The waitress stared down at him. Mitch handed her a crumpled bill and jerked his head toward the door. She nodded and left.

An old man wearing a shaggy Western vest and a white sombrero came over.

"L.A. *Times*, folks?"

Mitch shook his head, but Fitzgerald dug into his pocket and gave the old man a dollar for a newspaper. He waved away the change.

"Keep it, keep it."

"I've got the girl calling a cab," Mitch said as the old man shuffled away. "I'll bring your car in the morning."

Fitzgerald leaned forward, examining the newspaper. Mitch touched his arm.

"Scotty? Did you hear me?"

"Look at this!" said Fitzgerald. "Why is the writer always the last to know?" He jabbed his finger at a small advertisement on the theatrical page. "The Pasadena Playhouse is premiering a new play based on F. Scott Fitzgerald's short story, 'A Diamond as Big as the Ritz.' And they never even notified me!" He looked around. "Where's that waitress? Miss?"

She came over. "We'll have your cab in a few minutes—"

"Never mind that. I want a phone. A telephone."

She went to get one.

"This could be it, you know," said Fitzgerald. "It doesn't take much to make a writer hot again. If the play is a hit and the right producer sees it, I might be able to do something really good. Mitch, I can do it."

He pushed his martini back on the table.

"You watch, Mitch. One real break and . . ."

The telephone came and was plugged in. While Fitzgerald dialed, Mitch made writing motions in the air and the waitress went to fetch the check.

"Hello?" Fitzgerald said. "Honey? No. No, we're not there anymore. But I won." He paused. "No, I'm afraid he didn't like the story. What I meant to say was that I won fifty dollars at poker . . . Listen, I've got great news. The Pasadena Playhouse is premiering a play of mine tomorrow. Well, not *my* play exactly, but one based on one of my stories. Call Anton and hire us a Caddy and a chauffeur. No, you know we can't go in the Ford. I'll go black tie, and you can wear the new gray and red gown, and the silver fox. And we'll dine afterward at Chasen's. No, dear, I am *not* being extravagant. The major producers will probably be there, and we've got to put on a show." He winked at Mitch. "Yes. Yes, I heard you. I do *too*, but I can't talk, I'm in a restaurant. Oh? Well, Mitch Gardner's here. Jack was too, but . . ."

Slowly, he drew the receiver away from his ear.

"She hung up," he said.

Dorothy Parker adjusted one of her stockings. Mitch glanced at his watch.

"Come on, Dottie. We're going to be late."

"Curtains never go up on time," she said calmly. "Will you hand me my belt?"

"I should have met you at the theatre. What the hell am I doing acting as your dresser? I don't need any more angry confrontations with jealous husbands."

"There won't be any. Allan's staying at the Roosevelt. Listen, Mitch, are you sure about this whole thing? I listened around the studio today, and there wasn't any noise about the bigwigs going to a premiere tonight."

"I saw the ad in the paper myself. Aren't you ready yet? I've got a taxi meter running outside."

"Where's your Cord?"

"Spence stole it last night. I hope it blew up in his face on the corner of Wilshire and La Brea, so he had a long way to walk."

"Oh, hell, nothing helps," she said, studying herself in the mirror. "I suppose I'm as ready as ever."

In the cab, she moved closer to him and said, "I hope the play's good. The poor bastard needs it."

"He was as excited as a kid," said Mitch. "If nothing else, it's lifted his spirits a thousand per cent."

"I hope so. You might not have noticed, Mitch, because you never had a sensitive bone in your body. But when Scott was over at MGM with the rest of us—Anita Loos and Perelman and Ogden Nash—he'd come tippy-toeing past our offices like a little mouse, and sometimes he'd tap on the door, but when he opened it, he wouldn't come in. I'd say, 'Park her there, pal,' and Scott would shake his head and mumble, 'No, you're just being nice. You don't really want to talk with me.' and nothing you'd say would get it out of his head that he was intruding. This, from the same Scotty who used to throw his hat over the transom into an editor's office and barge in like he owned the joint." The tiny writer shook her head. "Hollywood took the guts out of him."

She fumbled in her purse and took out a silver flask.

"Want a nip?"

"Later. What are we drinking?"

"The finest scotch. I went to a party last night at John Huston's. When he wasn't looking, I filled my little life preserver." She laughed. "John's a dear, and if you don't watch your hat and coat, he's going to beat you out with his Dashiell Hammett film, and become the first writer-director in recent memory."

"I know," said Mitch. "There are enemies all around me, my flank is turned, and I am out of ammunition. So I shall attack."

She patted his leg.

"You do that."

As the taxi pulled up in front of the Pasadena Playhouse, Mitch leaned forward.

"That's funny," he said. "The marquee lights aren't on." He tapped the driver on the shoulder. "Park here."

The taxi pulled over to the curb.

"What time is it?" asked Dorothy.

"Eight fifteen. Curtain's at eight thirty. Dottie, there's something wrong." He slipped out of the cab. "You wait here. I'll check this out."

"I'll go with you."

"No. If there's some kind of a mess, Scott wouldn't want you to see it."

She sat back. "You're right. But hurry."

He crossed the street and entered the building. He was gone for a few minutes, then reappeared and hurried over.

Getting back in the taxi, he said, "Get us out of here."

"What's wrong?"

Mitch stared back through the rear window.

"I guess we didn't look at that ad close enough," he said finally. "It's not the Pasadena Playhouse presenting Scott's play, but only their undergraduate student workship. They don't even get to use the main theatre. They're upstairs in a loft, full of wooden benches. The kid at the door was all excited when I went in. 'Do you know who's up there, mister? F. Scott Fitzgerald! We all thought he was dead!' I sneaked up, and there they were, Scott and Sheilah. She's all gussied up in a beautiful gown and a silver fox jacket, and Scott's dressed to the nines in a full tux. Sitting on those goddamned benches, in a rear of a loft, with maybe a dozen kids in slacks and sweaters making up the rest of the audience."

"Oh, no!"

"He's playing it true blue all the way. When I came out, the kid on the door told me that Scott's sent word to the cast that he'll come backstage and talk to them after the performance. Just as if he knew all along what was going on."

Dorothy Parker leaned against Mitch and cried.

"Shit, shit, *shit!*"

8

Mitch met Clark Gable for a drink at the Brown Derby the next afternoon.

"How's it going, Mitch?"

"Pretty good."

Gable lifted his drink. "Well, buddy, you're on your way. Good luck."

Mitch drank. "Good luck. I hope I don't need it."

"You'll need it," said Gable. "In the history of Hollywood, no film ever got finished without spilling at least a pint of the director's blood. And when the director is also the writer . . . God knows what may happen."

Mitch checked the time.

"I'd better get moving. I have to call Charlie."

"That ought to be fun. Does he know that you've signed him to make a movie?"

"Not yet."

"He may just chew up your balls and spit them out," said Gable. "Jesus, I hope it works out, though. I'd like to see the old bastard again."

"So would I. But don't go quoting me."

Gable studied him.

"Why do you two keep it up? What did he ever do to you that was so unforgivable?"

"It's not what he did," Mitch said. "It's what he didn't do."

"Childhood trauma and all that crap?"

"Something like that."

"Say hello to the old fart for me," said Gable.

Over the crackling long-distance connection, Mitch told his father: "Clark sends his best wishes. He called you an old fart."

"Great. That's why you made a transcontinental phone call?"

"Well, no, Dad. I was wondering, how's the play doing?"

"Sellout. And in case you forgot the time difference, I'm due on stage in twenty minutes. I'm putting on my makeup right now."

"Don't forget the wart, Mr. President," said Mitch.

"Come on, boy, what's the big occasion here? Are you short of money again?"

"No, not that. In fact, I'm rolling in it."

"Good. In that case, you won't mind wiring me the last hundred I lent you. I lost at the Lambs last night."

"Sure," said Mitch. "Listen Dad, are you coming out this way anytime soon?"

"Not if I can help it. Why?"

"Oh, I just thought we'd talk about an idea I had for a movie I'm doing."

"Who are you writing it for?"

"Me, Dad. I've got backing from William Randolph Hearst, and Warners is producing it."

There was a long pause. Then, "Dad?"

"I'm here," said his father. "This connection must be bad. I thought I heard you say you had backing for a film from William Randolph Hearst."

"I did say it. I've written a screenplay about the Donner party."

"Who the hell were they?"

"A wagon train of settlers who were trapped in the Sierra Nevada mountains in 1846. Half of them died. The ones who survived resorted to cannibalism."

His father snorted. "I take it you'll be doing it as a musical comedy?"

"Be serious, Dad. It's a powerful drama, a real actor's challenge."

"Who's playing in it?"

"We're trying to sign Bogart and Judy Garland. Marion Davies is already set."

"That figures, with Hearst money involved. Who else?"

"Well, I was hoping for you."

"Me! What the hell gave you that idea? You know what I think of those galloping tintypes."

"You used to love them."

"That was before they hosed me. No more movies, Buzz. I mean it."

"Dad, I need you."

"Get Walter Huston."

"You'll play George Donner, the party's leader. It's a great role, Dad. I wrote it especially for you."

"You're wasting your—"

"Read the script."

"Why? I'm not doing any movie, and that's final."

"Dad, you can't let me down."

"How am I letting you down? Any part I could play can be handled by one of a dozen character actors who are already out there. Get Charley Grapewin. He was great in *The Grapes of Wrath*."

"Dad, listen to me. If you don't play George Donner, Hearst says he won't come up with the dough."

There was a long pause. Then, "How'd he get you boxed like that?"

"He wants Marion to look good."

"In contrast to an old fart like me."

"You got it, Dad."

His father made a quiet humming sound.

"I just can't, Buzz," he said finally. "I sure don't want to screw up your big chance, but I've had Hollywood, right to the top of my gullet. You can talk Hearst into someone else. What about Jack Barrymore? He's enough of a wreck to make that broad look young alongside him."

"Hearst was very specific about you, Dad."

"Well, get him to be unspecific. You have no right to mousetrap me into something like this."

"I've got every goddamned right! You owe me."

"I owe you nothing. Anything I owed I paid long ago and with compound interest."

"Not on my books."

"You little shit. You'll never let me forget sending you off to boarding school. Well, you're wasting your long-distance money, Buzz. I don't want any part of it."

"I'll mail you the script."

"Then you'll be wasting postage stamps."

"Air mail. You'll have it day after tomorrow."

"I won't read it."

"Damn it, Charlie, you owe me at least that much!"

There was a pause.

"All right. I'll read the goddamned thing. But don't get your hopes up."

"I won't," Mitch said.

"The clock is running, Mitch," said William Randolph Hearst.

"I know. But we're on schedule."

"What does your father say?"

"Charlie's reading the script right now. I ought to hear in a day or two."

"I have other matters to attend to," Hearst said. "Let's not waste excessive time on this one."

"We won't."

It had never occurred to Mitch that he would ever have reason to feel grateful to Louis B. Mayer, but the role of the mad Donner survivor, Keseberg, was an important one and Mayer had agreed to loan Wallace Berry out if Bogart wasn't available. Now Mitch had his eye on another MGM target. Again, he was in luck. As he entered the commissary, he heard a voice call his name.

"Mr. Gardner?"

Beneath a huge portrait of Norma Shearer sat a small, dark-haired girl. Mitch went over.

"Believe it or not," he said to Judy Garland, "I was just thinking of you."

"Are you meeting someone, Mr. Gardner?"

"Call me Mitch. No, I'm alone."

"Have lunch with me then. Mitch. That's funny. My tongue doesn't want to say it. I suppose it's because you're so much old—" She stopped and laughed. "Well, no, you're not *old*, but you're older than me."

"That's not hard. What are you now, fourteen?"

She stiffened. "I'm seventeen!"

"But—"

"Oh, you know Mr. Mayer. He doesn't want me to ever grow up. He's had the publicity people take three years off my age. Do you know, they had my—my chest so bound up during *Oz* that I could hardly breathe? I think it stunted my growth. Now I'm not developing there at all. Mickey says I should sue them. He says the Chinese girls bind their feet to keep them small, and that the same thing's going to happen to me—that I'm going to be flat as a wall for the rest of my life, and that it's all MGM's fault. But I couldn't possibly sue MGM, so what on earth *will* I do?"

"Wait a couple of years, and don't pay too much attention to Rooney. The problem will take care of itself."

He picked up the menu. "What are you having?"

"Do you think . . . Would the Charles Laughton sandwich be too much?"

"That's corned beef and kosher dill and turkey and God knows what else."

"I'd love it!" she said. "Please?"

"With it?"

"A milk shake! Strawberry."

"It's your stomach, Judy. I'll just have some coffee."

"Mr. Gardner—Mitch—could you do me a favor?"

"What?"

"You order the sandwich and the milk shake. I'll order the coffee and we'll trade."

"Why?"

"Please! Here comes the waitress."

"Calm down," he said. "Anything you say." He ordered and leaned back. His voice lowered. "Judy, did you ever think of making a picture where you didn't have to sing?"

"Oh, scads of times."

"Would you like to?"

"Could I be the femme fatale, with blond hair and a dress cut down to here and—"

"In a few years," he said. "But right now I have a part in my new film for an *actress*. A pioneer girl, lost up in the mountains in the dead of winter. I'd intended to talk with your mother before I suggested a loan-out to Mr. Mayer. But since you're seventeen—"

She bounced in her chair.

"Oh, it sounds so *dramatic!* I'd *die* to do something like that."

"Fine, then. I'll call Mrs. Gumm."

She hesitated. "When you do, please don't mention anything about the sandwich. You see, I have this weight problem."

"Eating a Charles Laughton isn't going to help it any."

"It's just this once. I didn't have any breakfast this morning. Mama was in a bad mood. Don't get me wrong, she didn't tell me I couldn't have breakfast, but I got nervous and couldn't eat anyway. But now I'm starving."

She was interrupted by a slim man holding a slip of paper. The waitress hovered, anxiously, behind him.

"Miss Garland," said the man, "you know better than this."

"Better than what?" Mitch asked.

"Mr. Mayer left strict orders. She is only to be served a small bowl of his special chicken soup."

"What the hell are you talking about?"

"Mr. Gardner," said the man, "I called the gate. You are here on a visitor's pass. Do not take advantage of the studio's hospitality."

"I still want to know why you're talking like this to Miss Garland."

The man's lips tightened. "You aren't the first visitor she's fooled this way. We used to feel sorry for her. One of the cooks would feed her in the kitchen. Mr. Mayer found out. The cook was fired. I had my salary cut ten dollars a week. That may not sound like much to you, Mr. Gardner, but it's important to me. So please, don't make a scene. We aren't cruel, but we have to obey Mr. Mayer's instructions."

"Okay," said Mitch. "Go back to your cash register. There won't be any scene."

"But I'm hungry!" Judy wailed.

"I'll make sure there's plenty of chunks of chicken in your soup, honey," said the waitress.

"God damn it, I don't want soup! I'm a *movie star!*"

"Come on," Mitch said, helping her up. "I'll drive you home."

"But Mama—"

"We'll leave word at the gate." He guided her out of the commissary. "And if you quit bawling, we'll stop along the way."

"You mean at a hamburger stand?" she said, brightening.

"Hamburgers aren't for movie stars. Mike Romanoff will feed us."

"Wonderful!" Then she made a face. "Oh, we can't. Mr. Mayer sent word to all the big restaurants that they weren't supposed to serve me unless Mama was with me or if I came in a studio car on a publicity date."

"Is that so." Mitch smiled. "I bet I know what Mike Romanoff sent back as an answer."

"What?"

"I'll bet he told Louis B. Mayer to go piss in his own ear."

The connection to New York was a bad one. Charlie Gardner's voice was barely audible.

"I told you that you were wasting postage, Buzz."

"Look, the script's not finished, Dad. I've got a lot of fine-stroking to do. We'll build up your part."

"That's a sure way to ruin the movie. This is a woman's story, Buzz. That Tamsen female has more balls than Errol Flynn and Clark Gable put together. George Donner sucks hind tit all the way, and that's how you ought to make the film."

"It's still the best male role in the story, Dad."

"Get Huston. Or here's an idea—talk Bill Hart into coming out of retirement. He's the right age, and he'd give you some class. You can't miss."

"Damn it, Charlie, don't you ever listen? I've missed already, if you don't play the part. Hearst won't take anyone else."

"I'm sorry, Buzz. You got yourself into this, don't look to me to bail you out."

"You miserable old bastard, you're throwing me to the wolves!"

"Give my best to Clark, and say hello to Mike Romanoff."

"Wait a minute, Charlie, don't—"

But Mitch was too late. His father had already hung up.

9

"What the hell am I doing at another Hollywood party?" Mitch grumbled. "I'm supposed to be waiting for Hearst's call."

"They'll forward it here if it comes," said Carole Lombard. "This bash is important to you. Now, don't make the mistake of thinking that because Louella is grotesque you can safely laugh her off. She's quick as a snake."

"Carole," Mitch said patiently, "Don't you think I know about Louella Parsons?"

"No, not really. But you're going to learn."

As they waited, both in formal evening dress, at the entrance to Pickfair, Mitch looked around. Maybe Mary Pickford's beautiful estate represented something forever gone from Hollywood, but, if so, he mourned its passing.

"I love your films, Miss Lombard," said the girl who took Carole's wrap.

"Thank you, dear," Carole said. Entering the huge living room, she added, to Mitch, "One more thing. This is important. If you see Louella get up from a chair, don't ever sit down there."

"Why?"

"Just don't."

"Come on, Carole. Does she have the clap?"

Carole giggled. "Oh, hell, I shouldn't be laughing at the poor woman. There's something wrong with her kidneys or her bladder or something. But for God's sake, she's married to a doctor. You'd think he'd treat her for it."

"What you're trying to tell me, Mrs. Gable, is that Louella Parsons piddles on the floor?"

"Constantly. Now that's an example of her power in this town. She's ruined more rugs than a battalion of poodles. It's worth your life to sit down after her, and yet to my certain knowledge, although everyone knows about it, this little flaw in her public decorum has never seen so much as an oblique reference in print."

"God damn it, here she comes. What do I say?"

"Congratulate her on that awful vaudeville tour she just got back from. 'Louella Parsons and Her Flying Stars.'"

"Sounds obscene," Mitch muttered. Then the columnist was upon them.

At 47, Louella Parsons was a bundle of flailing energy. Her hair was too black and her face too pudgy. Her hefty figure was bound up in a dark taffeta gown that groaned at the seams. But she moved with the sureness of a woman half her age. Her mouth stretched in what Mitch hoped was a friendly smile.

"Carole!" she lisped. "And this is Mr. Gardner. May I call you Mitch? Oh, I know your father so well."

Mitch took her hand and, feeling like Bela Lugosi, lifted it to his lips.

"Miss Parsons."

Louella giggled. "You didn't tell me he was a charmer, Carole."

"He's never kissed *my* hand," said Carole.

"Oh, well, Clark probably wouldn't understand. Dear, why don't you circulate and leave your delightful Mr. Gardner to me?"

"I'll be near the fountain," Carole said, leaving.

"Miss Parsons," said Mitch. "Did I mention, your show 'Louella and Her Flying Stars' was simply marvelous?"

"No. And I doubt you even saw it. Carole put you up to that, didn't she?"

"Yes. She said you were proud of it. You're right, I didn't see it. I don't go to the theatre much anymore."

"With your heritage? Why not?"

He shrugged. "Every time I do, Maxwell Anderson is spouting at me in blank verse. Or Clifford Odets is tugging at my social conscience. Hell, Miss Parsons, I always thought of the theatre as a place you went to enjoy yourself."

"Call me Louella. Yes, you're very much like your father. You speak what you think. You might have liked my little show. We had a delightful troupe. Cute Susan Hayward, you must know her."

"Beautiful girl."

"And little Jane Wyman, and that dear boy, Ronnie Reagan. We opened in San Francisco and toured simply everywhere. Do you know the melody to 'Oh, Susannah!'?"

"Slightly."

"Hum it," she ordered.

He did and, to his surprise she sang, in a fairly true voice

> Oh, Louella, won't you mention me?
> For a movie star in Hollywood
> That's what I want to be!

"Isn't that darling, Mitch? Then I pretended to write my column, and the girls all danced with Ronnie. Well, one of those girls absolutely *fell* head over heels for the boy. He's terribly handsome and dashing, you know."

"Which one was it?"

"Little Janie Wyman, of all the surprises!" she simpered. "I hear the wedding chimes will tinkle soon."

"How lovely."

"I'll give them a lead in my column." She smiled at him again. "I try to be kind to my friends."

"I hope you'll count me as one of them," Mitch said carefully.

"I hope so too, dear. After all, we both belong to the same family."

"What do you mean?"

"Mr. Hearst's, darling! Don't you realize he takes a great interest in *all* of his employees?"

"I'm not aware of being an employee."

"I'm afraid I don't understand you, dear."

"I'm directing a movie in which Mr. Hearst has a financial interest. But I don't work for him."

"Oh, that!" She waved one hand. "Perhaps not on paper. But you may be sure that he's keeping a close eye on your progress."

"That's good to know," Mitch said.

"Silly boy! Why do you suppose he's a multimulti*multi*millionaire? He didn't achieve such wealth by overlooking details."

Mitch murmured, "I thought he inherited most of it from his father."

He stepped back as she almost threw herself at him.

"Never say that! You don't know who might be listening! Oh, dear, I'm afraid I was wrong about you. How dare you judge your betters?"

"My *betters?*"

She looked around frantically—"Where's Docky? Docky!"—and hurried away.

"Miss Parsons—"

She had vanished into the crowd. He looked down.

Where she had been standing, a glistening pool was sinking into the red velvet rug.

Mitch scowled into the deep blue of Marion Davies' swimming pool, at the huge Santa Monica beach house. They were sipping tall rum drinks. The June sun was hot overhead in the cloudless blue sky.

"You're a mouse today," she said.

"Just tired," he mumbled.

"How's the revised script?"

"Finished," he said. "I'll send a carbon up to W.R. early in the week."

"Mitch, is s-s-something wrong?"

He had not noticed her stammer so pronounced in months. She was obviously under tension too.

"Nothing I can't handle. I didn't realize there was so much dog work to preparing a film. Most of my time for the past three months has been spent arguing about wardrobe and crap like that."

"D-d-daddy's getting uneasy," she said.

This was the first time Mitch had ever heard her refer to Hearst in this way, although everyone knew she did it frequently.

"Does he think I'm blowing his money on fast women and slow horses?"

"No. But somewhere he's picked up the idea that you're lying about your father being willing to play George Donner."

"I see," said Mitch.

"Are you lying?" she asked quietly.

"No," he said. Then, "Yes."

"*Why*, Mitch? You don't know what he can be like if he catches you in a double cross. I've seen him destroy men for less."

"Dad's going to do the film. I just don't have his John Henry on a contract. I'm flying East next week to see him about it."

"Are you sure? It's very important, Mitch."

"He didn't like the original script," Mitch said, conscious that he was lying again.

"Has he s-s-seen the new one?"

"No. I'm not going to take the chance of him turning it over to one of his buddies to read. I'm going to sit him down and read it to him out loud. That's all it'll take."

"Mitch, can you go up to Wyntoon this weekend?"

"Is that an offer?" he asked, smiling.

She did not return the smile.

"It's business. I think you ought to put Da—Bill's mind at rest. It would make things easier all around."

"Is he giving you a hard time?"

"No," she said. "But I don't like to see him worrying. Please, Mitch. The plane'll pick you up at Burbank, and b-b-bring you back. You won't even lose a working day."

"All right," he said. "I always wanted to see your little village anyway."

"Bring the script."

Mitch stopped himself from saying "Which one?" just in time.

Wyntoon, Hearst's lavish Bavarian village in the pine forests near the Oregon border, had originally been his mother's home. The old building burned in 1930, and Hearst instructed his industrious architect, Miss Julia Morgan, to begin construction on a village with a fairy-tale motif. She achieved it. Some said, cynically, too well. Others referred to the refuge as "Spittoon."

Hearst's private building was known as "Bear House." "The Bend" was another house, for guests, farther down the McCloud River. "Cinderella House" was prominent, with murals painted by Willy Pogany all over the outer walls. The central building was "The Gables," where guests were entertained. Cookouts and barbecues were the usual routine, unless the weather was bad.

In 1931, Hearst had been approached by a syndicate of British businessmen who inquired whether or not he would be interested in buying London Bridge. Hearst considered the offer seriously, and finally turned it down—the Bavarian architecture of Wyntoon was too far along to change, and it would have clashed with the ancient English landmark.

Hearst's private Fokker landed Mitch in early afternoon on Saturday, and a car was waiting. In half an hour, he got his first look at Hearst's northern enclave. He was put up at the Cinderella House. A huge painted clock dominated the center of the third floor. Below it was a mural of Cinderella fleeing the palace toward the magic coach. All around the main floor were other murals of scenes from the fairy tale. Mitch shuddered. Pogany's work fetched a handsome price, and here it was nakedly exposed to the ice and snow.

Hearst was waiting when Mitch was ushered up to the Gables. He gave Mitch a warm handshake.

"Glad you could come. Marion said you were flying East next week."

"Yes," Mitch said. "I've got the new script done. Here's your copy."

He gave Hearst a brown envelope.

"I want my father to hear it, and since the plane fare doesn't cost much more than a three-hour phone call, I'm going to recite it in person. Also, that'll give me the chance to catch up on what's new on Broadway."

"I envy the young. You leap into planes and speed off with hardly a moment's notice."

"I envy the rich," Mitch said, tempering it with a smile. "Especially those who *own* their own planes."

"Would you like to borrow the Fokker for your trip? I don't have any immediate use for it."

"Thanks, but no," said Mitch. "I don't know how long I'll be gone."

"Well, then, my home is yours. Dinner is at eight. I'd hoped to have a barbecue, but it wouldn't be much fun, just you and me."

"Oh? I just assumed Marion would be here."

Hearst shook his head.

"No. To be frank, I'm worried about the work load she's been carrying."

"But we haven't even started rehearsing. That's months away."

"You don't know my little girl," said Hearst. "She's been living in libraries, studying everything she can find about the Donner party. She's got a roomful of old tintypes and costumes. She wanted to go to Salt Lake City and examine the records there, but I refused. She's down at the beach house, and I've given strict orders that she isn't to stir outside its walls for at least a week. But I know in my heart that she's poring over some old book at this very moment."

"I didn't know a thing about this, Mr. Hearst. I certainly never put her up to it."

Hearst made a gesture with his hand.

"I'm not blaming you, Mitch. It's her way. She works harder than anyone knows. And the truth is, she's not strong. I would appreciate it if you would watch out for her during the shooting."

"I will, sir."

"While we're unburdening ourselves," Hearst said, "why don't you call me Bill? Or W.R.? I don't feel that we are in the usual employer-employee situation."

"Thanks." Mitch looked around. "This is something," he said. "Maybe I'll be able to swing a place like this one day."

"I shouldn't doubt it. You have many attributes working for you, Mitch. You're talented, you're honest, you're still young. There's no reason why not."

"Well," Mitch said, "this time next year we'll know."

"Because of *Donner Pass*? Don't make that mistake, Mitch. Don't pin everything on one effort, no matter how vital it may seem. The only thing that counts is the long pull. Consider your life's work. Ignore daily triumphs and despair. They don't count. I know."

He looked down at the brown envelope.

"I'll read this tonight. And I'm glad to hear that you've got Charlie Gardner firmed up. I've received some conflicting reports. It's good to know they're wrong."

"Bill," said Mitch, "what if things soured with my father? We could still get Huston or Grapewin, or even Bill Hart. What difference would it make?"

"To the film?" Hearst pursed his lips. "Perhaps none. But we have exchanged our word, you and I. The breaking of it would make a great deal of difference. A promise is like virtue. Once broken, there can be no repair."

Mitch stood. "Don't worry," he said. "I won't break my word."

Vivien Leigh was waiting for Mitch when he arrived at Burbank Airport. She tapped his shoulder as he left the waiting room.

"Well, if it isn't the Evil One," she said. "I've been waiting for you."

"Many thanks."

"Oh, don't mention it. You don't mind if I call you that in the privacy of my boudoir, do you? While I am squatting over the bidet, as 'twere? That is when I most often think of you."

"Jesus, Viv, you're smashed. Is Larry here?"

"Ask no questions—"

He sighed. "I know the rest. Do you have a car?"

"Yes."

"Good. I have to catch a train."

"To where?"

"I'm going up in the mountains, scouting locations."

"Here's my car, Evil One. If we hurry, we might even have time for a fast drinkie before your train leaves."

"I'll drive."

"A pleasure, Evil One."

As he turned the car downtown, toward Union Station, Mitch asked, "Why do you keep calling me that?"

"Because I know what you've been up to. You are the very root of my evil, Mitch Gardner."

"When I figure out what it is you're saying, I'll come up with an answer."

"This may help you: Three months ago, you promised me the lead in *Donner Pass*. You spent an entire weekend promising it to me, during which much of the time I was staring at the ceiling in that Godforsaken cabin in the mountains. And since then, I have broken my Cockney ass helping you get your film under way. I interceded with David Selznick. I spent an entire evening with his drunken agent brother Myron, and did everything but go down on him to try and get him to put a package together. I even had lunch with those dark Italian brothers at the Bank of America, and, my friend, that is devotion above and beyond the call of duty."

"You know that I appreciate it, Viv."

"Do you?"

She slapped him squarely across the face. He flinched from the blow, and the car swerved.

"Watch it! Do you want to smash us up?"

"*How* much do you appreciate it, Mitch? Enough to make an under-the-table deal with Jack Warner? Enough to kiss ass with

William Randolph Hearst and talk him into guaranteeing negative costs and studio overhead?"

Mitch frowned. "Who have you been listening to?"

"A little bird! A little Lolly bird, who informed me that you've been fucking the eyes out of Marion Davies in every hotel from here to San Francisco! But that isn't what disturbs me, Evil One. If you have to sleep with old bags to raise your precious production money, who am I to point the finger? But God damn you, Mitchel Gardner, you *promised her my part!*"

He drove in silence for a moment. Then, "I thought we were going to have a fast *drinkie.*"

"Watch the sarcasm, Mitch. I know what kind of a drink I'd like to give you."

"All right," he said. "I plead guilty to everything. But be fair, Viv. Now that you've won your Oscar, you know that you don't really want to go up in the snow and ice to do a film on location. You've just been looking for a way to get out of the deal. Admit it. And I wouldn't have blamed you."

He saw her teeth flashing at him in the dimness of the car interior.

"Well, dear," she said, "we will neither of us ever know now, will we?"

"No, love," he said softly. "I suppose we never will."

Mitch parked the car in an all-night garage near the railroad station. He looked at his watch.

"We're early. Do you still want that drink?"

Vivien looked around, frowning. The storefront restaurant bore the unlikely name of "The Stop 'n' Chop." Painted across its plate glass front was the menu:

>3 large pork chops—30¢
>Oxtail goulash—20¢
>Spinach and eggs—20¢
>Pig's head with red cabbage—25¢
>Veg. dinner—10¢

And, beside the restaurant, a red and white striped barber pole revolved, an internal light illuminating the wares of Sammy the Barber:

> Shave, bay rum and towel—10¢
> Haircut and Shave—30¢
> Single Haircut—20¢
> Ladies Hairbob—30¢
> Children Buster Brown—30¢

Mitch grinned. "Hungry?"
She sniffed. "Hardly."
"How about a hairbob, then?"
She turned on her heels.
"I'll take a drink. If we can find one."

They walked beneath the marquee of a movie theatre offering Ed. G. Robinson in *The Last Gangster*. A banner promised: "Always 20¢—2 good AMERICAN Features—Always 20¢."

"Why don't you put your railroad terminals in a decent part of town?"

"Like Waterloo Station?"

She giggled. "Oh! Why can't I stay angry with you?"

"There's a place." He indicated a dimly lit "Beer and Free Lunch" sign over a building that squatted on a deserted corner.

Inside the barroom was musty. Its sawdust-covered floors were damp and littered with cigarette butts. An old Atwater-Kent radio blared near the cash register, its semicircular dial lighted and the horn speaker helping Bonnie Baker sing her way through, "Oh, Johnny, Oh, Johnny, how you can love!" The bartender, wiping beer mugs, squinted over the pile of free lunch. Stacks of rye bread, rolls of sausage, chunks of liverwurst, and heaps of dripping kosher dills, nestled on a bed of sauerkraut.

"Just about ready to close, folks," said the bartender.

"One beer?" asked Mitch.

The bartender nodded. "A short one." He drew two and slid them down the bar.

The heavy mugs spun to a stop directly in front of Mitch, who handed one to Vivien, hoisted the other, and blew off the suds.

"Good luck," he said.

"God bless," she answered, and drank.

He put his mug down, half empty.

"What are you going to do next?"

"I want to appear in a play on Broadway but you know how

impossible David is." She sipped at her beer. "Ugh, how do you put down this dreadful stuff? It's as cold as ice cream."

"The American way," he said. "We like our beer frigid and our women boiling. So you think Dos is stalling you?"

"I don't know. I think that it's just that once he feels he owns something ... or someone ... that he resents their having any additional life or emotions of their own. I don't know what I shall do. Sit and wait, I suppose."

"You're still marrying Olivier?"

"Oh, certainly. Once he gets rid of Jill, that is." She pushed her beer away. "Let's not talk about me any more, Mitch. Tell me, do you think your arrangement with Warners will come true?"

"If Hearst gives his blessing. But that takes some doing."

"Still, you'll get *Donner Pass* done?"

"You bet I will."

"In spite of anything, or any one? Not even if it kills you?"

His jaw tightened. "No matter *who* it kills."

Back from his mountain trip, Mitch planned to meet Jack Warner for lunch and make an informal report. Instead, he found himself talking with columnist Hedda Hopper.

"Hello, Genghis Khan," she said. "I hear you're trying to commit suicide."

He shook his head. Hedda was slim and tall. She wore one of the outrageous hats that were her trademark. Her nose was long and pointed. She had on too much rouge. And her breath smelled of brandy.

"Jack's going to be late," she told Mitch. "He wanted me to chat with you anyway. After your love fest with Louella, he thinks you need all the help you can get."

He held a chair for her.

"Are you drinking?"

"Are you *serious?*" She waved at a nearby waiter. "Jose! Two of the same."

"What are the same?"

"I don't know. The bartender flatters himself that he remembers everybody's favorite drink. I always order 'the same,' and I never get it twice in a row."

Mitch laughed. He liked this outgoing, lusty woman.

She leaned on one elbow and studied him.

"Did you really say those gawdawful things to Lolly?"

"I disagreed with her about my being an employee of William Randolph Hearst."

Hedda nodded. "That would do it. If the boat were sinking and there was only one life preserver between Louella, Docky, and Hearst, she'd make sure it got tied around W.R.'s ribs."

"Frankly," he said, "when I read her column, I thought of suing."

"Never, *never* try to sue a columnist, dear. It only gets the canard repeated in open court where everybody can quote it, and you'd never win anyway because all your friends and supporters would abandon you to the wolves, which is to say, us. You see, they need us more than they need you."

"Doesn't Louella realize that I'm trying to make a good film? I'm not some fast-buck hustler, cashing in on Marion's name and Hearst's money. But she treated me like a beachboy trying to sneak into the main house."

"That's Louella all the way. No class."

"Well, what do I do?"

"My advice is to send her the most expensive present you can afford along with the most abject *mea culpa* letter you can compose."

"And *that's* the way it's done?"

"My dear, that's exactly the way it's done. Do you know what they say about me? That I use my column to punish the business because it never made *me* a movie star. That I hate men, particularly the young ones who give me a poke every so often. That I'm a terrible snob. And they're right. But there's more to me. I love this lousy business, and I stick up for it. I never betray a friend. So, Mitch, your view of me very much depends on which side of the bed you're standing on, doesn't it?"

Intrigued, he asked, "What do they say about Louella?"

"That she only has her job because she knows the truth about the William Ince death aboard Hearst's boat. That she's the greatest freeloader the world has ever seen. That she's a lush who starts the day with four fingers of Old Panther Piss. That all of her copy is marked 'MGAI,' which means 'Must Go As Is.' And you already know about her deplorable urinary habits."

"What's the good side?"

"She's a shrewd old biddy. The scatterbrained bit is just to get your guard down. She's intensely loyal, but you have to pay your dues."

"And you two run this town," Mitch said wonderingly.

"It's a tough world, baby. I've got news for William Saroyan. Every whore does *not* have a heart of gold. Ask Lolly. Or me."

"Okay, I'll pawn my cuff links and send her a silver-plated cocktail shaker."

"Good. Accept her thank-you with good graces. And from then on, stay the hell out of her way. She's got a short memory. Pretty soon she'll only remember you as that nice Mitch Gardner who got a little out of line and made up for it with a lovely gift. Don't give her another look at the original tapestry. Because there's no way in the world you and Louella will ever get along. You are *in*compatible!"

"And you and me?"

Her lips surrounded by wrinkles only half hidden by the makeup, her eyes boring straight into his, Hedda smiled.

"Why don't you come up and poke me some time?"

Her imitation of Mae West was very bad, but Mitch forced himself to laugh anyway, and then Jack Warner arrived to rescue him from his misery.

10

After getting lost twice, Mitch finally found Clark Gable's new ranch in Encino. It sprawled over twenty-two acres, surrounded by a white board fence.

Mitch, who had been nipping at a flask of Jack Daniel's, was in fine shape. He parked his car between the house and a new camping trailer which was set up on blocks. The back door opened and Carole Lombard peered out.

"Mitch? Is that you?"

"One and the same."

"You know, the party was Sunday."

"What's today?"

"Wednesday, idiot. Come in. You look like you need some coffee."

"No, no, I'm sorry."

He started the engine; Carole ran over, reached through the window, and turned off the key.

"You'll kill yourself! Come on, we've got plenty of room."

"Where's Clark?"

"He had to work late. Spence is putting him up."

Mitch reached for the key again.

"That means there'll be a poker party. I'd really better get back, Carole."

"Over my dead body. Get out, buster."

He staggered into the kitchen.

"I don't think this is such a good idea," he mumbled. "Think of what Louella could make out of it."

She laughed and poured him some black coffee.

"Mitch, where have you been? We've gone frantic. You dropped completely out of sight."

"Up in the mountains," he mumbled, sipping the coffee. He burned his tongue and swore. "Scouting locations."

"I thought you were going to shoot everything at the studio."

"That's what Jack Warner thinks. I never said we would. I never said we wouldn't. Anyway, he knows I plan second-unit location work. I'll sneak the actors up there."

"Jack won't like that, Mitch. He's very much a get-it-down-on-paper man."

"You know what paper's good for, don't you?" Mitch laughed. "Speaking of that—"

"In the hallway, first door to the left."

When he returned, she had scrambled some eggs and fried thick slices of Canadian bacon.

"Eat," she commanded.

"Sure, I'll eat. What are you getting so upset for?"

"Eat!"

"I'm eating, I'm eating." He shoveled the eggs into his mouth, then scraped the plate.

"When did you have your last meal?" she asked him.

"I drank an olive over in Burbank before I knew it was in the glass," he said. "Carole, I love you."

"I love you too, stupid. But it'll be posthumous if you don't start taking care of yourself. Damn it, Mitch, what's wrong with you?"

"Nothing a good lay wouldn't cure."

"If I thought that was all you needed, you'd have it," she said softly.

"Always promises."

"Mitch, don't joke. You've almost pulled it off. You did the impossible. You're going to direct your own film. Can't you ease up for a couple of weeks and give the liquor industry a chance to retool?"

"I don't know," he said, sipping some more coffee. "I guess I'm just scared, Carole."

"You? Scared? Ha!"

"No, it's true. I don't know how to explain it, honey, but when you get up close to something you've always wanted, and it's so near you can actually reach out and touch it, all of a sudden, the fear comes over you. You get *scared.* I don't know how to handle that, so I drink."

"Balls," she said. "As long as I've known you, you've had a glass in your hand. The difference was, before, you always handled it. Now it's handling you. If this is what directing a film can do to you, maybe you'd better give up the job."

"No way," he said. "Charlie would never let me hear the last of it if I folded up my tents."

"Is what he thinks so important?"

"Of course it is! Carole, I'm going to show that old son of a bitch that I'm somebody other than Charlie Gardner's son."

"Then what?"

He hesitated. "I don't know. Maybe once I've proved what I have to, maybe me and the old bastard can start getting along again."

"I hope so," she said.

There was a long pause. Then he said, "Carole?"

"What, Mitch?"

"I can trust you. The truth is, I don't have Dad set for the role Hearst insists on having him play. And I'm worried about Marion. I had to sign her to get Hearst interested. But now it's just no good. I can't have her in the film."

"Why not?"

"For one thing, she's too old. I keep trying to tell myself that acting will overcome that, but you ought to see her. Carole, her eyes look a hundred years old."

"You should have thought of that before you dragged her into it. You've used Marion to raise your money. You're honor-bound to deliver what you promised."

"I know," he said miserably. "I'm not trying to bail out. I'm willing to try anything. But as things stand, we're going to deliver a dog."

"Well, rewrite her part."

"It doesn't help. If we go the way Hearst wants, serving her up like Jean Arthur in *The Plainsman,* they're going to laugh us right out of the theatre. The role only works if she'll do it in the rough. No makeup, no special lighting, play her as old as she really is. And you know we won't be able to do that."

"Why not?"

"Hearst would hit the roof. He doesn't see her that way."

"How do you see her?"

He spread his hands.

"I guess I don't know anymore."

"Cheer up," she said. "After all, it's only another movie."

Mitch stared at her.

"That's easy enough for you to say. You don't have the responsibility of delivering a salable product to the box office. You just have to give the film cutter enough sexy footage to sneak into the one scene that'll drag the teen-aged crowd into the theatre. You can come home at night and forget about everything."

Carole pressed both hands on the table and leaned forward.

"Now, you listen, Mitch Gardner. Nobody, *nobody* in this whole goddamned world can talk to me like that. I've paid my dues, I've earned my place in this rotten business. I do my job, and then some, and right now that's more than anyone could say for you. So don't come bleeding to me about not being able to take care of your own responsibility and blaming it, in some oblique way, on my not being a director too. Whoever promised you it would be easy? They don't hand out screen credits for being somebody's uncle. Oh, the assistant-producer ones, sure. Nepotism Gulch. But not for the real work. You deliver, or you get out. So all you have to do now, my friend, is to make up your mind which one it is you're going to do."

He stared down at his coffee cup.

"Carole . . . I just don't know."

She sat near him and stroked his face.

"Yes you do, baby. You're just tired and lonely. Mitch, why don't you get yourself a girl?"

"I've got more girls now than I can shake my prick at."

She slapped his face tenderly.

"I don't mean broads. I mean somebody to depend on. Why do you keep that kind away?"

"I haven't got time to get married. Maybe if Jean hadn't died . . ."

"But she did," Carole said harshly. "Anyway, who said anything about marriage? You need somebody good for you, that's all."

"Let's skip it," he said. "Can I have some more coffee?"

"Can your kidneys handle it? You're staying over, aren't you, Mitch?"

"Seriously, baby, I'd better not."

"Oh, shit, Mitch, don't be put off by the stuff I've been saying. I like to play Jewish mama every now and then. You can turn queer for all I care."

As she refilled his cup, he asked, "Are you really happy, Carole?"

"Yes," she said. "Paw and I make jokes at each other in public, but he's my man. Do you know what he paid Ria to get clear of her? Every dime he had in the world. He gave the preacher in Kingman, Arizona, a hundred dollars and then, in the hotel room, he asked me if I had any cash. I said I had fifty dollars or so, and he grinned and said we'd need it. I asked why, and he told me he had just given his last hundred to the little man who married us."

She leaned forward and kissed Mitch on the forehead.

"That silly bastard," she said. "He paid half a million for me."

In the rearest rear booth of the Trocadero, on Sunset Boulevard, Carole Lombard hugged her martini closer to her lips and grinned in an evil fashion that would have struck terror into the heart of Peter Lorre.

"Tonight," she whispered. "We get that no good son of a bitch."

Mitch, still wearing his casual studio clothes, contributed an ominous heh-heh-heh. "Tonight!"

"He deserves no mercy," Carole said. "All in favor?"

"Tonight," Ben Hecht agreed. He celebrated the decision by biting into the bowl of his cocktail glass and chewing the fragments. Hecht was skilled at this trick. The one time Mitch had tried it, he cut his tongue and lips so badly that he looked like a mad dog frothing red.

"Tonight!" repeated Harpo Marx. Without his frazzled wig, the comedian was rarely recognized outside of Hollywood circles.

"David's really a nice guy," said press agent Russell Birdwell. "Why don't we just lay for him and beat him up? This is too mean."

"Revenge!" said Carole. "Besides, it's time we got him again."

"But, Carole, I thought you and David were friends."

"What's that got to do with it? He's still a pompous ass. Are you with us or are you a fink?"

"I'm with you," said Birdwell. "But I'll deny everything if we get caught."

"Mitch?" Carole asked.

"All the way."

She turned to the last person at the table.

"Spence?"

Spencer Tracy nodded.

"I'll bring my camera," he said.

"All right," said Carole. "Now, we know he'll suspect Clark. But Paw's up in the mountains hunting with Hemingway, and everybody knows it. We have good weather forecast for tonight, and the stuff is already on a truck, parked behind David's house." She looked at her watch. "It's ten of one. Let's go. He and Irene are down in San Diego at a sneak preview. They won't be home for a couple of hours at least."

"I'll meet you there, Carole," said Tracy. "I'll stop at the neighborhood delicatessen for a supply of liquid refreshment."

"Forget it. There's two cases of beer on the truck. Let's go."

"This is work." Mitch groaned, tearing open another fifty-pound bag of Knox Gelatin and, with Tracy's help, dumping the powder into the pool.

"Shut up and pour," said Carole, stirring with the pool skimmer. "We're running out of time."

In an hour, they had poured almost a thousand pounds of gelatin into David O. Selznick's kidney-shaped swimming pool. It was starting to thicken. Since it was colorless, no difference could be seen in the pool's consistency—except when Carole stirred.

"He'll be out here at dawn, like always," she said. "Nude as a prawn. Healthy David'll prance out on the diving board, jiggle his ass, and dive in. Kerplop!"

Hecht broke up. "I'm sorry," he croaked. "I've got to be here to see it."

"He'll nab you, Ben."

"I don't care. It's worth a month's pay."

"We're all crazy," said Mitch. "Where but in Hollywood would people like us be filling their *boss's* swimming pool with gelatin?"

Carole was struggling with the skimmer.

"I think that's enough. We don't want to get it so thick that he can walk on it."

"I'm with Ben," said Harpo. "I'm staying around. We'll hide in the pool house."

"He'll make you pay for having the gunk cleaned out," Carole warned.

"So I'll pay."

"They're right," said Tracy. "This is too good to miss."

"You can go on home, Carole," said Mitch. "We won't implicate you."

"Like hell," said the blonde. "You think you're going to have all the fun? Anyway, if David sticks in the goo like a cork, one of you guys can pull him out."

She took a wad of bills from her purse and went over to the truck. Money passed hands, and the truck pulled away.

"Hey," said Mitch. "There goes the rest of our beer."

"David never locks his back door," said Carole. "Hide those empty bags and clean up the mess. I'll get something to drink and be right back."

In five minutes, the pool was immaculate. There was only a slight glistening sheen to its surface.

Carole joined them in the pool house, a large pitcher of martinis in her hand.

"What time is it?" Mitch whispered.

"Ten of three. They ought to be home soon."

"Jesus. He won't get up until nine in the morning."

"Wrong, Mitch. He's got a picture shooting. That means he'll be out here around six, maybe earlier."

"Listen," said Hecht. "There's no reason for *all* of us to take the rap. Let's cut cards and the loser pulls Selznick out of the gelatin while the rest of us take it on the lam."

"You sound terribly sure you're going to win, Ben," Mitch said.

"That would only be fair. We're using my cards."

The conspirators drew cards. Hecht and Tracy tied with fives. They drew again and Hecht lost.

"I'll pay any one of you a thousand dollars to take my place," the writer offered. He was answered with a chorus of catcalls.

"Shhh," Carole whispered when the laughter had died down. "I hear a car. It's them."

They waited, nipping at the martinis. Lights went on inside the house, and, after a few moments, went out again. The pool lights flared.

"Jesus," said Mitch. "He's coming out here."

Selznick appeared, in a bathrobe. He stood staring up at the night sky, breathing deeply.

Carole groaned. "It's not hard yet."

"Well, David is." Hecht pointed at an obvious bulge beneath the producer's robe. "I don't think he's going swimming tonight."

There was a sound from within, and Selznick turned, stretching his arms toward the night sky. He disappeared inside, closing the heavy glass doors.

"God bless you, Irene," said Carole.

Dawn crept over the stucco roof. Carole, huddled in Mitch's arms, stretched and yawned.

"Jesus, it's cold!"

Harpo looked up.

"Fine. The gelatin's *solid.* Look, I just tossed a dime out on it."

Carole peered straight out from the pool house and saw the coin resting on the apparent surface of the water.

"He'd better not see that."

"With his eyesight? He's lucky to find the pool, Carole. Okay, Hecht, get ready. I see somebody moving around inside there."

"I think I just changed my mind."

"Too late, chicken," Tracy said. "But for Christ's sake, whatever you do, don't let him drown."

"I can't even swim," Hecht pointed out.

"So who's going to be swimming in a pool of jello anyway?" asked Marx. "Here's some rope. Lasso the mamser."

"Here he comes," Birdwell whispered. "And there goes my job."

Selznick opened the towering glass doors and stepped through them. He tossed aside his robe and took down a deep breath.

"Hell," said Carole, examining his nude body. "He's only got one just like everybody else."

Selznick bounded up on the pool's diving board, bounced twice and threw himself into what he presumed was the water.

He hit the gelatin with a slithering, plopping sound. At first his body skidded along on the surface, but then it broke through and he began to flounder, flailing at the quivering mass with his arms. He made mad incoherent sounds which were obviously cries for help.

"Hecht to the rescue!" yelled Harpo, shoving Ben and the coil of rope out onto the poolside.

Hecht ran along the edge until he was even with their struggling prey. He threw one end of the rope out, and Selznick caught hold of it. Grunting with exertion, Hecht dragged the exhausted producer to the edge of the pool and helped him, slimy with gelatin, up to dry land.

"Good morning, David," said Hecht, resplendent in his white dinner jacket and black tie. "I was just passing by and happened to hear you sinking."

11

New York.

Mitch had tickets for the Earl Carroll *Vanities,* and a supper date with his father after final curtain of *Abraham Lincoln.* He had made a courtesy call on Ethel Barrymore to give her John's respects and, to his surprise, heard himself inviting her to the *Vanities.*

"Oh, wonderful!" she said in that delightful foghorn of a voice that could fill a theatre without amplification. "I've been simply *dying* to see all those undressed beauties, and I didn't quite have the nerve to go by myself."

They had an early dinner at Lüchow's, and Ethel told him about the new play she was taking into rehearsal in a few weeks, Emlyn Williams' *The Corn Is Green.* "Oh, I know you remember Williams as that nasty Welshman who wrote *Night Must Fall,* with murders and all. But this is a beautiful play, Mitch. I portray a spinster who moves to a Welsh village to devote herself to the education of the coal miners. I have the chance to help one dirty-faced boy, and be oh, so self-sacrificing." She laughed. "Never give an actress the chance to be self-sacrificing. It's the one irresistible impulse."

They spoke quietly of her brother John, and Ethel revealed her own concern over his health.

"He just closed on the road in *My Dear Children,"* she said. "He worked himself to the bone on that show, merely to earn a little money. And when it was all over, do you know what his share was? Five thousand dollars. He could have gone into bankruptcy in 1938 and started clean, but he's paid every nickel, dollar on the dollar, plus interest, and he's honorably clear of all his debts. Yet they snicker at his name." Her hand crumpled the napkin. "Come on, Mitch, let's get out of here before I say what I'm thinking and someone calls the police."

The *Vanities* was what they'd expected, raw, vulgar, distinguished by a great display of undraped limbs and baggy-pants comics. They both loved it.

"I'm meeting Charlie at the Astor for supper," said Mitch. "Do you want to come along?"

"No, dear. Just stuff me into a cab, and God bless you for dropping by."

Mitch let her keep the taxi, and got out at the Astor. He bent down and kissed the lean cheek.

"I'll come back to see your play," he promised.

"Please do. We like you so very much, you know."

He went up to the roof garden and joined his father at the bar.

"You're late," said Charlie.

"I was making pash love to Ethel Barrymore."

"You should be so lucky. What are you drinking that I can't afford?"

"A light scotch," said Mitch.

Charlie raised his eyebrows.

"You're reforming?"

"Work. I can't enjoy martinis the way I used to. Hurts my head in the morning."

"Will wonders never cease?"

"Oh, I'm a new character these days."

His father's smile widened.

"Well, whoever you are, it's goddamned good to see you, Buzz."

"Same here. We ought to get together more often. Have fun together."

Charlie snorted. "Like, for instance, on a movie set somewhere?"

Mitch looked away.

"Afraid to bring it up until we'd had a couple of drinks? Damn it, Buzz, be a man!"

"It's still the same isn't it, Charlie? You don't give a solitary damn what happens to me."

Charlie finished his drink and waved for another.

"I feel for you, son, but I can't quite reach you. I haven't heard one good reason yet why I should give up doing what I like doing to do what I *don't* like."

"Maybe you owe me a favor."

"I owe you nothing!"

Mitch stared down at the table.

"All right. Let's say you owe it to Mama."

"Your mother's been dead for thirty years."

"And she died happy, because I never told her about you and that singer from the *Follies.*"

Charlie Gardner stood up.

"You little son of a bitch. You're blackmailing me."

"No I'm not. I'm only reminding you of a debt unpaid."

"By God, maybe there's hope for you yet," Charlie said, sitting again. "You'd peel off my hide and use it for scenery if it'd push your project a day closer."

"Without even blinking."

"Now, that's more like a man talking. Maybe..." Charlie paused, shook his head. "No, damn it. I am not going to let you buffalo me."

"Please, Dad. Just this once. You've got to."

"I don't *have* to do anything, son," Charlie said quietly.

"No. But if you don't, I'll never get another chance. I told Hearst you were in the boat. If he finds out I lied, he'll cut me off at the knees."

Charlie swore. "You did that deliberately, didn't you? Just to pressure me. Well, it won't work."

"You don't even know what you're turning down. Dad, it's the best role of the year. I've got the script right here"—he touched his briefcase "—just let me read it to you."

Charlie looked down at the polished bar.

"No," he said. "You couldn't get me out there with promises of a million dollars, an Academy Award, and blondes every night. And I resent your putting this kind of pressure on me. You're my son, Buzz, and, no matter what you think, I love you. But you have no right to put me in this position. If I do what you want, I violate my own beliefs. If I don't, I'm the old shit who let his son go down the drain because he didn't care enough to help out. I ought to beat the crap out of you."

"I wish you would. Look, Dad, this wasn't my idea. Hearst brought your name up, and I had no reason to think you'd let me down so I agreed. Now things have turned out differently, and W.R. won't back off an inch. It's itchy for both of us. But who loses the most? If you do the film, you'll make a hell of a lot of money, I'll see to that. You'll have the fattest expense account west of the Mississippi. You'll probably win a goddamned Oscar, and then Zanuck will hire you for even *more* money and, first thing you know, you'll be rolling in dough and I'll be sneaking around hitting you up for another hundred because I can't get backing for my second film. That's what happens on your side if you do the film. But if you don't I have to go back and tell Hearst that I lied. He puts a pox on me, I go around town with spots all over my ass, nobody will even give me the time of day. I finally end up pimping for the hustlers down on the strip, and one night, a boogey boy friend sticks a knife in my heart. Goodbye Hollywood, hello Forest Lawn."

Charlie groaned and waved for the waiter.

"I want oysters Rockefeller," he said. "You should have them too. Your tastes run in that direction. Oscar, did you hear that? The oysters Rockefeller, and a thick steak, and some red wine, and coffee and brandy and cigars from the good humidor?"

"In other words, Mr. Gardner, the usual?"

Charlie nodded.

"First class all the way."

Mitch was reading the script aloud. "Then you tell your wife, 'Take the children. Try to get through.' And she—"

His father waved his hand. "No, wait a minute."

"Dad—"

"Shut up. I'm thinking. Buzz, it's wrong. The relationship between them is too close. He wouldn't insult her that way."

"But he's trying to *save* her."

"He's trying to save the children. He knows goddamned well she wouldn't go off and leave him alone to die. He might try to trick her into going, but he wouldn't lay it out naked like you do in this mess you call a script."

"Okay, I'll make a note of it."

Mitch scribbled a hurried "Rewrite" on the margin of the page. At the same time, he sneaked a glance at his father.

Charles Gardner was leaning forward, his eyes bright. By God, thought Mitch, I'm getting to the old bastard!

He went on. His voice was hoarse, and he sipped at a half-empty brandy and soda.

"Okay, you're dying. You know it. Tamsen knows it. You plead with her to send the children on to Sutter's Fort. She agrees. There are some men in camp who sign on to do it, for money. But Tamsen flat out refuses to leave you."

He choked a little on his drink.

"Now, in your last scene together you call up memories of Illinois . . . of the cool green of the river, flowing beneath the willows. For a brief moment, the snow and ice vanish, and we're back in a happier time, a happier land—where birds fly and flowers grow. You promise her it'll be like that again, as soon as you reach California."

He paused.

"*Well?*" Charlie said. "What happens then?"

"Why, you die, of course."

Charlie threw down his cigar.

"Jesus Christ, it's about time. I thought I was going to lay there coughing in that log cabin until Judgment Day."

"Well?" Mitch asked. "What do you think? Do you want to hear the rest of the script?"

"Please God, no. Don't read any more, Buzz. You sound like a crow, cawing up in the trees. I'm too tired to take it anymore. You got yourself a George Donner."

His hands trembling, Mitch put the brandy down on the table. He stared at it.

"Thank you."

"Don't thank me," said his father. "I'm doing myself a favor. You're right. I can win an Oscar. Thank yourself, you've written one hell of a script. But, boy, you're sure taking one hell of a risk."

"Now that I've got you—"

"What do you think Hearst is going to say when he sees what you've done to Marion Davies? You know, and this is straight, you might be better off to go back and tell him that you couldn't sign me. Then he'd only be mad at you for falling down on the job. This way, he can accuse you of betraying him, and I don't think he'll take it kindly."

"I'll take the risk," Mitch said.

They were having a last drink in the Oyster Bar at Grand Central.

"The train?" asked Charlie. "I heard you were the press agent for the aerial age."

"Only when the weather's good, Dad. When the fog rolls in, I follow the pigeons' example. I walk. Or maybe take the train." He looked at his watch. "And that's in forty minutes."

"The length of a good third act." He sipped his martini. "I ought to have my head examined, letting you talk me into going back to that rat race."

"You drove a hard bargain. *I* can't afford to put you up at the Beverly Hills Hotel."

"Is it your money?"

Mitch laughed. "Okay. Screw Jack Warner."

"*And* William Randolph Hearst. Me in my way, you in yours."

"You'll be available for costume tests in September, maybe late August?"

"At my regular per diem."

"Crook."

"Director!" said Charlie. And he smiled.

Mitch smiled back. "It's been great, you know."

"For me too," his father said. "I'm glad you finally saw the play."

"You're better than Raymond Massey."

"Don't badmouth Ray," said Charlie. "He's my gin rummy victim at the Players every Sunday night. Why don't you write a play for both of us, then—"

"I don't think I'll be writing any more plays. They're such small potatoes, compared to what you can do on the screen. Films just haven't come of age yet."

"They never will," said Charlie.

"How can you say that? Think of the great movies that have already been made. The batting average is as good as that of the theatre."

"Maybe so, but only because there's so much money to spend that quality somehow leaks through, in spite of the people who control the film industry."

"*Donner Pass* will be a good film," Mitch said. "How do you account for that?"

"I account for it because you're putting your own personal ass on the line, and you're cheating William Randolph Hearst, and lying to Jack Warner, and God knows who else, just to shove through your personal idea of what's good. I applaud you, son, and I'll even back your hand. But I don't think you can win in the long run. Consider this: All over the world, movies are probably the most important single cultural influence. Yet their production is controlled by men who consider their form, their content, their quality, as being completely unimportant. They just don't care. Nothing matters as long as they can hold their jobs. And yet *they* decide what the world will see."

"Nothing's perfect." Mitch said.

Charlie sighed. "Go on, climb on your train. Get out of my sight before I change my mind and back out of this mess. I can see you turning into one of those no-goods, right before my eyes."

"We've got time for another drink," Mitch said, checking his watch again.

"Have it by yourself. I'm due at the theatre."

Mitch hugged his father close.

"Give a good performance."

"You'd better do the same," said Charlie. "The tab's a little higher in the game you're playing."

12

Mitch ordered a martini, shuddered when the club car attendant poured it from a tiny bottle, and retired to a lounge chair. The first sip was not so bad as he had imagined. He stretched out his feet and watched the Illinois countryside slip past the window of the Super Chief. He had intended to fly on from Chicago, but the weather forecast was still bad and he could not see himself spending the weekend in some Kansas field.

Well, at least the screenplay's done, he thought. Now Warners can complete their budgets.

This was the side of film-making that he hated, the constant creation of plans that would lock you in, tie you down to shooting a certain number of shots of a particular actor in a predetermined location on a day that had been decided six months before. It might be convenient for the accountants, but it did not necessarily make for creative film production.

Mitch finished the martini, and waved for another. The black bar attendant smiled and waved back; began clinking ice cubes into a glass.

"All right, dahling," said a deep voice behind Mitch. "Drink alone and ruin your liver. Ignore your old friends."

Mitch spun around in the chair.

"Tallulah! Where did you come from?"

She stroked her body with both hands and stretched.

"This," she announced, "is no time for a nature lesson."

The bar attendant brought Mitch's martini and smiled.

"The usual, Miss Bankhead?"

"Gin, straight up. This bastard's on his second. I've got some catching up to do."

"It's been a long time," said Mitch. "How've you been?"

"Not long enough. I'm still mad at you. It was a rotten trick to play on an old drinking buddy."

"I don't know what you mean."

"The hell you don't! You sent that cute blonde to my dressing room last spring. It had to be you, Mitch. You were in town, and that automatically makes you guilty."

"I thought you liked little blondes."

"I do, dahling. But your little blondie turned out to be a *boy* in drag. You can imagine my surprise when I groped 'her' and found all that equipment."

"It must have been quite a shock. I'm sorry it ruined your plans for the evening."

"Oh, you know us hillbillies," she said. "We can always make do. But I still hold a grudge, Mitch Gardner. When I saw you back there in your car, I would have fixed you then and there, with the little container of *eau de lapin* I always carry, but—"

"*Eau de* what?"

"Water of rabbit, you pinhead. Bunny piss, to you. I have saved it, ever since my last pregnancy. It smells Gawd-awful."

"Thank you for not using it. I presume you dump it on unsuspecting enemies."

"Right down their necks." Tallulah smiled, sipping her gin. "But, naturally, I couldn't do that to Charlie."

"To who?"

"Your father. Some of it might have spilled on him."

Mitch leaned forward.

"Tallulah, I don't know what the hell you're talking about. Where did you see my father?"

"Have you lost your memory? He was sitting right beside you."

"Tallulah," Mitch said slowly, "I don't know what kind of joke you're pulling, but my father's in New York, finishing up his contract in the Lincoln play."

"Don't kid a kidder. I saw the old bastard."

Mitch shook his head.

134

"You couldn't have. Nobody's sat in that seat but me since we left Chicago. I'm serious, Tallulah."

She put her drink down with a trembling hand.

"Oh, shit, *no!*" she said. "Not again."

"Not what again?"

"Never mind, Mitch. I must have been seeing things."

"Has this ever happened to you before?"

She nodded. "Several times."

"Hallucinations?"

"Hallucinations, hell! I *see* them. I don't know why or how, but I do."

"See what?"

She lowered her voice.

"Ghosts."

He choked on his martini.

"Come on. I'd rather have the *eau de lapin.*"

"I'm not joking with you, Mitch. This isn't the first time I've seen someone who . . . wasn't there."

"But how can Dad be a ghost? He's alive and drunk in Manhattan."

"I'd rather not say."

"Tallulah, fun's fun, but—"

"Forget it, dahling. But, Mitch, you tell *him* to be careful."

"I will," he promised. "What takes you to the Coast?"

"We closed *The Little Foxes*. I'm going to take it out on tour in September. But I thought I'd look up some old friends before I buckled down to work again."

"Friends like David Selznick?"

She flared, "Don't even mention his name! That bastard!"

"A fairly universal reaction."

"Listen, honeychile, he looked *me* up! I didn't ask to be tested for *Gone with the Wind.*"

Mitch laughed, gesturing for two more drinks.

"Then you're the only female actress under forty who didn't."

"Dahling," she said, "believe me. I was touring in *Reflected Glory*. David saw me and immediately telephoned George Cukor, who was scheduled to direct. 'We've found our Scarlett O'Hara,' he told George." Tallulah fluttered her eyelashes. "And, dahling, who was *I* to suggest that David was wrong? Wasn't I a genuine Southern belle myself? Didn't I have a reputation for being a hell-raiser, just like little old Scarlett? And, between two old friends, wasn't I willing to do anything—and I do mean *any*thing—to get the part? How could I lose?

"I lost because an old London chum of mine, Larry Olivier, had to bring that bitch Vivien Leigh over here with him. I was thirty-four, darling. Leigh, and I *do* mean to pronounce that *Lay*, had five less years on me. Still, I'd bet she really had to put out to persuade David to give her the part."

"Yes," Mitch said. "But if you'd played Scarlett, you never would have gotten *The Little Foxes.*"

"Who *cares?*" Tallulah yelled. "Who the Christ wants a supporting role in a play on Broadway when I could have been Scarlett, God damn it, O'Hara, for MGM?"

"Selznick International," he corrected.

"Don't mention that bastard's name, I said!"

The bar attendant, slightly uneasy at her outburst, gave Tallulah her new drink. He looked at his watch.

"Dining car's opening soon," he said. "Want me to see that you-all get a good table?"

"What's the matter with you, Rastus?" Tallulah demanded. "Afraid I'm drunk?"

"No, ma'am, but we're crowded this trip and—"

"Oh, all right, is there anyone important traveling?"

The bar attendant thought for a moment.

"Miss Joan Crawford and Mr. Franchot Tone."

"Lovely," Tallulah said. "Put us at their table."

"I don't know, ma'am. I think they asked to be alone."

Tallulah nodded at Mitch.

"Cross his palm," she ordered.

The attendant took the five-dollar bill held out by Mitch.

"I'll give this to the steward, sir. Maybe he can fix up what Miss Bankhead wants."

"He fucking A better," said Tallulah Bankhead.

Joan Crawford was sipping her soup when Tallulah led the way to their table, secluded at one end of the crowded dining car. Franchot Tone was chewing on a celery stalk and staring out into the darkness.

"Dahlings," said Tallulah. "How wonderful to find you here. You both know Mitch Gardner?"

Joan Crawford, who had met Mitch once, nodded. Tone shook hands with him.

"Never had the pleasure," he began, "But I—"

"—Knew my father," said Mitch. "Sorry to disturb you, but you know Tallulah. She insisted you'd want company."

"Well," Tone said, hesitantly.

"Sit *down*, Mitch," commanded Tallulah. Since Joan was seated across from her husband, both near the window, Tallulah took the aisle seat and left Mitch beside Franchot Tone. "What looks good to eat?"

"I'm trying the fillet of sole," said Joan. "Franchot's having a steak."

"Blood rare like you used to?" Tallulah leaned forward toward Joan. "I never could get him to eat his meat cooked."

"Oh?" said Joan. "I didn't know you were old friends."

"Friends? Dahling, you *must* know, your husband and I had the *wildest* affair. But that's all over. You know, sweets, you're simply divine yourself. You could be my next."

Tone almost dropped his coffee cup. Mitch cleared his throat and tried to think of something to say.

"That's very nice of you, Miss Bankhead," said Joan. "But I'm afraid I only love men."

"Oh, well," Tallulah said lightly. "If you should ever change your mind, please give me a ring." She put down the menu and stood. "Mitch, since you seem to be all that remains, I suppose you're in luck. Are you coming?"

And, without looking back, she walked out of the dining car.

Mitch sprawled in his compartment, making minor changes in pencil on the master copy of his shooting script. It was nearly midnight when he heard some one try the door. He reached over and flipped it open.

"Come on in."

Before he could see who was entering, cold liquid was flung in his face. He threw himself back, spluttering.

"What the hell?"

"That, dahling, will teach you to stand up a lady! You poltroon!"

"My God, that wasn't your rabbit soup, was it?"

"I wouldn't waste it on you," said Tallulah. "All you got was cold water, courtesy of the cooler in the aisle."

"Well, close the door," Mitch said, brushing tiny puddles off the surface of the script.

Tallulah seated herself on the bed.

"Where the hell have you been?"

"I had a nice dinner with the Tones," Mitch said. "And since then I've been working on my script."

"That's not what I meant. You were supposed to follow me to my compartment."

"Sorry, Tallulah. I like to chase tail. But I don't want it chasing me."

She threw back her head and laughed.

"Mighty proud, aren't you? Or is it that you're afraid you wouldn't be man enough?"

"That never entered my mind. I was embarrassed by the way you treated Joan. You don't seem to know when to stop."

"If you don't make calls, dahling, you don't get orders."

"What does that mean?"

"Simply that one never knows about another lady until one asks her."

"Come on, Tallulah. You're a married woman. You've got a reputation for cutting a wide swath through everything in pants. Don't try to convince me you're *really* a lesbian."

"Who says I can't enjoy both?" She took a tiny compact from her purse. "My father exacted a promise when I left home to try and become an actress. He warned me against men and booze. I told him I would be careful with both." She leaned forward. "But he forgot to warn me against women or dope." She took a tiny pinch of a white powder from the compact and delicately sniffed it up her nose.

"What the hell is that?"

"Cocaine, love. Try some?"

He shook his head. "No, thanks. Are you crazy? That stuff's murder."

"Oh, crap. Dahling, I've been sniffing coke since I was nineteen.

I still have my wits and most of my looks left. Look what liquor did to Helen Morgan. Not that I have anything against drinking, you understand. But variety, there's the spice to life."

Mitch sighed, put the script back in his briefcase, took out his flask.

"Do you want some bourbon?"

"Not while I'm snorting. Dear me, Mitch, I seem to have overestimated you. I assumed you knew all about Congressman Bankhead's little girl."

"I thought I did. But I guess I was wrong."

"Disappointed?"

He thought for a moment.

"No, not really. But I am surprised."

"Why? You surely must have heard the stories."

"I did. But you hear so many. I dismissed a lot of them."

She kissed his cheek.

"Thank you, dahling. That was kind of you. But, you see, you were wrong. They're all true. And there's more, believe me."

Mitch finished his drink and made another one.

"Tell me."

She stretched out on the Pullman bed.

"Only if you promise me that I can stay here tonight."

"Why?"

She hugged the pillow to her.

"I don't like to sleep alone. Promise?"

"All right. But talk."

"Where shall I begin?"

"Well, did you really get your first part by sleeping with Jack Barrymore?"

"Of course not, dahling! Oh, I was madly smitten with Jack. I was living with my Aunt Louise at the Algonquin Hotel. It was 1917, that awful war was dragging on, and life was so dreary and dull. Frank Case ran the hotel then, and when my aunt went back to Alabama, he promised to watch out for me. Otherwise I would have been obliged to return to Montgomery. I had an allowance of four dollars a week."

"Come on, Tallulah, nobody could live on that, not even in 1917."

"You're right. My grandfather sent me fifty dollars every week, that was the agreement when I got permission to come to New York. But, you see, the room cost twenty-one dollars."

"That's only twenty-five. Where did the other twenty-five go?"

"Why, that's what I had to pay my maid."

"*What?* You spent half the money you had each week—"

"—On a private *French* maid. And not for the nasty reasons you're thinking. A French maid in those days meant you were somebody. I had to put up a good front, didn't I? Anyway, it took a while, but in 1918 I got my first walk-on in a turkey called *The Squab Farm*. That led to a silent film that Samuel Goldwyn shot called *Thirty a Week*. I don't even remember what it was about, but for weeks at the Algonquin I was in demand as a dinner partner, because naturally everybody was terribly interested in movies."

"Well, that hasn't changed," Mitch said.

"No, it hasn't. But I often wonder why. How can a flat image on a screen ever compare to the life and excitement of the real stage?"

"The movies took that life and excitement to small towns which had never seen a live show."

"That still doesn't explain, dahling, why New York and London and Paris should have turned to motion pictures the way they have. At one time I thought it was because of the universality of the silent film. There were no language problems to overcome. But with the coming of sound, pictures became even bigger business. Yet, what are motion pictures, really? Nothing but shadows on the wall, mummified memories of a performance someone gave long ago. They have no life of their own, no breath. They do not even exist until we turn on the electric switch. In a way, they are like a storage battery. It will power your car and turn on its lights, but only after someone has first put the electricity into it."

"I agree," said Mitch. "But that's the very appeal of the film to me. What's put on a stage lives only that one night. But once a film is put together, it will never change, not in a hundred years."

"And *that*," Tallulah said, "is why I hate them."

"Do you? Is this the same actress who would have done *anything* to play Scarlett O'Hara in the movies?"

"Oh, crap!" she said. "Don't expect me to be consistent. My overall feelings about movies have nothing to do with my personal ambitions. Where was I? We were talking about New York in 1918. Well, my dear, that was the hottest summer in human memory. I had an older friend, an actress, Estelle Winwood, from England. She was a dear, but she had such great cow eyes that I still always think of her when I see Elsie on a milk bottle. Anyway, she and I went to Atlantic City in hopes of escaping the heat wave. On our way down, I met Jack for the first time. He had a drawing room, and Estelle knew him, so we were invited to share it. All the way down, I mooned at him shamelessly, and once, when I was on my way out to the biff, I overheard him say to Estelle, 'What a pretty girl your friend is.'"

Tallulah took another sniff of the white powder and sighed.

"It's almost like coming, when it hits your bloodstream. You really ought to try it, Mitch."

"I prefer the real thing."

"Oh?" she said. "We'll see."

"Did you shack up with Jack at the beach?"

"My dear!" she said. "Whatever can you be thinking? I wasn't that kind of girl. In fact, although you won't believe this, I was still a virgin." Tallulah roared with laughter. "Yes, it's true. But it wouldn't have taken much for him to persuade me out of that office. Except he didn't even try. Oh my God, Mitch, you can't imagine how *beautiful* he was then. That's why it's like getting kicked in the stomach by a horse every time I see him now. Lord, he really did look like some kind of god. His wit was bright and fun, not bitter the way it is now. I didn't sleep all that night, and if you laugh, you bastard, I'll kick you in the crotch. I got up at dawn and went out on the boardwalk in hopes that he might be taking his morning exercise. But he wasn't there. He was taking his exercise, all right, up in the sack with some broad he'd wired to meet him there. And, you know, although I haunted the boardwalk and even the beer garden, I never saw him again on that trip."

"I wouldn't laugh at you, Tallulah," Mitch said. "I love Jack too."

"You? You love nothing but your name on the credits." She sniffled a little and dabbed at her eye. "You louse, you've got me ready to cry. But I always do, when I remember Jack as he was then. He was my first true love. It was from afar, I'll admit, but it struck me all the way to the heart. I used to skulk around the Algonquin, looking for him. And every time I caught up with him, he would brush me off. He was appearing in a play called *The Jest*. Jack's role was that of a soft, feminine man, oppressed by another, played by Lionel. I saw the play ten or fifteen times, and developed a hatred for Lionel Barrymore that was hard to overcome when I actually met him. Then, one day, Jack invited me back to his dressing room. He told me that he was going to make a film of *Dr. Jekyll and Mr. Hyde,* and asked me if I would like to be his costar. I was ready to leap at the chance, then I noticed that he had locked the door, at which point he threw aside his robe and leaped at *me.* This being the first time I had ever been seriously in danger of being ravished by a man, my innate modesty overcame my true desire to find out what it would be like, particularly with Jack. I screamed, and he got back in his robe with the speed of light, and that was the last I heard about the movie, and the last I saw of Jack for a very long time."

"So it wasn't Jack who deflowered you after all?"

"No," she said sadly.

"He always claimed he did."

"I know. I wish he had. But instead . . . " She paused.

"Yes?"

"Come to bed, Mitch. I'm tired of talking."

Toward morning, in the darkness, she pressed herself against him.

"Thank you, Mitch. You're very kind. I bet you don't know what it's like to be so terribly lonely."

"You lose your bet," he mumbled, half asleep.

13

On his first night back in California, Mitch had dinner with Clark and Carole at the ranch. He was tired from the long train trip, and his voice was hoarse with weariness.

"It's all set," he told them. "Dad will leave the play early. He agreed to play three extra weeks during the summer, so they're letting him out of the contract without penalty."

"It'll be good to see the old buzzard again," said Clark. "He really brightened up this town."

"I'm glad for you, Mitch," Carole added. "I don't know anybody in this town who's worked harder than you have. You deserve it."

"If only those cheapskates at Warners don't cut the budget so tight that we ruin the film," said Mitch. "I'm economizing everyplace I can but we can't skimp on production. I want to put that terrible winter up there on the screen, and it won't work on a sound stage, using bleached corn flakes for snow. Plus we can get a lot of publicity out of actually going to the original locations."

"You don't have to convince me," Clark said. "I never did hold with building it on the back lot if you could find the real thing."

"Paw, maybe we'd better introduce Mitch to Paul Mantz."

"The pilot?" said Mitch. "I've heard of him. Isn't he the guy who runs the *Honeymoon Express*?"

"Among other activities," said Clark. "Paul's done most of the really good flying sequences you may have seen in pictures."

"Warners has a staff pilot I'm supposed to use."

"Don't make that mistake. Use the studio plane for hauling film and stuff, but if you want good aerial photography, you'd better get Paul. I'm not kidding, partner. He'll actually save you money in the long run."

"You're really sold on him?"

"He's the best. I worked with him three films in a row. *Test Pilot, Love on the Run,* and *Too Hot to Handle.* Take my word for it, Mitch, you can't do better."

"I'll give him a call. And thanks for the tip."

"Just don't come bleeding to us when you get his bill," said Carole, serving Mitch some more mashed potatoes. "He'll nick you around two thousand dollars a week. But like Paw said, you'll know you've had the best."

"At those prices, I'd better schedule him for only one week."

"Don't tell me Jack Warner's managed to make you budget-conscious," said Clark.

"He gave me exactly enough money to make the film under ideal conditions. If one light bulb blows out, we'll go over budget."

"It's good for you," said Carole. "You need the discipline. Remind Paul about that weekend he spent with me and Paw down in La Gulla. Maybe he'll give you a discount."

Mitch groaned and pushed his chair back from the table.

"I've had it. Another bite and I explode."

"You're staying over, aren't you?" asked Carole.

"If it isn't too much trouble."

"None at all. We've got plenty of room. When guests overflow, I put them up in Paw's trailer."

Mitch grinned. "I've heard all about that trailer."

Clark laughed. "Word gets around. Well, this time the stories are true. We had a big party to celebrate Carole's getting it for me, and we went out there to spend the night. The party was still going on, and some jokers shoved it off the blocks."

"I heard another version," said Mitch.

"The one you heard is right," said Carole. "Paw was feeling his oats that night. He climbed on top the minute we turned in and got to bouncing so hard it shook that damned trailer right off its supports."

"Now, Maw, that's not the kind of thing you talk about to friends."

Carole smiled. "I've knocked your lovemaking so often in front of Mitch, it's about time he heard some reports about the times you've been good."

Clark got up.

"How about a brandy?"

"Just one."

Mitch followed the actor into the sprawling living room. A fire was blazing in the stone fireplace.

Clark handed him a large snifter.

"Napoleon," he said. "I stocked up with half a dozen cases. The way that idiotic war is going, for all we know, there won't be any more brandy out of France for a hell of a long time."

"What's the word on the French army?" Mitch asked.

"That's right, you've been on the train for three days. Well, it isn't good. I think Hitler's going to take Paris."

"I refuse to believe that!" said Carole. "The Kaiser couldn't take Paris, so where does this slimy little paperhanger get off thinking *he* can? Wait until the British get into action."

"*We* ought to be over there," Clark said.

"Roosevelt said we aren't going."

"I think he's lying."

"Easy," said Carole. "You're talking about the man I love."

"The *other* man you love," said Clark. "Seriously, Mitch, all you have to do is look around. We're going on a war footing, I can sense it. The question is, will we be tooled up in time? Once we lose our foothold in Europe, it's all over. The British can't hold after that, they'd be bombed into rubble and overrun in a month."

"Speaking as an Irishman, I never underestimate the English. They're not inclined to give up."

"Stop it, you two!" said Carole. "I don't want to hear all this nonsense about war. President Roosevelt said our boys won't fight in foreign battles, and that's that. Come on, let's assassinate the character of one of our friends, or tear apart the new Gary Cooper movie, or, for Christ's sake, just get drunk. Only don't talk about war!"

Her voice was ragged. Gable touched her hand.

"Don't get all riled up, Maw. I'm too old to fight anyway."

"If we *do* go to war, you fat old bastard, you'd *better* fight."

He studied her.

"Maw, you mean that, don't you?"

"I never meant anything more," she said. "It makes me sick,

listening to the talk around the studio, how L. B. Mayer and Harry Cohn and all the other big sticks are wheeling and dealing to get the movie industry declared essential to war production, so they can go on making money while the ordinary men are out there in the trenches bleeding."

"They don't fight in trenches anymore," Mitch put in.

"Shut up, smartass! I'd better not see *you* slinking around in civies, either. This country has been goddamned good to all three of us, and don't you forget it."

"Carole, I promise to volunteer the moment war is declared. If and when."

She sat down, blinking her eyes.

"You're lying. But I don't blame you. I don't think it's fair, the way the men have to go off and be wounded or killed, while the women sit at home rolling bandages."

"I'll roll bandages," Clark said. "And you can go in my place."

She held his big hand in her own. "Maybe I will at that."

Although Mitch had spoken to Humphrey Bogart at occasional parties and studio functions, he did not really know the actor. He was surprised to discover how cultured and dryly witty the Warners "tough guy" really was. Gone was the snarl, the rasping slang—except in occasional deliberate jokes Bogart turned on himself.

He and Mitch were seated at the far end of the long Malibu pier, sipping beer and watching the old men fish in the moonlight.

"I like to come down here at night," Bogart said. "Maybe it's from having been in the Navy, but I never like to be too far from the water."

"One of these days I'm going to buy myself a boat," Mitch said.

"Don't wait too long, keed," said Bogie. "Enjoy it while you can, that's my motto."

"I wish you'd reconsider being in my film," Mitch said. "It's a crucial supporting role, Keseberg. He's feeble-minded, but he *survives.*"

"I can't do it," said Bogart. "Raoul Walsh is finally giving me a chance to break out of playing backup man to Cagney. He and John Huston have a terrific script, *High Sierra*. George Raft turned it down." He laughed. "Maybe that's my slot. Picking up the parts Raft, or Eddie Robinson, or Cagney won't do."

"We're not shooting until snow flies," said Mitch. "I hope I've got Judy Garland. And L.B. will lend me Wallace Beery for Keseberg, but I'd rather have you."

"Wally's good box office," said Bogart. "So is Judy. Go on, pack the marquee with big names. But that's not enough. Make the best picture you can. Make it to please yourself. Do you know that new director, Nick Ray?"

"Only by name."

"He said something I've gotten stuck in my head. He said, 'There's no sure formula for success. But there's one for failure. Try to please *everybody*.' You know, Mitch, we bitch about how many salaries we've got to carry on our backs, but in spite of all the waste, we still, by God, make some damned good movies. Why? Because every so often there's a guy who doesn't care only about the money, he's out to do the best job he can. Get enough of that kind together with a good idea and you wind up with a good picture."

"Yeah," Mitch groaned. "But what happens when I try to get one of those guys? He tells me he's making a different picture with John Huston!"

"Did you know he's writing another version of *The Maltese Falcon?* He wants me and Peter Lorre to do it."

"It's died at the box office twice already. Why the hell would anyone want to revive it again?"

"Remember Nick Ray's formula for failure?"

Mitch looked at his watch.

"It's nine o'clock. Weren't you supposed to take Mayo out for dinner?"

"Slugsy knows better than to believe me," said Bogart. "Besides which, I'm mad at her."

"What for?"

"I got home from the studio last night tired. I'd been chasing Barton MacLane over rooftops all day. And it's hot, right? So I flop down on the couch and say, 'Get me a drink. It's hotter than hell.' 'Oh,' she says. 'It's hot. Call the NBC Blue Network. Humphrey Bogart, the terrific movie star, announced that it's hot today.' This," Bogart pointed out, "is only average for the course, you understand. I thought I was safe, the real danger flags weren't flying yet."

"How do you know when they are?"

"When Slugsy starts humming *Embraceable You,* that is the time to dive for shelter. But this time, without so much as a hum, she dumps a pitcher of iced tea over my head. And do you know why?"

"She found lipstick on your skivvies?"

Bogart laughed. "That wouldn't upset her. No, she'd been reading Louella Parsons, who mentioned us in passing, something like, 'Also at the party were Warner Bros.' tough guy, Humphrey Bogart, and his wife, former actress Mayo Methot.' Bam! That's all it took. 'Former actress!'" Bogart finished his beer and crushed the can between his fingers. "I guess I should be glad it was iced tea. Usually it's worse. Do you know who lives in our house now? Four dogs, four cats, six canaries, and one doctor on permanent house call to patch up my wounds."

"I noticed the sign in front of your house," Mitch said helpfully.

Boggie nodded. "Slugsy Hollow. We don't try to hide it. We couldn't. Our bills for bandages are almost as high as the ones for booze." He looked down at the water and frowned. "Maybe that's not funny. I think Slugsy's got a real booze problem. Maybe that's why we fight so much. She gets a few in her, her fuse is so short it doesn't even hiss. Just, *bang!*"

"Maybe you ought to cut down, both of you, for a while."

"What the hell for? I don't get plotzed. She does. Why should I stop doing something I enjoy, just because *she* can't handle it? And, believe me, there's nothing worse than— Hell, you'll see. It's a barrel of monkeys up there in Slugsy Hollow."

Mitch felt embarrassed. "Well, the later we are, the worse it'll be."

Bogart shrugged. "It's nine o'clock, right? She's already in the bag, so there's no hurry. She never passes out. She'll be no more drunk in an hour than she is right now."

"Why on earth did you marry her if she's so tough to take?"

"How was I supposed to know how tough she was?" Bogart laughed. "But, my friend, she *is* tough. One night in New York, we were coming out of '21'. We hit some autograph collectors, mostly kids. They always grab at me, and that spooks me, so I guess I got a little nervous and jumped in the car before Mayo. Mitch, you should have heard that blond broad. She called me every name in the book—at a volume I thought would break the car windows. Plus which she threatened to kill *me,* to take those little bastards outside and cut them up for soap, and burn down New York City in the meantime. I heard one of them. He forgot all about me and asked for *her* autograph. One of his buddies asked why, and he said, 'Because she's even tougher than *he* is!' How about that, pal? Can I pick 'em, or can I pick 'em?"

"Well, maybe you're not scared of her, but *I* am. Let's get going."

The private bar in Bogart's Horn Avenue home was decorated with caricatures of the actor and his blond wife, Mayo. A gimbeled ship's lamp hung from one wall. On another was a studio publicity shot of Mayo and Bogart, toasting glasses with a bottle of milk prominent in the foreground.

Mayo was all charm as she welcomed him. He could see no sign of inebriation.

"Bogie was just showing me the boat," said Mitch. "And it's my fault we're late. I've been bending his ear, trying to get him to do *Donner Pass* with me."

"And he turned you down, poor baby? You must need a drink."

"I'll get them," Bogart said. "Are you drinking, sweetheart?"

She whirled on him.

"What exactly is that supposed to mean?"

"Only whether or not you want me to mix you a drink. Yes or no?"

"Oh, all right," she said. "But make it light. I haven't eaten, you know."

"I'm sorry, babe." He mixed two scotches, then a martini for Mitch. "Why don't we jump in the car and go out somewhere?"

"It's too late now," she said.

"Romanoff'll feed us."

"What's the point? You'll only get in another fight with him."

He gave her one of the drinks. It was, Mitch saw, much lighter than the other one. Mayo noticed, too.

"How come you're so perfect?" she said. "How come you always know when to quit drinking?"

Now Mitch could sense the imbalance. She did not slur her words, nor did she move unsteadily. But there was an odd twist to her words, to the thrust of her meanings.

"Mark Hellinger taught me how to drink scotch," Bogart said, more to Mitch than to his wife. "Up to then, I'd been drinking like a boy. Mark really handled the stuff himself and he knew how to teach me. Some people have a little thermostat in their heads, just like the one that runs the furnace. Some guys don't. I do. It doesn't matter what time of the day I start boozing, that thermostat keeps the old body metabolism perking at just the right level to burn up the alcohol as fast as I pour it down. If it slows down, *I* slow down. So at the end of the day, I feel good, and I've felt good all along, while some poor guy who doesn't have a thermostat may have thought he was only matching me drink for drink, and suddenly he's flat under the table."

"Meaning *me,* you son of a bitch!" Mayo threw her now-empty glass at Bogart. He tilted his head slightly and it flew past, smashing against the wall. Mitch now noticed a number of discolored patches along the walls.

"Mayo's just teasing," said Bogart. "She's a lousy shot. If she really wanted to get me, she'd come after me with a meat cleaver. But she doesn't. She's really crazy about me. She knows I'm braver than Jimmy Cagney and Eddie Robinson put together."

Mayo shrieked something unintelligible and made a dash for the kitchen. Bogart finished his drink.

"Maybe we'd better go play chess with Mike," he said. "I get the feeling she's in a bad mood."

"Oh, you noticed too? Come on, let's get moving."

She caught them at the door.

"Where are you two bastards going now?" she screamed.

"Just down to Romanoff's. Why don't you take a nap, baby?"

"I'll nap *you!*"

Mitch ducked through the door; Bogart followed him. Just as the door closed, Bogart yelled, "Hey!"

It slammed behind them.

"What happened?" Mitch asked as they went down the stairs toward the car.

"Slugsy tried to break my neck," Bogie said. "Only she missed. My shoulder feels busted."

Mitch laughed. "After all, you *did* say she was tough."

He spun the wheels driving off. They turned up Sunset.

"You're going to be better off with somebody else," Bogart said thoughtfully. "There are plenty of good actors around. Besides, nobody would believe me as a cannibal."

"Who said anything about cannibals? That's not in the film."

"The boys in mimeo slipped me a copy of the real script. It wasn't too smart, having it run off at Warners."

"Oh my God," said Mitch. "It never occurred to me they read the stuff they printed."

"Are you kidding? Every kid down in mimeo has dreams of becoming Ben Hecht. They all want to write movies. Why do you think they're working for twenty bucks a week?"

"God damn it, this could screw everything up. I didn't want Jack Warner to see that version."

"He won't. Nobody runs to the front office. Besides, how's anyone to know it isn't the authorized version? But I'll give you this, keed. You've got balls. If this thing flops, it'll be your neck. You can't get an okay for one script and shoot another, not unless you've got a sure hit."

"That's what I'm gambling on."

Bogart shifted, groaned.

"What's the matter?"

"My shoulder still hurts. She really gave me a clout. Where the hell did you get the idea, anyway? Ringing in a phony script? That's crazy."

"A few of us did it to David Selznick on *Gone with the Wind*, and nobody thought twice about it. The words were on the script, so Sam Wood shot them, and the editor cut them together, and the projectionist screened them for David. Only then did the shit hit the fan."

"And you think you can get all the way to preview on *Donner Pass* without anyone catching you?"

"Why not?"

Bogart laughed. "Stranger things have happened." He shifted position again and gave a small gasp. "Buddy," he said in a strained voice, "something's not right. My shoulder's hurting worse than ever and I'm getting dizzy."

Mitch hit the brake and pulled over to the curb. He switched on the inside light.

"Jesus Christ!" he said. "You're bleeding all over the seat."

"Good old Slugsy . . . She must have stabbed me."

He smiled, slipped to one side, and passed out with his head on the open window.

"No publicity," Mitch told the doctor.

"Not a word."

The physician was in late middle age, bald, and the white coat he wore had seen better days. He had just finished taking five stitches in Bogart's right shoulder. "But your friend's lucky. Only the tip of the knife penetrated. If the incision were deeper, he would have needed hospitalization."

"Or an undertaker," mumbled Bogart. "Thanks, Doc. Any more stabbings come my way, I'll make sure you get the business."

The doctor fingered the five hundred dollars Mitch had given him.

"Always glad to be of service, Mr. Bogart."

"The name," Bogart said, "is George Raft, in case anyone asks."

The doctor smiled.

"Certainly, Mr. Raft."

14

"What do you mean, the left-hand column?"

Mitch's Warners producer, Sam Freeman, explained.

"Some people call it 'above the line.' That's what we spend for development of the property."

"I'm still lost," Mitch said. This was his first meeting with Freeman, and he wanted it to go well. But there was no point in pretending to knowledge he lacked.

His honesty did not go unnoticed.

"Hell, sometimes it confuses me, Mitch. Don't be afraid to ask questions. As long as we work together, we'll bring this baby in on schedule and under budget, and Jack Warner will let us both live another year."

"Okay," Mitch said. "Take me through it slowly."

"Above the line," Freeman said patiently, "is where we put the costs of acquiring the property. The cost of writing a screenplay, or even several screenplays. You've worked with producers like Selznick. He'll go through five, six versions, and as many writers. All that dough goes above the line. Then there's the director's fee. And mine, the producer's. And the stars. All of these costs are incurred before the picture's begun. That's why we call them 'above the line.' "

"Wait a minute. There's no property cost in *Donner Pass*. I wrote the screenplay from research I did myself."

"Wrong," said Freeman. "We may have to pay George Stewart for the use of his *Ordeal by Hunger*. Not much, but enough to keep the author and his publisher happy."

"But why?" Mitch said. "I never even opened Stewart's book. I didn't have to. I got most of my information from original sources. I spent weeks up at U. of Cal's Bancroft Library."

"So did Stewart," said Freeman. "Believe me, Mitch, this is the right way to do it. It's inevitable that you'll duplicate some of the material he's got in his book. It's cheaper and smarter to buy the rights."

"And take the dough out of my screenwriting fee?"

Freeman smiled. "Some producers would do that. But the word has been passed, Mitch. You're to be treated with kid gloves. You seem to have a friend in high places. So you get paid the full price due on screenplay. And the same goes for your director's fee. That's all out in front, my boy, less what you've deferred to earn your points-of-profit ownership. And even there, you'll be okay. You'll get a fair shake, which is somewhat more than standard. Do you know how many ways there are for a studio and a distributing company to hide profits? The mind boggles. But, within reason, whatever Warners makes, you'll make too. So count your blessings, and don't forget to pray for Mr. Hearst."

Mitched considered. "It looks to me like the system is designed to make sure all us boys close to the bone get fat, no matter what happens to the picture."

"You learn fast," said Freeman. "Screw the stockholders. Let's say *Donner Pass* is a dog. The new Bogart film will take up the slack for the studio. You and me—and Jack Warner—won't hurt any. We've already got our money out in front and the rest is gravy."

"What about the players?"

"That depends," said Freeman. "Most of them are on contract, so they get paid whether or not they work. Merely by using them in your picture, you've saved Warners a chunk of dough. As for Marion Davies, she's getting a straight fee. That's charged directly to the film."

"Now I can see why a picture costs so much."

"That's only the beginning. If we cancel at this moment, all those above-the-line costs must still be absorbed, and Warners is out that much. Except, of course, it's stolen right back from all the films now in production or release."

"And from San Simeon," Mitch said.

"That too," Freeman agreed. "Or you might never have gotten

this far. But these costs are small, compared to what we'll spend below the line. If you ever dreamed of snatching a baton from your knapsack and commanding an army, you've just arrived at your glory. Here's a list of the people who will be working for you during the next two months. They go where you tell them, do what you order, eat when you let them. And, when they collect their paychecks, the money will be charged against *your* picture."

Mitch took the long, legal-sized sheet of paper, and scanned the work categories printed there.

He read:

>Director of photography
>Camera operator
>Assistant camera operator
>Clap stick boy
>Film loader
>First, second and third assistant directors
>Second unit director
>Second unit camera operator
>Second unit assistant cameraman
>Production secretary
>Production manager
>Personal assistant to the producer
>Personal assistant to the director
>Production accountant
>Script clerk
>Dialogue coach
>Music composer
>Music arranger
>Music conductor
>Orchestra (24 performers plus one contractor)
>Sound editor
>Dubbing editor
>Sound engineer
>Boom man
>Sound mixer
>Film editor
>Assistant film editor
>Art director

Assistant art director
Special effects photographer
Special effects assistant
Scene painters
Prop makers
Prop man
Carpenters
Plasterers
Painters
Plumbers
Gardener or greensman
Gaffer (electrical supervisor)
Electrical best boy
Electrical operators
Grip foreman
First grip
Second grip
Assistant grips
Drivers
Mechanics
Still photographer
Film publicist
Publicity secretary
Costume designer
Costumers

Hairdressers
Makeup artists
Wardrobe men and women
Special advisers
Choreographer

Mitch handed the list back.

"I don't think we'll need a choreographer," he said, choking down the anger in his voice. "Other than that, you haven't forgotten anybody in town."

Freeman grinned. "Don't you have a square dance sequence?"

"Two minutes, with one broken-stringed banjo. Listen, what the goddamned hell—"

"You'll need a choreographer," said the producer. "Don't argue."

"*Mr.* Freeman," said Mitch. "It looks to me like the whole system of making pictures is a self-perpetrating racket to ensure that all of us who have jobs keep on getting our salaries. Producing the movie itself is only incidental."

"Like I said. You learn fast."

"Featherbedding is pretty easy to recognize," said Mitch. "If Warners can shoehorn a man onto the payroll, you will. If you can use two men instead of one, you will. If you can charge my film for a service it really doesn't need, you will."

"Wouldn't you, if you were Jack Warner?"

"No!"

"You've been honest so far, Mitch."

Mitch looked away.

"Shit! Okay, maybe I would. Who the hell knows? But it's no wonder pictures lose money."

"Ah," said Freeman. "There you've got it. Pictures may lose money. But the studio never does."

15

The August sun beat down heavily as Mitch waited near the airport's fence. The plane from New York had just landed, and passengers were climbing—stiffly—down the ramp from the American Airlines DC-3. Although coast-to-coast air travel was frequent enough now, it was still anything but comfortable.

He saw his father, waved and shouted.

"Dad! Over here."

Charles Gardner came toward him, scowling.

"You and your big ideas. *Fly*, you said. Why waste time on the train. Well, I flew. And never again."

"It's a long haul," Mitch admitted. "But you saved two days."

"And cut two years off my life. Do you know what those air pockets over the Rockies were like?" Charlie shook his head. "Come on, let's get my suitcases and go find a drink somewhere."

"Right, Dad. I've got a cottage for you at the Beverly Hills. And a rental car. Like you said . . . first class all the way."

"We'll see."

They waited while the baggage cart was rolled in. "I don't see my suitcase," Charlie complained.

"It's probably underneath."

But it wasn't. Soon the cart was empty, and Charlie still had no suitcase. He glowered at Mitch.

"Maybe they threw it out to save weight. We were scraping some of those mountains so close, I wouldn't be a goddamned bit surprised."

"I'll ask someone," Mitch said. But before he could, a uniformed attendant came in, carrying a tattered wreck that had, at one time, been a suitcase.

"Does this belong to anybody here?" He asked the question as if he did not want an answer.

"That's mine!" yelled Charlie. "What the hell did you do to it?"

"It, ah, must have happened somewhere along the way," said the attendant. "It arrived here like this."

He put it on a counter. Charles Gardner pawed through the contents. The clothes were oil-spattered and torn. He made a growling noise in his throat.

"We'll pay for the damages," the attendant hastened to say. "I just don't know how this could happen."

"Come on, Dad," said Mitch. "I'll let the studio's lawyers handle the claim. They'll get everything replaced."

"Who the hell's going to replace my dressing robe? I had that robe since 1904, when I played with Joe Jefferson. It's my lucky robe. And look at it!"

"Maybe we can get the oil off," Mitch said. He looked to the attendant for help.

The man shrugged.

"We don't have much luck with oil, sir."

"But you have a lot of *experience* with it, don't you?" Charlie yelled.

"Sir, I am just as appalled as you by this... accident."

"Leave the kid alone, Charlie." Mitch took his father's arm. "He's not to blame. Let's just go get drunk. What the hell, it's only money, right?"

"*And* my lucky robe," Gardner grumbled.

But he followed Mitch, who drove directly to Romanoff's. The prince threw his arms around Charlie.

"It has been so long!" he said. "We thought you did not like our town anymore."

"I don't. But my boy promised me so much money that I couldn't turn him down."

Romanoff nodded at Mitch.

"Yes, we are all proud of him ... Sit, sit. I'll order your drinks. The usual?"

"It's been eight years, Mike. How the hell would you remember the usual?"

"Bourbon and soda with lemon peel," said Romanoff.

Charlie shook his head.

"Leave it to a Russian. Okay, Mike. But you'll join us?"

Romanoff nodded. "For a moment. Later, when the crowd starts arriving, I must play genial host to all."

"You sound like a madam of a fancy house."

"Some evenings, I feel like one." Romanoff hurried away.

"I think Mike's missed you," said Mitch.

"With you here to give him trouble? Not likely." Charlie looked around the restaurant. "He's doing fine."

"That's because he's a bigger phony than anyone in town, and they all enjoy it. It's hard for a producer to find anyone to look down on."

"I never heard you talk like that before, boy. What's the matter? You getting a swelled head?"

Mitch shrugged. "Not that I know of. I just don't kid myself."

"Well, if that's all you think of Mike, you'd better not let him hear it. I know these Russians. He'll stick broken glass in your martini and laugh while you bleed to death."

"Oh, you know what I meant, Dad. With the whole world going to hell around our ears, worrying about ninety minutes of celluloid seems—selfish. Who the hell cares?"

"*You'd* better care," said his father. "Otherwise, we're all in big trouble. Look, I've been through a couple of wars, and you had a piece of one, back in 1917. There's nothing fair about them. A few people suffer terribly, and the rest of us make sympathetic noises, and some of us even get rich. That's the way the world goes, boy. You do what you can, and you stick up for your own. Well, like it or not, Mike's one of our own, and so is this town, and when you badmouth them without thinking, you're cutting your own feet out from under you. If you want to go fight, fine. Volunteer. but don't sit around drinking martinis and eating T-bone steaks, and complaining because you don't feel like a hero."

"Knock it off, Dad. Message received."

Romanoff returned with their drinks and, for himself, a slim glass of white wine. He sat.

"Just for a minute," he warned.

Charlie toasted. "Good luck, Mike."

Romanoff clinked glasses. "Good luck, Charlie. To your son."

"My son," said Charles Gardner, drinking.

Mitch nodded slightly and sipped. The martini seemed to choke him as it went down.

"Why don't you billet your people in Reno?" asked Harry Breen, the Warners production estimator. He and Mitch were standing on top of a hill, staring down into the Truckee Flats.

"Too far," said Mitch. "We'd lose hours every day just moving them back and forth. Better to pay for the trailer rental."

"But it's going to be *cold* up here," said Breen. "Hell, it's only August, and it's cold *now.*"

"Compromise. We'll stick the crew in private homes along Route 80. Cisco, Emigrant Gap, Blue Canyon, Soda Springs. Cast, we'll put the occasionals and the bit players in Truckee and Floriston. But Marion and Dad, and Wallace Beery, at least, will have trailers here with me and the key crew—camera, sound and makeup."

"That's better," said Breen. "But you'll still need gas furnaces going in the trailers. It's going to be rough."

"That's the way I like it," Mitch said. "If it's rough enough, maybe we'll get some of it on film."

29 LONG SHOT—TAMSEN—THE SNOW-COVERED HILL—DAY 29

She staggers through the drifts. Her clothing is torn and she is nearly frozen. She looks up at the sky and as she does, we:

PAN UP TO REVEAL a hawk flying.

TAMSEN
(Crying out in anguish)
Fly, damn you! If I had a gun you wouldn't be so high and mighty!

CUT TO:

30 MEDIUM SHOT—A TREE—DAY 30

A wildcat looks down and snarls.

CUT TO:

Mitch and Harry Breen listened as Mitch's assistant, Dennis Wayne, read the two scenes from a bound copy of the shooting script.

"Hold on," said Breen. "That's two different shots."

"But we can get them both at once," Mitch said.

Breen shook his head.

"We budget one shot at a time. You might get rain. You might have your cat escape."

"Shit! The sky might fall, too, but I don't think it will."

"We'll take shot 29 first," Breen said calmly. "Why the hell did you have to have sync sound? That means bringing the entire sound crew up on this mountain, just to record two lines of dialogue."

Helpfully, Dennis Wayne said, "Why don't we shoot it MOS and dub it later?"

"What's MOS?" Mitch asked.

Wayne laughed. "It means silent. They say it comes from an old Erich von Stroheim gag. 'Mit Out Sound.' MOS. How about it?"

"Hell, no! It's that studio phony baloney I'm trying to get away from. When you dub dialogue it never sounds right."

"You're the director," said Breen. "Okay, we'll have working sound. That's a boom man, mixer, and recordist."

"How come we need three guys? The goddamned recordist just sits there while the other two do all the work."

Breen was writing figures down on his estimate sheet.

"Union requirement, and you'll need grips to lay the dolly tracks. Do you want a crane, or can you get by with the crab dolly?"

"Why can't we mount the camera on a wheel chair and just shove it along? What the hell do we need a dolly and fifteen guys to push it for?"

"Because that's the way it's done," said Breen. "Then makeup."

"Marion's not wearing makeup."

"Makeup works anyway. And script girl. Gaffer..."

"For what? We don't have any lights."

"Eye highlight on the camera."

"Holy shit." Mitch threw his script down in the snow. "Do you mean we have to bring a full lighting crew all the way up here just to turn on one fifty-watt dinky to put some sparkle in Marion's eyes?"

"That's what the union says," Breen told him.

"Well, I say no."

162

Breen jotted some more figures on his pad.

"You can't say no."

"Whose side are you on?"

"The studio's. Listen, Gardner, if you get up here and start pushing your crew around, they have a perfect right to shut down production. That would cost Warner Bros. thousands of dollars every day. It's my job to make sure things like that don't happen."

"Please, Breen. We simply don't *need* all those men."

"We're paying them anyway. You might as well put them to work."

Mitch threw up his hands.

"The hell with it!" he shouted. "Go ahead, load them on me. Pile up the overhead. That's the idea, isn't it? This film's going to get charged for every deadbeat you've got on the payroll."

"What lens do you think you'll need for this shot?" Breen asked. "A fifty?"

"How the hell do I know?"

"Well, *I've* got to know so I can be sure it's included in the camera package."

"Bring one of everything."

"There's a write-off charge for each lens. Per shot. If we included them all with every setup, it'd shove the budget for photography out of sight."

"What the hell do you plan to do with those extra lenses when we aren't using them? Are you going to have a special plane to fly them back and forth to Burbank between shots?"

"Please stop fighting me," said the production estimator. "You may not realize it, but I'm giving you a break. I'm putting you in for the minimum, all the way down the line."

"All right." Mitch scuffed his foot in the rich mountain earth. "I guess I'll use a thirty-five-millimeter wide angle."

"Good move," said Breen, jotting it down on his pad.

When the operating budget for *Donner Pass,* Warner Bros. Production #1204, was completed, it included:

Direction	$ 51,000
Cast	72,885
Story and continuity	32,500

Overhead	229,000
Photography (motion picture)	23,500
Props (rental and purchase)	31,250
Extras (Screen Extras Guild)	19,300
Sound	28,900
Film editors and projection	10,620
Producer's unit fee	92,000
Production staff	25,015
Still photography	8,200
Picture film and processing	12,377
Sound film and processing	6,930
Music	8,500
Makeup	9,150
Wardrobe	8,689
Vehicle rentals	13,780
Travel expenses	6,120
Meals and lodging	21,365
Location fee and expenses	13,900
Misc.	17,500
TOTAL:	$742,481

From the $72,000 allocated for cast, Marion Davies would receive $20,000 in front, plus a deferred salary of an additional $10,000. Wallace Beery would be paid his regular MGM salary, which for the five weeks scheduled for him would amount to $15,000. However, canny L. B. Mayer had charged Warners $25,000 for the loan-out, so MGM was $10,000 ahead.

The rest of the cast money would be divided among minor players. Since Judy Garland's mother had declined to let her daughter appear in *Donner Pass*, none of these players commanded more than $1,000 a week.

Mitch was to receive $12,000 plus another $18,000 in deferred salary. These deferments would be paid out of first money after production costs had been earned.

In addition, he owned ten points, or 10 per cent, of "profits." However, under the unique Hollywood system of computing film costs, the half a million-plus actually spent shooting *Donner Pass* would be multiplied two and a half times to come up with a negative cost of $1,300,000 which had to be earned before one dime of "profit" appeared. Added to this negative cost would be the costs of prints, advertising and promotion, shipping, plus a straight 35 per cent of gross to Warners for releasing the film. This moved the "profit" even further away, so that the film would have to earn around $4 million before Mitch collected any of his 10 per cent.

One item in the budget breakdown caused Mitch to smile and swear. The studio caterer had been written in for some $13,500 in box lunches.

"I hate those goddamned box lunches," Mitch said.

That night Mitch dined with his father at Chasen's.
"Are you all set to go?" asked Charlie.
"Yes." Mitch picked at his steak. "I've done all my homework. I can't think of a thing I've overlooked."
"Then why aren't you eating?"
Mitch pushed away his plate and looked down at his trembling hands.
"Because I'm scared," he said. "Shitless."

PART THREE

Shooting Schedule

"It's like that bad night in Egypt. The dark angel is making his rounds."

—DOROTHY PARKER,
to Mitch Gardner

16

Mitch found shooting in the Warner Bros. studio less confusing than he had feared. He was surrounded by assistants, who anticipated every problem before it arose. They deferred to his judgment, but there was never any question as to what they had scheduled to do next. Dennis Wayne, Mitch's young assistant director, was always at his elbow, asking questions, suggesting, relaying instructions. Mitch found that each day's shooting schedule was prepared so carefully that he had only to speak with the actors, direct their performances, okay good takes, and move on to the next shot. He was pleased that this baptism had been so painless.

His only rough moment during the first day came when his father stormed out of a dressing room and rushed up to Mitch, screaming. "All right, where *are* they?" His voice was oddly sibilant, and he sprayed spit with every word. "God damn you, Mitch, you did it! I know you did!"

"Good morning, Dad. I like your makeup."

"Screw the makeup! *What did you do with them?*"

"Do with what?"

Gardner pointed at the empty cavity that was his mouth.

"My fucking false teeth," he lisped. "They're gone!"

"No kidding. Well, Dad, that's all right. I like you better this way anyway."

"You stole them!"

"Dad, I don't see what you're getting so upset over. Clark Gable's got false teeth and look how *he* makes out with the women."

"God damn it, Gable doesn't *perform* without his teeth! I'm warning you, Mitch. I'm not too old to kick your ass right down the street! This isn't funny."

"And I'm not joking."

Mitch took his father's elbow and guided him over to one side of the set.

"I didn't mean to get you upset, Dad. All right, I hid your teeth. I've asked you to work without them for a week, and all through the rehearsals you've ignored me. Believe me, you're *better* without them. It suits the time period you're supposed to be living in. Please, Dad, try it my way."

"Like hell!" yelled Gardner. "I quit! I'm going back to New York where I can turn my back without having my choppers stolen!"

He hurried back toward his dressing room, ripping the air with curses.

"Jesus!" said Dennis Wayne. "Maybe we'd better give him back his teeth."

"Set up the first shot with Marion," Mitch said calmly.

He made three takes before he had one he was satisfied with, and then began preparing for another sequence with Marion and Beery. He glanced up and saw his father, still in costume, watching from the shadows outside the lighted area.

Mitch gave no sign of having seen him. He briefed the actors, rehearsed, shot two takes, approved the second. When he looked again, his father had moved in closer.

Mitch instructed Wayne to prepare a third scene, this time with two of the Donner children playing with homemade toys in the squalid log cabin. As he worked on it, he was aware that his father was now hovering directly behind the camera. When Mitch went back and ordered the take to begin, he saw that Charlie had eased himself into one of the folding chairs directly behind the sound man's console. It took three takes to satisfy Mitch; during the third one, he crouched directly under the camera and, with motions of his hands, drew a touching performance from the children through the signals he gave them.

"Cut," he said.

There was a smattering of applause on the set, most of it from the crew. Mitch was pleased that he had passed their unspoken test on this first day of shooting.

"How about *me*, C.B.? Don't I get to work too?"

It was Charlie, standing up and lisping out his toothless anger.

"Dennis," said Mitch. "Set up for Charlie's big closeup. We'll start in a long shot and push in slowly until his face fills the screen."

"Teeth working, boss?" Wayne said with a straight face.

"No, God damn it!" yelled Charlie. "Teeth are *not* working. That pea-picking Illinois farmer couldn't have afforded false teeth in 1846. Don't you know anything about history?"

"Mitch, I don't know if I can help you out," said Paul Mantz. "My schedule's fatter than a Christmas turkey."

"You wouldn't abandon me up there in the mountains at the mercy of Jack Warner's staff pilot, would you?"

Mantz shrugged. "I've got to take care of my regular studio work. RKO wants me for *Men Against the Sky*. Paramount's already booked me for *For Whom the Bell Tolls*—"

"Carole said you'd help me."

The pilot sighed and rubbed one calloused hand across his sunburned face.

"You would have to pull that on me, wouldn't you?"

"Just give me one week. Paul, I need some really good aerial shots, it's mountain flying. The roughest. You're the only one who knows how to get me those shots."

"One week, maximum?"

"I promise."

"I've got a new camera plane, a Lockheed Orion," Mantz said thoughtfully. "It was originally an Altair mail plane, then Jimmy Doolittle flew it for Shell Oil. Jimmy put in a big Cyclone engine and for a while, it was the fastest plane in these parts. I'll do the job, Mitch. It's got six camera mounts, and the photographers work inside, out of the slipstream."

"And I can have her for one week?"

"You've got my word. Give me your schedule as soon as you've got it firmed up."

In late November, the studio work was finished. Plodding along at the rate of three or four script pages a day, Mitch had captured nearly fifty minutes of good footage in twenty-one days of shooting. This was slower than the usual pace at Warners, but he was still well within the original budget, and only now did he appreciate the latitude the friendly estimator had given him.

One morning, just before lunch, he called Wayne over.

"Dennis, can they set up the camera so I can run it just by pressing a button?"

"They could, but they won't. Why?"

"Never mind. Look, it's worth an extra day's pay to every man on the floor. I want to be left in here alone with Marion for half an hour. Lights on, camera loaded and ready to go. Wide-angle lens, so I won't have to worry about focus. Set it up, will you?"

Wayne shrugged. "The union shop steward won't like it. But I'll try." He went off to discuss Mitch's request with the crew leaders.

Mitch sat down near Marion.

"You're doing great," he told her. "I can't tell you how glad I am you're working with me on this."

"Stop greasing the pig, Mitch. I know you'd much rather have had Vivien Leigh."

"At first," he said. "Not now. You're fantastic. Hearst is going to be very proud of you."

"I hope so. This isn't turning out exactly the way your script did."

"If it didn't develop as we went along, that would mean we'd stagnated."

"Are we breaking for lunch?" she asked.

"Maybe. Dennis is asking the crew if you and I can stay here alone and do one shot after the rest of them leave."

"Why alone? Can't we make it with the full crew?"

"I don't think you'd want to."

"What the hell do you want me to do now? I made that sickening take of tying up your father's jaw after he d-d-died, didn't I?"

"This is different, Marion. I want to get a shot of you seminude."

"You *what?*"

"In profile, shadowed, very moody and very beautiful. You know the scene where Mrs. Murphy dies? Well, she's left the baby, Catherine. I want a shot of you holding the baby, comforting it. And when you realize it's starving—"

"Jesus Christ! You want me to n-n-nurse it?"

"That's what I want."

"Well, I won't do it. You can't make me."

"I wouldn't force you, Marion. But take a moment and think about the scene. What greater expression of beauty and love is there than a woman nursing a baby?"

"That shows how much you know about women. I wouldn't have any milk."

"You would if you'd lost a baby of your own shortly before," he said.

"But I didn't. Anyway, if I'd been pregnant, it would have showed."

"Not in those baggy dresses you wear. Remember the sequence we shot where you're in terrible pain from cramps? All I have to do is add a few words of dialogue in a cut-away, and we're in business."

"My God, you're serious. You really want me to show my tits to the world."

"I want a softly beautiful shot which just barely reveals your breast, Marion. Breast, not tit. The difference between art and vulgarity. You don't have to do it. But if you do, we'll have a scene that no one has put on the screen before."

"Well, we can't anyway. We don't have a baby."

"We have a doll mock-up. We can dub in its cries later."

"And there won't be anybody on the set but you and me?"

"Not a soul."

"You know," she said, "you're as tough as D-d-daddy. You both know exactly what you want and you go out and get it."

"Then you'll do the scene?"

"*One* take."

"That's all we'll need."

"I ought to have my head examined. Going naked, for God's sake. I thought only Hedy Lamarr did stuff like that."

"Marion, Hedy's whole body isn't as beautiful as one glimpse of your breast. That's why this scene will be so great."

"Stop flattering me. I said I'll do it."

Dennis Wayne returned.

"I'll be damned," he said. "I guess money talks. We're breaking for lunch, Mitch. You stay here. The camera's ready, and so are the lights."

"Thanks."

"You want me to hang around and help?"
Mitch smiled at Marion, who flushed.
"No, thanks, Dennis. I can handle it myself."

When all the studio work was finished, Mitch and his father went to Dave Chasen's for dinner. They shrugged off all the others who wanted to join them. Neither wanted to share this evening with a third party.

"I'm proud of you, son," said Charlie. "You've made mistakes, but they've been good mistakes. You made them because you were trying to do something special. I guess you were right. This picture might just turn out to be good."

"Thanks." Mitch stared down at his plate. "Of course, the going gets rough now. It won't be any picnic up there in the mountains."

"What the hell?" said his father. "Every year I pay out a thousand bucks or so to some guide for the privilege of sleeping in the snow while he tells me that the moose were moving last week, and I should have been there then. I guess I can stand it while getting *paid* twelve hundred a week."

"Don't mention that price around town, Dad. You ought to be getting a lot more, and everybody thinks you are. Don't let them know how cheap you worked for me, or they'll try to cut your price."

"Nice business we're in."

"Don't blame me," said Mitch. "You're the one who started it all. If you'd gone into banking like your brother, we'd both be getting our fingers green from counting other people's money now instead of trying to outwit Jack Warner."

"Right. But we wouldn't have had anywhere near as much fun."

"I'll drink to that." Mitch raised his glass.

"Down the hatch." Charlie took a swallow, then put his glass down. "It sure has taken us a long time to start getting to know one another, hasn't it?"

"I guess it's been my fault," said Mitch. "I hated you for being so successful, so rich, so happy."

"Balls! You know how long it took me to be 'successful'? I played more one-night stands in Scranton, Pennsylvania, than any living creature, and that is cruel and inhuman punishment right there. As for being rich, when have I ever had two quarters to rub together except on payday? Happy? That's all you know. Getting drunk and chasing around and having lots of 'friends' who would sell you out for a dollar, you call that happy?" He paused. "Of course, these last few months, I guess you had your own chance to find out what that's like."

"That I have. It isn't what I expected."

"It never is. When you go after what the next fellow has, you have to be careful."

"Well, when this is over, we'll both have what we want," said Mitch. "We know we're doing good work. Nobody can take that away."

"Don't be too sure. Doing good work doesn't necessarily mean getting rich."

"I don't care about being rich. I guess I did, once, when I hated you because I thought *you* were rich. But it wasn't anything I wanted because it was good, I only wanted it because you had it."

"We both screw things up, wouldn't you say? We wasted all these years. We've been nothing but strangers, standing back and walking around each other stiff-legged like two stray dogs fixing to fight. What a crying shame. All that time is gone, and we can never get it back."

"There's plenty of time left. Dad, you said you're proud of me. Well, that makes me feel good. I mean it. But let me tell you this: I'm prouder of you than I thought anyone could be. You wouldn't believe how proud I am. You're an *actor*, Charlie Gardner! I don't care how many years you hacked around in tab shows and playing second banana to George Jessel at Chautauqua. Or how many musicals you do. You're great!"

"Tab shows? I suppose my *Cyrano* was chicken liver! *Abraham Lincoln*? And is it my fault I can sing and dance as well as act?" Charlie, mock-angry, was shouting now. "You can bet your ass Raymond Massey wishes *he* could sing and dance!"

Dave Chasen came over. "Hold down the noise, will you, Charlie? I've got enough trouble around here."

Charlie waved toward an empty chair. "What happened, Dave?"

"You know Orson Welles?"

"Of him," said Mitch.

"Well, he was having an argument with his partner, John Houseman, in the back room. I don't know what it was all about.

Anyway, Orson up and throws a flaming chafing dish at Houseman. Houseman ducks, but the dish hits my draperies and it's instant five-alarm. The whole place nearly went up in smoke."

"Welles must be having trouble with his new script," Mitch smiled.

"What makes you think that?"

"Because whenever *I* have trouble with a script, my first impulse is to throw flaming chafing dishes at the nearest producer," Mitch said.

"Buzz," said Charlie, "I don't know when I had a better meal. And I don't know when I felt happier. Thanks."

"Let's get a brandy at the bar."

Mitch ordered two Martells, and when the large snifters came, they rolled them between their hands and smiled without speaking.

"Is this private?" asked Paul Mantz, coming over from a nearby table.

"Drop your landing gear." Mitch waved for another drink.

Mantz shook hands with Charlie. "Like your work. I saw everything you did for the screen. And most of the Broadway stuff."

"Paul Mantz, Dad. He flies airplanes."

"Ha!" said Charlie. "Fly the Airline of the Stars? Wiley Post, Will Rogers, Knute Rockne, to name only a few who are no longer with us?"

Mantz grinned. "So we've dropped one here and there. It's still safer than driving."

Over his brandy snifter, Mitch saw a familiar face.

"Excuse me," he said. "I see somebody."

He went down to the end of the bar and joined Judy Garland.

"You missed your chance," he told her. "If you'd done my film, we'd be drinking brandy together every night."

"Oh, Mitch!" she said, delighted. "How nice to see you."

"You look wonderful, Judy." This was no forced compliment. She had slimmed down. Her face was lovely. "What have you been doing?"

She lifted her glass. "I'm eighteen now," she said. "Scotch. And I got my own apartment, with a girl I knew at the studio."

"Terrific."

Judy made a face.

"That's all you know. I found out she's really working for L.B. and every week she gave him a list of what I ate, and the friends I saw."

"That's terrible. What did you do?"

"I cried," Judy said. "But it wasn't that much of a surprise. The studio seems to be everywhere."

"Well, you didn't lose weight just by crying. What happened?"

"Oh, pills."

"What kind of pills?"

She giggled. "Nice pills. The studio nurse gives them to me."

"What kind of pills, God damn it?"

"When I'm shooting, an hour or so before lunch they give me amphetamines. Guess what? By the time we break, I'm not hungry. It doesn't take will power at all. Of course, they make me awful nervous, and I can't sleep, so I take a couple of red devils at bed time. And the weight just melted off."

"Does Mayer know about this?"

"I guess so. He knows everything that happens at the studio. I couldn't work without pills. But everything's so much more fun now."

"Yeah, it sounds like a ball. But watch it, will you? Those pills can give you trouble."

"Oh, I will," she said. "But I know Mr. Mayer would never do anything that might hurt me."

17

"Thanks for coming, Mitch," said Scott Fitzgerald.

"Glad to." Mitch sat down in the booth of the Brown Derby and scowled at the drink before Fitzgerald. "Aren't you ever going to learn?"

"The pot calling the kettle black? Have one, Mitch."

"Just a beer. I'm cutting down. We go on location in a couple of weeks."

"God, I wish I could go with you. Don't you need a dialogue writer?"

Embarrassed, Mitch said, "Dialogue won't help me. I'm stuck with a story that has people crawling around in the snow shaking their fists at God."

Fitzgerald swallowed two quick gulps of his drink and laughed.

"My own sentiments exactly."

"How are you doing these days?"

Fitzgerald coughed.

"The old T.B.'s acting up."

"Crap. You haul that out every time you fall off the wagon."

Fitzgerald's mouth curved in a half smile.

"You think you have me all figured, don't you? Well, don't take another kick at me while I'm down."

"I think I'll switch to scotch." Mitch called out his order to the bartender. "If you're going to wallow around in self-pity, I'd better dull my senses."

Fitzgerald gripped his wrist.

"Don't be sarcastic, Mitch! I need your help."

"You know you've got it anytime you want. But don't go paranoid and start lumping me in with the rest of your imagined enemies."

"I won't," Fitzgerald promised. "It's just that suddenly there doesn't seem to be anyone I can turn to. You know about the script I did from my short story, 'Babylon Revisited,' don't you? I call it *Cosmopolitan.*"

"You wrote that for Lester Cowan over at Columbia?"

"Right. We needed eating money. I sold the story rights for a lousy eight hundred bucks. But my daughter's tuition bill was overdue, and there weren't any other buyers in sight anyway."

"Christ, Scotty, I've told you a dozen times, I'm always good for a loan."

Fitzgerald finished his drink and held the empty glass up to his eye like a telescope.

"Yes, and I've called that promise already. Have you forgotten that I owe you five hundred now?"

"So make it another five hundred. Listen, if money's all that's bothering you—"

Fitzgerald held the glass up and the bartender nodded. Then he put it back down on the table and began rolling it between his two hands.

"No, that's not it. Oh, I'm always short these days, but we're getting by. I wanted to ask if you could help out over at Columbia."

"You know how little Harry Cohn thinks of me. Anyone I recommended to him would get the kiss of death."

"But you know Lester. He's a straight Indian, isn't he?"

"As far as I know, Scotty. What was your arrangement?"

Fitzgerald pushed the empty glass away.

"Kind of half and half. Half money, half spec."

Mitch groaned. *"Never* work on speculation."

"I said it was half and half. He paid me five thousand for the first draft, with a promise of more money if the project went further."

"Well?"

"I delivered the best script I ever wrote, Mitch. It's got everything I've learned about the movies as its foundation. And Cowan liked it very much. We spent almost two months doing rewrites, tailoring it for Shirley Temple. Then, all of a sudden, they put it on the shelf."

"Why?"

"Their story is that they want to rush through a film for that brave hero, Laurence Olivier, so he can hurry back to fight for merry old England."

"I think that's true, Scotty. I heard he's enlisted."

"Well, hooray for patriotism. But, Mitch, couldn't you go to Cowan? Tell him you've read the script and that he's making a mistake to shelve it?"

"But I haven't read it."

"You can take my word. It's good."

"Of course it is. But no, Scotty, I'm sorry. I'd do anything in the world for you except put my recommendation on a script I haven't read."

"I'll send it over, then. It'll only take a couple of hours."

"Can you do it soon? I don't know how I'll make time, but I'll read it."

Fitzgerald smiled down into his drink.

"Listen to me, pleading with a punk like you to read my homework and give me a passing grade."

"Come on, Scott. I don't mean to offend you. And I would like to help, if I can. But as a writer, you know that I can't possible lie about anything as important as whether or not I think a script is good."

"I know, Mitch. Forget it. It was a lousy idea anyway. Besides," Fitzgerald said, brightening, "when my novel comes out, it'll be the same as it was before. They'll be sending their top brass around to plead with me." He laughed. "And, brother, will they pay!"

"I didn't know you were working on another book. That's great."

"It's about this town. Don't I know it? And how do you like *The Last Tycoon* as a title?"

"Sounds terrific."

"Oh, I know what you're thinking. Another of those dog-in-the-manger indictments of the movies, full of worms and sour grapes. Well, that's not so. Because, Mitch, in my old age, I've lost my bitterness. I now accept Hollywood with the resignation of a ghost assigned to a haunted house."

"How far along are you?"

"I've got four good chapters, and notes for the rest."

"I'd like to read it when you're done. As for the script, why don't I drive you home, and you can give it to me? And if I can, I'll put a bug in Lester's ear."

"No, let's forget it," said Fitzgerald. "You're involved in your own film, you don't have time to play agent for me. Don't worry, Mitch, I'll work things out with Cowan."

"All right, if that's what you want. Need a lift?"

"No, I've got the old heap outside."

Fitzgerald finished his drink and smiled. His eyes were deep in the hollows of his pale face.

"Do you know, Mitch, every one of my books is out of print? Max is talking about one of those twenty-five-cent paperback editions of *Gatsby,* but I'm not sure. Somehow it doesn't seem dignified."

"Don't look down on them. The important thing is to keep on being *read.* And, let's face it, Scotty, people just can't afford to pay three dollars for a novel."

"I hope you're wrong."

Fitzgerald got up and held out his hand. Then, suddenly, he sat down, clutching at the table.

"Scotty!"

He did not answer. Mitch hurried around the table and caught him by both shoulders.

"Are you all right?"

Fitzgerald nodded.

"Just let me rest a minute."

"What happened?"

"It was the oddest sensation," Fitzgerald whispered. "Everything seemed to go *away.* It was as if I were attached to my body by a long rubber band, and it stretched, so long and thin, as things ... receded. Then it snapped me back."

"I'm taking you to the hospital," said Mitch.

"No! I'm all right."

"Are you sure?"

"Yes," Fitzgerald said. "My doctor's giving me a checkup tomorrow. I'll mention it to him." He took the glass of water the bartender had brought over, sipped at it, tried to smile. "It was just a dizzy spell. I've had them before during a hangover."

"I'll drive you home," said Mitch.

"No, I said I'm all right. Besides—"

"You don't want her to see me."

"You got it. If she does, she'll know for sure I'm back on the sauce. And I promised. I promised ... "

"Where's your car?"

"Outside."

"Can you make it?"

Fitzgerald managed a laugh.

"I'm no invalid, you Irish Galahad. Let's have one more nip before we go."

"Don't be a fool, Scott. Come on."

Fitzgerald stood up. He was hunched down inside his coat, his head bowed. At forty-four, Mitch realized, he looked like an extremely old, enormously tired man.

"But I'm too busy to go East," Mitch told Jack Warner. "Hell, we're right up to our ears getting ready for location."

"You can bow out for a few days. I want the sales people to meet you. I want you to tell them the story. See how much interest you can stir up. The trip's important, Mitch, believe me. It's the difference between a regular booking and a road show."

"Why don't they wait until we've got it all on film?"

"It'll be too late by then. They firm their schedules up early. We're booking June and July of 1941 right now."

"Jack, can't one of your promotion men do it? I don't like to walk away from things at this stage."

Warner shook his head.

"You're the only one they'll believe. I built you up good. Besides, things won't dry up and blow away while you're gone. If you're going to wear two hats, it's about time you learned that moviemaking is 80 per cent *deal* making. That's where you spend most of your time."

Wearily, Mitch nodded.

"I'm already finding that out. All right. When do I leave?"

"How about tomorrow morning?"

Mitch fought the urge to pop inside the Paramount Theatre and see *Dodge City*, which starred his friend Errol Flynn. He sighed and headed off for his meeting at the Warners New York office.

This was his first meeting with the Skouras brothers. Half an hour later, his head was whirling. He had listened to what seemed insane babbling about first and second run, about print costs, advertising allotments, shipping charges, screening fees for foreign censors, dubbing charges for Spain, midnight-showing surcharges for projectionists, and what Spyros Skouras referred to casually as "breakage."

"What the hell is breakage?"

"Breakage," Skouras explained, "is what we call everything we can't fit in another column."

Mitch spent three days conferring with various executives at Warner's. He promised the publicity men all the cooperation they wanted during location filming. He told worried insurance specialists that every precaution would be taken to protect the cast and crew from frostbite. He assured lawyers that all was well with regard to survivors of the Donner party, that he was sticking to history and that this was attested to by the California Historical Society. He had only one minor setback, when an angry young man burst in on him in his temporary office and demanded to see his card from the Screen Directors' Guild. Mitch had not joined yet, and the young man, quivering with indignation, signed him up on the spot.

At last it was Friday morning. The work he hated was done. Location shooting lay ahead of him. The thought made the flight back to California almost comfortable.

18

The weather was lousy. The clouds were actually *below* the Truckee Pass. Paul Mantz sat in his trailer, sipping at a bourbon.

"Only a week, he told me. A promise, word of honor, gentleman's word." He slammed the glass down on the table. "Thirteen-day weeks we have now."

Mitch said, "I'm sorry, Paul. The weather isn't cooperating."

"Do you know what I had Terry do?" Mantz asked. "I had her check with the Bureau of Weather, and guess what she found? During no December on record have there ever been more than four good flying days in and around the Donner Pass."

"How about that?"

Mitch flipped through the heavily marked pages of his script, searching for more scenes he could shoot while they waited for the weather to clear.

"Who's Terry?" asked Dennis Wayne.

"My wife, you klutz."

"Gee," said Wayne, "it's too bad nobody thought to have her check that out earlier, while we were still arranging the shooting schedule."

Mantz glared at Mitch.

"Do I kill him, or will you?"

"It does no good to kill assistant directors. They reproduce by fission, and killing them only accelerates the process."

"Then let's send him down the mountain for some more booze," said Mantz.

"Hey, Paul," said Mitch, "this weather could lift at any time. Shouldn't you be in shape to fly?"

"Anytime you think I'm not fit to do my job, boss man, just let me know. I can be out of here in thirty minutes."

Mitch waved at Wayne.

"Drive down and get another case. And while you're there, call the Weather Bureau, see what the long-range forecast is."

"It was for continued cloudiness and rain on the coast side, snow up here," said Wayne.

"That was this morning. Check it again."

The assistant director left.

Thoughtfully, Mitch asked, "Paul, have you ever read Antoine de Saint-Exupéry?"

"I glanced at *Night Flight*. So?"

"I just wondered, does he tell about flying the way it really is?"

Mantz considered.

"Well, he's a real pilot himself. Maybe a little more introspective than the rest of us. Hell, most of us, we're just bus drivers with wings."

"I was just thinking of something I vaguely remember reading in one of his books. He said that there was no such thing as real fright during a storm, or a crash. He said that it was something you make up after it was all over."

"I'd say he's right," said Mantz. "I've never thought about the consequences during a midair emergency. I've always been too busy trying to keep them from happening. It's only later that you get the shakes."

"But you still go up again."

"Sure you go up again. It's your job."

"There are safer jobs."

"None that I'd have," said the pilot. "Do you think I'd like *your* job? I don't mean to put you down, Mitch, but my experience with directors so far is that they take something that's easy and make it look hard. Now, me, I'm just the opposite. I like to take the hardest thing I can find, and make it look easy."

Mantz pulled on his drink, slowly.

"Mitch, can I ask you something?"

"Sure."

"You aren't fooling around with Carole, are you?"

"That's some question. What business is it of yours?"

"I like those two. You know, Gable's some kind of man. But he's gentle. He wouldn't punch you out if he found you screwing around with his wife. He'd be too hurt. But, believe me, *I'd* let you have a couple."

"Paul, I know you're very close to Clark and Carole," said Mitch. "That's the only reason I've sat still this long." He stood up.

"Does that mean you want to fight?" asked Mantz.

"If you force me to."

Mantz jumped from his seat.

"Jesus, it's been dull around here. Come on, let's go outside."

"Why not?"

But before either man could move, the door to the trailer burst open. Dennis Wayne stood in the door.

"The weather's clearing!" he yelled.

Getting the first aerial shot Mitch wanted involved some intricate radio communications between camera plane and cast and crew on the ground. All cameras and technical personnel at the rebuilt Donner camp had to be hidden from aerial view. Mitch had four cameras rolling at the same time, each sheltered within a cabin or under a ceiling of boughs. There would be three additional cameras working inside the plane itself.

Mitch had a Moviola set up permanently in his trailer. On it, he reviewed the scenes that had already been shot in the studio. Paul and the cameraman joined him in watching as the bulky coils of thirty-five-millimeter sound and picture film threaded their separate ways though the intricate mechanism, combining to give a tiny three-by-five-inch picture accompanied by sound track.

Marion's Tamsen Donner was confronting the two men she hoped were rescuers. The men swilled precious coffee in the barren cabin and stared at her.

"I'll give you all the gold we have," said Tamsen. "But in God's name please take the three little ones out to Sutter's Fort."

She placed her hands on two of the children's shoulders.

"They're good children. This is Georgia, and Frances, and here's little Eliza."

"I don't know, ma'am," said one of the men. "That's a hard trek, with the snow and all."

"You got in!" Tamsen cried. "You plan to go out. They won't be much bother. They're strong. And they'll mind you. They'll do everything you say. Won't you, children?"

The children cast frightened looks at each other.

"Yes, we will," said Georgia.

"Sure you ain't got a little more of that gold, ma'am?" the largest of the men asked.

"We're giving you everything. *Please* take them."

"Well," said the big man. "I reckon so. But we got to leave right now."

"Give me half an hour," said Tamsen. "I've got to get them ready."

"Done," said the man. "Just make sure you get the gold ready, too."

There was a break of blank leader on the Moviola, then another scene began. In this one, Tamsen was dressing the children in their finest winter clothing.

"You got to look good when you get to Sutter's Fort," she told them. "They mustn't think you're dirt-digging farmers."

"Mama," said Eliza, "I don't want to go. The men scare me."

"They're our friends," said Tamsen. "You listen to them and do like they say, do you hear me? It's very important. Georgia, you see to it, you're the oldest."

"I'll see to it."

Frances spoke for the first time.

"Mama, we don't want to leave you."

"I've got to stay with your father, don't you understand? He's got the gangrene in his leg. Someone's got to nurse him."

"But we'll be all alone! We'll—"

"Hush up, now, and wrap that muffler real good."

The men arrived. Tamsen gave them the gold coins, wrapped in a bit of cloth. They spread them, clinking, on the table, and counted.

"Right enough," the big man said. "Let's get moving."

The two younger children were crying as Tamsen and Georgia

shooshed them toward the door. When it opened, the wind and snow wailed in and filled Tamsen's hair with glistening white particles.

"Goodbye, my dears," she whispered, staring out into the storm.

Mitch's voice, in the sound track's background, called, "Cut! Marion, that was terrific!"

Marion Davies looked up, surprised, and in the tiny voice that William Randolph Hearst loved so well, said, "Why, thank you very much."

19

"What we want now," Mitch said, briefing his cameramen and Paul, "is the departure. We'll only shoot it once, so no matter what happens, keep rolling. We'll cover any fluffs with cutaways later. Paul, here's where you come in. We show the men and the three girls climbing the hill, apparently on the verge of reaching safety. Then we sweep in over the cabins, right down on top of the trees, and, as if we were somehow leaping forward in time, the camera will look ahead and see miles and miles of the worst goddamned snow and ice ever put on film. Mountains covered with it. We'll keep going until the magazines are empty. I'm going to hold that shot on the screen as long as we can get away with it. Questions?"

"Where do I go once they start climbing the hill?" Marion asked.

"Follow them for a few yards. Then sink down in the snow. You've fainted. And don't move again until the camera plane has gone over. Everybody got it?"

"Got it," said Mantz.

"It's two ten now. We'll need half an hour to get down to the plane. We'll radio Dennis when Paul takes off. We should be approaching the location around twenty to three."

"We'll be waiting," said Wayne.

The actors began to move. Just as the two renegades and the three girls plunged through the snowdrifts on top of the hill, and Tamsen Donner fell prostrate in the snow, Paul Mantz's camera plane came roaring over at treetop level. From his position in the nose of the Lockheed Orion, Mitch looked over the cameraman's shoulder and saw the tiny figures below, black against the snow. Then Paul pulled up slightly and sped past them, just yards overhead. The bleak wilderness stretched below and as far in front as the eye could see.

"Great," Mitch yelled. "Keep going, this is fantastic!"

The plane swept between two rock faces and, its wings brushing snow from a pair of tall spruce trees, retraced the hundred-year-old path of the Donner party.

"Keep those cameras rolling!" yelled Mitch.

He sat there, watching the snow and ice whirl past, and it was like going back into the last century.

"Christ," he muttered. "They'll never forget *this* shot!"

That night, Mitch awoke with a start. He had heard something. He sat up in his bunk, listening.

There it was again.

A distant cry: "Fire!"

He rolled out of bed and jammed on his trousers, stuck naked feet down in his boots, threw on a jacket. When he opened the trailer door, the snow was bright orange with the flames.

Men were running around in the flickering glare. One of them caught Mitch's arm. It was Dennis Wayne.

"It's the camera truck!" he yelled.

"Jesus! The film's in there!" They had not been able to send the day's shooting to Hollywood, because the mountains were so fogged in that the studio plane could not land.

"I know. They're trying to get it out."

As they talked, they had been plunging through the latest snowfall, moving toward the burning trailer. Three crew members were spraying clouds of carbon dioxide from portable fire extinguishers.

Mitch rushed toward the door. Two men caught his arms.

"Don't go in," one of them warned him. "That nitrate raw stock's on fire. It makes poison gas."

"Today's *shooting* is in there!" Mitch yelled.

The men held him back.

"We don't want to lose you too. One guy's already in there, and I don't think he's coming out."

"Who?"

Before the other crewman could answer, there was a shower of glass as something hurtled out a window. It was an octagonal metal film can. Two more followed it, and then someone dived out the window and landed, curled, in the snow. His clothing was on fire.

Mitch and his two crewmen heaped snow on the burning man.

"Thanks," said a muffled voice.

Mitch hauled the man to a sitting position.

"*Paul?* What the hell were you doing in there?"

Mantz stripped himself out of his smoldering leather jacket.

"I've never lost a reel of film yet. I knew today's rushes were in there, and I was closest to the door."

"You need a drink." Mitch helped Mantz up. "I could use one myself."

"I thought you'd never ask," said the pilot.

On the morning of December 22, the last half day of shooting before breaking for the Christmas holiday, the studio plane brought Mitch's mail. He skimmed through it during a coffee break while the camera crew was lining up a shot.

One envelope was addressed in an unfamiliar hand, with "1403 North Laurel Avenue, Hollywood, California," written on the flap. Mitch tore the envelope open and skimmed down to the signature. He smiled.

December 18, 1940

DEAR MITCH:

I have been lying on my ass, listening to football games and reading, and somehow that combination caused me to think of you. I don't suppose you were able to pick up last week's Harvard-Princeton game on the radio, locked in by the mountains as you are. The old songs spun me back twenty-five years, and caused me to reflect on the mysteries of time. Is it, as Tom Wolfe wrote, a river? Flowing past us, forever, to the sea? Or is it only an illusion we carry within us, a mechanical clock that dictates our every movement and, more importantly, our beginning and our end?

Such vagaries are, I am sure, profoundly stimulating to you, neck-deep in snow. Courage, Camille, this too shall pass.

My daughter Scottie sent me Wolfe's final book, *You Can't Go*

Home Again, and I like to think that it is not overly competitive of me to see its flaws along with its greatness. There is no doubt that Wolfe had a fine, penetrating mind. He wrote like a streak of lightening, illuminating every detail of his life with each flash. But, alas, Mitch, the flash also shows up only too clearly the glaring flaw of this work:

HE HAD NOTHING TO SAY! Don't take my word, pick up the book yourself (if you can! It is longer than *War and Peace*!) and see if, behind all the recapitulations of Walt Whitman, and Nietzsche, and Milton, Wolfe has added one single thought that is new. Yes, the Carolina Kid threw great gobs of raw life, brightly colored with his own viscera, up there on the pages. And I'll give him this: he didn't hold back, he didn't try to "pace himself." He went full out, all the way, like a fire horse on its way to the blaze. But energy isn't everything as you must know. I am sure that directing a film isn't unlike writing a novel. You must constantly juggle a thousand details, knowing where each and every one fits into the great jigsaw puzzle you are assembling. And the one thing you cannot allow yourself is that compulsive passion to "pour on the steam" and race, pell mell, toward the finish line. Because it does no good at all to lead the field for half a lap and then fall out and never finish at all. We old professionals know that one secret, which more than makes up for our flagging energies.

When are you coming down off the mountain, Moses? When you do, please drop by. I plan to take a New Year's vow. I am going to stop hiding my old friends. We will march together in the Rose Parade. By then my novel will be at the typist, and maybe I can peddle it to that successful young director, Mitchel Gardner, to star John Garfield as Irving Thalberg—sorry, I meant Monroe Stahr... (Star, Stahr, do you know, this is the first time I have noticed that unconscious echo of words? Perhaps I will change his name. What do you think?) and with Spencer Tracy as me, and we'll get Cole Porter to write the background music. Or am I dreaming?

I know what you're into, Mitch. But surely you must be coming down off your perch for Christmas. If you do, please call.

Always your friend,
Scott Fitz

Mitch read the letter twice. No mention of the episode in the

Brown Derby, but Mitch had since heard reports that it had been a minor heart attack. Now, however, Fitzgerald seemed cheerful and active, and was obviously planning far ahead.

Dennis Wayne came over.

"The shot's ready, Mitch."

"How does it look?"

"You'd swear this was the blizzard of '88."

He was referring to shot #123 in the revised final shooting script of production #1204.

123 LONG SHOT—EXTERIOR—DAY   123

A lone horseman comes over the ridge. His animal shies and falls in the snow. The rider tumbles clear.

1 horse, stunt, with tack	$150.
1 stunt man, costumed, to provide 3 falls @ $35 ea. Additional falls, $50 ea.	$105.
1 backup horse	$50.

CAMERA working
SOUND working (wild track)
MINIMUM crew

TIME estimated for shot: One hour, including strike.
ESTIMATED BUDGET for shot: *$1,850.*

The script girl made a note on her clipboard. "First take started at 10:47 A.M."

"Roll camera," said Mitch.

"Roll camera!" yelled Wayne.

"Sound," said Mitch.

"Roll sound!"

"Speed," said the assistant cameraman.

"Sticks."

The slate boy clapped the zebra boards.

"Okay," said Mitch. "Everybody settle down. Let's get this one on the first take. *Action!*"

The horseman came over the hill. With a concealed trip rope, he caused the animal to shy. The horse fell, and the rider tumbled into a snowbank.

Mitch nodded. *"Cut!"* shouted Wayne.

"Okay for camera," said the assistant cameraman.

"Mitch," said the sound mixer. "I got some wind blast in my mike."

"Well, put a baffle on it."

The rider got up, brushing off snow. He took his horse's reins, and the animal struggled to its feet. Mitch went over.

"That was perfect for action. I'm going to print it, but we had some sound problems. Want to try one more?"

The stunt man shrugged.

"You're paying me for three. I owe you two."

"Fine, Dusty. This time, do you think you could make him rear a little more?"

"Mr. Gardner, I can make him rear right over backward. But you're only paying me for a fall."

"Do the rear, I'll okay another hundred bucks. After all, we already have one good fall."

"You're the boss," said the stunt man.

The angle of the camera had been changed slightly so that the old tracks in the snow were out of its viewing field. Mitch stepped up to the boom-suspended microphone and spoke directly into it.

"Okay for wind blast now?"

"Perfect."

"All right, let's go again."

The slate boy held his black-and-white slate with its familiar clap sticks in front of the camera.

"Roll camera!"

"Roll sound!"

"Speed."

"Sticks!"

The slate boy shouted out, "Production twelve oh four, scene one twenty three, take two."

He clapped the zebra-striped sticks together and leaped back out of camera range.

"All right, Dusty! Make this one count."

The stunt man rode slowly over the hill. The camera operator, peering through the finder on the side of the Mitchel BNC thirty-five-millimeter camera, turned the wheels of the Huston pan head to keep the action in the center of the picture. Out of camera range, halfway down the hill, the rider did something to his horse. The animal shrieked, stood up on its rear legs, flailing with its front hooves, and then fell backward against the mountain. The stunt man threw himself clear just in time and rolled away from the plunging horse. The animal struggled to its feet and ran down the hill. The stunt man did not get up.

"Cut!"

Mitch rushed out from behind the camera and jumped through the waist-deep snow to the side of the stunt man, who was now crawling around on hands and knees. He helped him up.

"Are you all right, Dusty?"

"Yeah. Just got the breath knocked out."

"That's worth another fifty bucks." Mitch clapped him on the shoulder. *"Great* shot." He turned to the crew. "That's a wrap! Let's all go home."

"Did you see that?" the cameraman told Wayne.

"What?"

"Dusty just did it to your boss."

"Did what?"

The cameraman laughed. "The old 'warrior-injured-in-the-line-of-duty' number. He tries it at least once on every new director. Nearly always gets him a bonus."

The Warners plane landed just after four in the afternoon at Burbank Airport. Most of the cast had come down the day before, including Charlie Gardner.

Mitch phoned the Beverly Hills Hotel, but his father had already gone out. Checking his address book, he dialed Fitzgerald's number. No one answered. He let it ring eight times, hung up, then tried Sheilah Graham. Someone picked up on the third ring.

"Hello? Sheilah?"

"No, sir. This is the maid. Miss Graham isn't home."

"I'll speak to Mr. Fitzgerald, then . . . Hello? Is Mr. Fitzgerald there?"

"Didn't you hear, sir?"

"Hear what? I've been out of town."

The voice broke.

"Mr. Fitzgerald died. He had a heart attack yesterday and died."

Mitch found a cab and told the driver to take him to the Garden of Allah. As the taxi worked its way through the rush-hour traffic, Mitch sat, staring out the window. Once, he took Fitzgerald's letter from his pocket and, without opening the envelope, held it in his hand for a while.

At the hotel, he went directly to Dorothy Parker's cottage and tapped at the door. She opened it immediately. She had been crying.

"Oh, Mitch," she said. "I knew you'd come—"

"I just heard."

"Come in." As he did, a tall, handsome man rose. "You know my husband, Allan Campbell, don't you?"

"We've met," said Campbell. "Everyone knows the famous Mr. Gardner. Do you want a drink?"

"Thanks. Anything will do."

"I left a message for you at the studio," Dorothy said. "They said you were out on location."

"Typical Warners efficiency. I never got it."

"Allan, make that two," Dorothy called. "I'm sorry, Mitch. I just can't stop crying."

"What happened?"

"He was talking to Sheilah yesterday morning, just standing there near the fireplace talking, and then he went, bingo. At least he didn't suffer."

"No. Not from that." He was staring down at the floor. "The last time I saw him he asked me for a favor. It wasn't much, I could have done it. But I—"

Dorothy held one of his hands between her palm.

"Don't, Mitch. None of us could help him. We all tried. But it was already too late when we began."

Allan brought their drinks and then sat in a chair, apart from them.

"Where is he?" Mitch asked.

"Down in L.A. on Washington Avenue. I don't know who had that bright idea."

"There probably wasn't any money," Allan said gently.

"Are you going?" Mitch asked.

"We were just leaving when you showed up," Dorothy said. "Talk me out of it, Mitch. I don't really want to go."

"Neither do I. But we can't leave him there all alone."

She fumbled in her purse.

"He knew he was dying, Mitch. Listen to this. He sent it to me only last week. It's a kind of poem." She smoothed a sheet of paper, and read:

> Your books were in your desk
>   I guess and some unfinished
> Chaos in your head
>   Was dumped to nothing by the great janitress
>   Of destinies.

She folded it carefully and put it back in her purse. "That's the lousy part, Mitch. He died thinking he'd failed. But that's not true. We all know that."

Mitch stood up.

"Come on, if we don't go now, I'll chicken out."

During the long ride to the funeral home, no one spoke.

Fitzgerald was laid out in a back room labeled the William Wordsworth. Garishly made up, he looked like a mannequin ready to be placed in a window display featuring the Roaring Twenties.

Dorothy sucked in her breath.

"Jesus, look at his hands."

There, the cosmetician had either overlooked or been unable to conceal the wrinkled, worn claws that had once written about the reckless exuberance of the Jazz Age. They were the hands of a sick old man.

Dorothy swayed and gripped Mitch's arm so hard that pain shot through him.

Staring down at what remained of Francis Scott Fitzgerald, she repeated a line one of his characters had uttered at Gatsby's funeral:

"The poor son of a bitch," she whispered.

They got back to the Garden of Allah late, and more than a little drunk. Mitch and Dorothy did most of the drinking. Allan drove.

There was a small gathering at the edge of the pool.

"Who the hell's having a party tonight?" said Dorothy.

"Looks like Sid Perelman."

"Let's shove the son of a bitch in the pool! Doesn't he have any respect?"

She headed toward the gathering, Allan and Mitch following.

"What the hell kind of crap is this?" Dorothy demanded. "Scotty's in his coffin and you creeps are drinking by the pool?"

"Shhh, Dottie," said Perelman. "We know about Scott. But there's been an accident."

She staggered slightly and sat down in one of the pool chairs. "Who?"

"Nat and Eileen. Over on Ventura Boulevard . . . They're both dead."

"Oh my bleeding Christ!" she whispered. "When's it ever going to stop?"

"I'm taking them East," said Perelman. "I just came over to let everybody know. In case you wanted to visit before we leave."

"Who's got a drink?" she asked.

John O'Hara, visiting the Coast in an attempt to sell *Pal Joey* to MGM, handed her his glass.

"Watch it," he warned her. "That's straight bourbon."

Dorothy poured it down as if it were water.

"Sid, Sid," she whispered. "What can I say?" She looked at Mitch. "It's like that bad night in Egypt. The dark angel is making his rounds."

"Amen," said O'Hara.

Allan Campbell said, "Dottie, let me take you to bed."

"You? Take *me* to bed? Get lost, Cyrano. Your sword is blunted."

"I only meant—"

"Leave me the hell alone!"

He stared down at her silently for a moment, shrugged, and walked away.

"You shouldn't treat him like that," said O'Hara.

"Shut up, mick. You're no paragon of virtue yourself. Do you want me to spill a few of your little boudoir beans?"

"Hold it down, Dorothy," Mitch said softly. "Or I'll knock you on your mean little ass. This is no time for your usual shit."

She pressed one trembling hand to her forehead.

"No, I suppose it isn't. Why doesn't somebody sew up my mouth, stop me from talking? I'd be all right, if only I wouldn't talk." She gripped his hand. "First Scott, and now the Wests. Mitch, I'm superstitious. These things come in threes. Who's going to be number three? You? You're going back up in those mountains, with snow and avalanches."

"I won't be number three," he said.

"How do you know?"

"I just know."

"They're taking Scott back to Baltimore on the train," Mitch said, staring down at his navy grog. His father, not drinking, sat near him.

"Are you going to the funeral?" Charlie asked.

"No, I hate funerals. Besides, we've got to get back up in those frigging mountains."

"I saw the rushes, you know. I'm impressed. And you were right—taking my teeth out may win me my first Oscar. Except it's going to hurt me in the starlet department."

"Tell them it's makeup," said Mitch. "Well, anyway this time poor Scott doesn't have to fly. God, how he hated it. I remember something he told me, about those lonely little airports in Kansas. You'd land at four in the morning and sit around in a crummy waiting room like the ones they have at railroad stations in small towns. Nothing to eat, nothing to drink. Nothing to do but wait. Well, Scott doesn't have to wait anymore."

"Stop crying over it," Charlie said. "He was your friend, but he's gone now. There's nothing you can do."

"It's been a lousy week for funerals, Dad." Mitch hoisted his glass. "You know about Nat West and his wife."

"I read *Miss Lonelyhearts*. The boy was talented, all right. Too bad he wasn't a good driver too."

"What a rotten thing to say!"

Charlie spread his hands.

"Son, what do you want from me? So suddenly all of your friends are getting killed, or dying of heart attacks. Is there anything either one of us can do about it?"

Mitch was quiet for a long moment.

"Eileen's sister, Ruth, has a play opening in a couple of weeks," he said finally. *My Sister Eileen.* Do you think they'll cancel it?"

"Why?"

"Well, Eileen's dead now, and—"

Charlie bit the end off a vile black cigar and lit up.

"Why the hell would they do that? Son, life and theatre aren't the same thing. You go out there on that stage and give them their show, no matter what private grief you got."

"Sure," said Mitch. " 'The show must go on.' Immortal words, spoken by some fucking theatre manager who didn't want to refund the ticket money."

Charlie shrugged. "Buzz, I don't really understand you. Here you've been in this business, man and boy, for most of your life. And you still haven't waked up to the fact that when we're up there on the stage, or on the screen, we aren't *real.* We die at every matinee, then get up and take the makeup off and go home. The audience doesn't care about our ulcers, or our piles, or our deaths."

Mitch looked at his watch.

"Why do you keep doing that?" Charlie asked. "You got an important date somewhere?"

"I promised to stop over later and see Dorothy."

"She's too old for you, son. She's too old, and she's got a husband. Of course, she's not all that exclusive."

"What the hell are you talking about?"

"I'm talking about a woman who's got two floor mats on either side of her bed, both with the word WELCOME on them."

"How do you know that?" Mitch said sheepishly.

"Used her john one night at a party."

"I just want to cheer her up. She's feeling low."

"Bullshit," said Charlie. "She's trying to upstage death—she's that kind of broad. Center stage fancy all the time, she can't even grieve honestly. She has to use it to attract attention."

Mitch shook his head.

"You're a cynical old fart, aren't you? I didn't remember that in you."

Charlie smiled. "Oh, that's not going to make me mad, son.

Because I know the difference between truth and those old pipe dreams?" He laughed. "Isn't that a gasser? You have a reputation all over town for being a no-good hard-ass, and the truth is, underneath, you're as sentimental and soft as a girl."

"And, you, naturally, are as hard as nails and never shed a single tear over a friend."

Charlie looked down at his smoldering cigar and smiled again, but this time it was a sad, wan smile.

"No," he said. "I cried over a few in my time. I guess whatever you've got, it runs in the family."

20

"I don't like it, boss," said Dennis Wayne. "The weather's getting worse."

Mitch was rummaging through a stack of shirts looking for one he had not worn yet on location.

"Where the hell's that suede?"

"You wore it Monday," said Wayne.

"And we're out of opera capes, too. I hate to say it, Dennis, but we may have to go home soon. I'm running out of wardrobe."

In the weeks on location, Mitch had made it a very obvious point to start each day's shooting in a new outfit, the more flamboyant the better. At first his choices had been greeted with laughter and derision. By now, however, the attitude of the crew and cast had changed to one of anticipation and admiration.

Even Charlie granted him a grudging nod of approval.

"I hate to admit it, Buzz," he said one evening, "but you got everybody on your side with your goddamned morning fashion show. Everybody but the weather, that is."

They were alone in Mitch's trailer, having a predinner drink. The sky outside was bulging and leaden. Mitch had been forced to wrap up shooting at three that afternoon.

"If I can finish up Marion's stuff tomorrow, we'll send her down," said Mitch. "That'll just leave the long sequence where you get into the fight with Beery, and the one where you try to get out on your own before you hurt your hand."

Charlie groaned. "I'm not one to complain, but if you wanted

Doug Fairbanks to jump around from tree to tree, why didn't you hire him?"

Mitch laughed. "You're doing just fine, you old fraud. I bet you haven't had this much fun since—"

He paused, searching for an image.

Charlie finished for him: "Since I last got my prick caught in a zipper."

Snow sifted from the dark-gray sky. Marion Davies kissed Mitch's cheek.

"I can't believe I'm finished."

She was shivering in the wind even through her heavy mink.

"Two more days with Dad and we're wrapped for good."

"I'm glad. You know, he puts up a good front, but he's terribly tired."

"We all are," Mitch said shortly.

The studio car pulled up. Mitch glared at the driver.

"You're late."

The driver shrugged. "Don't blame me, mister. Those roads are like glass. The road sander's stuck down in the valley. If you want my advice, you'd better get your ass out of here while you can."

Mitch kissed Marion again.

"See you in a few days. You were wonderful."

"Again, Charlie!" Mitch called. "That wasn't quite right. You didn't look like you were really falling."

His father was perched on the side of an icy hill.

"Damn it," he yelled back, "if I let myself really fall I might not stop sliding until I hit Salt Lake City."

"One more time. Roll 'em, Dennis."

Wayne turned to the crew.

"This is a take," he called. "Quiet!"

On cue, Charlie missed a handhold, scrabbled for balance, then tumbled down the icy hill, clawing at handfuls of snow and ice all the way. He banged into a spruce tree and half a ton of snow fell from the branches, a good bit of it covering Charlie.

"Cut!" Mitch yelled. "Great. Print it."

He made a mark on his script and turned to the next shot. Then, aware that Wayne was no longer at his side, he looked up.

The assistant director was helping Charlie out of the snow.

"I'm okay, God damn it. Just knocked out my breath."

Wayne looked around him, then shouted, *"Lunch!* One hour."

"Hey," said Mitch. "It's not even eleven thirty—"

The cameraman leaned toward him and said, "Let it go, Mitch. The old man's worn out. We'll make up the time on setups this afternoon."

"If we don't get a blizzard," Mitch complained. But he started down the hill.

"You're sure you've got it straight now?" Mitch was leaning over the studio car.

The driver, a new one who had arrived more than an hour late for the morning's shipment of exposed film, nodded.

"I'll have your secretary go down to that place on Sunset, the one that makes fancy awards. They're supposed to take these"—he touched a paper-wrapped packet on the seat beside him—"and gold-plate them, then fix them up on top of a big award just like the Oscar."

"The wording for the inscription is inside," Mitch said. "And, please, keep quiet around the studio. I don't want anybody finding out about this in advance."

"Mr. Gardner, I wouldn't open my mouth. I don't even *know* what's in this package."

The tire chains clanked against the thickening ice as the studio car slid down the highway. Mitch headed for his trailer, stamped the snow off his boots, and went in. His father was pawing around on the cluttered table.

"Lose something, Dad?"

"My goddamned teeth," Charlie grumbled. "You didn't steal them again, you bastard, did you?"

"Why would I do a thing like that? All the rest of your scenes are in long shot, so why should I care if you wear your teeth or not?"

At nine minutes after twelve in the snow-filled afternoon of December 30, 1940, Mitch Gardner leaned forward and said, quietly, "Cut."

There was a long pause. Panting, Charles Gardner looked up from his position on the ground.

"What next?"

204

"I don't know," Mitch said. "I seem to have run out of script."

His father stared at him.

"You mean this fucking thing's finished?"

Dennis Wayne threw his fur-lined hat up into the air and yelled at the top of his voice, *"It's a wrap!"*

The crew cheered and began packing up the equipment.

"God damn it," said Charlie, "I don't believe it. We won't have to spend New Year's Eve on this lousy mountain after all."

Mitch did not hear him. He was listening to the assistant, who had just rushed out from the nearby generator trailer. He nodded, then turned back to his father.

"What was that all about?" asked Charlie.

"Storm's nearly got the road closed down below. We'd better haul ass out of here. Forget packing. They'll have to send the rushes with the next load."

"Let's go."

Charlie headed for the nearest car, but the warning had come too late. Half a mile down the mountain, the driver pulled over.

"I'm sorry, Mitch. I can't even see the road. It's suicide to try and drive in this."

Mitch cursed. "Okay, let's head back to camp."

The driver tried to turn around. The car hesitated, broadside in the road. Wheels spinning, it started to slide toward a guard rail.

"Jesus Christ!" shouted Charlie. "Your wheels—"

"She won't take hold," said the driver.

The engine missed, sputtered, stalled. The driver ground the starter.

"Hand brake," Mitch suggested.

The driver pulled it on, but the slide continued.

"Let's get out of this bastard." Charlie threw open his door and leaped out into the gathering snow, followed by Mitch.

The driver cast a frantic glance over his shoulder at the approaching abyss, weighed the balance between his own self-preservation and his duty to Warner Bros.

Warners lost. He leaped to safety.

The car banged against the guard rail, which held for a moment. Then a weak section of board splintered and the sedan forced its way through. It hesitated on the brink, toppled, and crashed out of sight into the wall of pines below.

The driver cleared his throat, spat.

"There goes my job."

"Don't worry about it," said Mitch. "At least we didn't have the film with us. Let's get back to camp."

Two hours later, they staggered into the small compound of trailers. They were caked with snow, their hair frozen solid.

The lights were on in Mitch's trailer. When he opened the door, Dennis Wayne looked up. He and several of the crew were sitting on the floor.

"Mitch! We were hoping you made it through."

"Not a chance. What's going on here, a crap game?"

"We thought we'd better conserve heat," Wayne said. "The power lines are down. So are the phones."

"No sweat. Jack Warner won't leave us up here long. He'll have a rescue party out first thing in the morning."

"You're kidding."

"Am I? Remember, we've got the ending to his fucking film."

"Glory to be God," Charlie said, lying exhausted on the floor. "Then we're saved!"

Wayne's idea of conserving heat had been a good one. The storm that swept over the Truckee Pass that day was one of the worst in half a century. Hundreds of farms were cut off for days. Whole communities were isolated. Nineteen motorists, stranded along the mountain roads, died of exposure.

The *Donner Pass* crew made the best of it. A marathon poker game evolved. Outside, the snow fell and the wind buffeted the trailer walls.

Once Mitch thought he heard a plane and held up his hand for silence. But the sound, if it had been there at all, was gone.

"You and your lousy planes," Charlie grumbled.

"Cheer up, Dad. When we get out of here, I'll throw you the goddamnedest party you ever saw. We'll close Chasen's down for the night. What do you say?"

Charlie was massaging a sore left shoulder.

"First we've got to get back to civilization," he said. "Or Hollywood, whichever one is closer."

The long night passed, and a longer day, distinguishable from the night only by a pale-gray light. By now, on the battery-operated radio, they had learned how bad the storm was. Jokes about Jack Warner's rescue party ceased.

"It'll take a week for them to clear the roads," said Charlie. "At least."

"We've got plenty to eat," Mitch said. He and Dennis Wayne had been putting together a list of their supplies.

"We damn well better have. You other bastards might be able to cook Dennis here and eat him, but I'm down to my bare gums."

Mitch almost told his father, then, about the oblique honor he had bestowed on the now-famous false teeth.

Midnight.
The *Donner Pass* modern-day party hoisted glasses.
"Happy New Year," said Wayne.
"Happy New Year," said Mitch.
His father grinned toothlessly.
"Chin chin," he said.

With dawn came the sun. It was pale and lifeless, but the wind had died and the snow was no longer falling.

"Anybody know how to ski?" Mitch asked, looking out the window.

"Shhh," said Charlie. "I hear something."

"Me too," Wayne said. "Engines?"

Mitch listened. From the sky came a sound not unlike the one which might be made by some giant egg beater.

He ran outside.

A strange, ungainly machine was settling down in the clearing. Wingless, its airframe only a skeleton, its huge propellers whipping around directly overhead, it was like something from another planet.

Paul Mantz leaned out of its cockpit, holding a brown paper bag.

"Liquor store!" he called. "Where's the lady who phoned?"

Mitch lunged through the deep snow.

"What the hell *is* this thing you're flying?"

"My twenty-six-thousand-dollar helicopter," said Mantz. "You should see the bill I'm sending Warners."

"You're kidding. Did Jack really send you up?"

"You bet your ass he did. He said you had some film that belongs to him. You boys ready to get out of this ice-cream parlor? I'll have to take you one at a time. Hop on, Mitch."

Mitch hesitated. "No," he said. "Take Dad. I'll come later."

"Anything you say." The pilot paused. "Good to see you," he added. "Everybody got a little worried."

"Thanks," said Mitch, wondering why he felt no relief.

21

"That lazy bastard!" said Mitch.

"Did you call the hotel?" Bogart asked.

"Hell no. Why should I call? It's his party."

Bogart shrugged. "Charlie could be tired, a little boozed up. He might have flaked out and missed the wake-up call."

"God damn it, he knows how important this is to me."

"How about Charlie?" asked Bogie.

"What about him?"

"Is it important to Charlie too?" Bogart sloshed his scotch around in its glass and sipped. "Hell, Mitch, everybody in town heard about the gold-plated false teeth award you figure to spring on him. Maybe he decided he'd rather curl up with a cold martini and a warm blonde."

"But the party isn't only for me. It's for the good of the picture."

"Screw the picture," said Bogart. "You can make pictures any day of the week. But they only give you one old man." He turned to his wife, who was animatedly trading gossip with Margaret Booth, MGM's head film cutter. "Hey, Slugsy, shut your trap for a minute. Zip into the powder room and call the Beverly Hills. Get Charlie Gardner on the horn. Tell him his crazy son's getting pissed off, and is he coming to the party or not?"

"Just tell him to get his ass down here," said Mitch.

Mayo smiled. "Play nice, Mitch. Don't get Charlie mad at you too. You ought to keep at least *one* friend in this town."

As she headed for the ladies' room, Louella Parsons, sensing a story in the tense, nervous Mitch Gardner, hurried over. In her dark dress she was like a blacked-out battleship crashing through the surf of the crowd.

"It's a beautiful party, Mitch," she said, sprinkling his shirt front with droplets of old-fashioned as she waved her hand to indicate the crowded room. "Everyone, but everyone is here." She sipped. "Even Hedda. Oh, don't worry, dear. I know you had to ask her too. But she didn't have to accept. She knew I'd be here." Another sip, a little cough. "Where is dear Charlie hiding himself? I wanted to tell him that I've heard he's simply *mar*velous in *Donner Pass*. How utterly clever of you to cast your own father as a cannibal! But darling, why on earth did you have to go all the way up in the *mountains?* Oh, I realize Hollywood isn't as gay as it should be because of that terrible war in Europe, but—"

"Louella," Mitch said quietly, turning away from her, "why don't you be a nice Lolly and go sit down on a sofa somewhere and have a quiet pee? That is, if you haven't already." He walked away without looking back.

Bogart looked down into his glass.

"I've run dry," he said. "How about you, Louella?"

"That bastard!" Louella began to sniffle. "This is only his first picture. Who the hell does he think he is?"

"That's his big trouble," said Bogie. "He doesn't know."

"Mitch's night has been completely ruined," said Myron Selznick, "and it couldn't happen to a nicer guy. Do you know what he paid his father for *Donner Pass*? For climbing up that goddamned mountain and freezing his ass off? Twelve hundred a week! Peanuts."

"Oh, stop being such an *agent,*" said Carole Landis. "Mitch didn't set the salaries, Jack Warner did. Anyway, I think he's cute."

"You're lucky I'm running interference for you, baby," said Myron. "Because you're a lousy judge of character. Mitch Gardner would sell his own father for an Oscar nomination. And I think that's just what he's done."

"He's still cute. Not only that, he's lonely. It makes you want to reach out and help him."

"Go ahead," said Selznick. "Join the ranks of thousands who've tried. Jesus, I'll never understand women."

"Stop skimping on the booze," Mitch told Dave Chasen. "Are you afraid we'll drink up all your hoarded scotch?"

"Settle down, Mitch. The guests are getting them the way they like. This may surprise you, but not everybody *wants* to get blasted by midnight."

Mayo joined them. "Mitch, your father's bungalow doesn't answer. They even sent a boy over to tap at the door."

Mitch glared at Chasen.

"Dad's one you were wrong about, Dave. It's not eleven o'clock yet, and that old bastard's passed out cold."

"You're wrong about Mitch," Spencer Tracy told George Raft. "Your trouble is that you haven't worked with him since 1937. You're right, back then he wasn't anything more than a nice guy to get drunk with. Jesus, did Clark and I booze it up with that hollow-legged bastard! But he's settled down recently."

Raft scowled at Mitch, who was arguing loudly with Chasen.

"Yeah, so I see. He's certainly being the gracious host tonight. I've had enough, Spence. I'm going home."

Tracy touched his shoulder.

"No, don't. Charlie Gardner's late, and this party was supposed to be in his honor. That's why Mitch is being such a bastard. I guess this was the first time he ever felt really able to show his old man how much he likes him. And now it's going all wrong." He looked at his watch. "I hope Charlie shows up soon."

"He'd better," Raft said. "Or the police will."

Tracy squinted at him.

"Why's that?"

"Because unless I miss my guess, your buddy Mitch is keyed up enough to sock somebody if they so much as blink."

"Now," said Errol Flynn, "would you mind repeating that slur again? It's bloody noisy in here."

"Gladly." Robert Taylor rubbed his hand across his neatly trimmed mustache. "I said Mitch Gardner is the most reckless man in the business. To which I will add: he's absolutely uncaring about anything except the world's image of Mr. Mitchel Gardner. Who the hell else would show up on the set wearing an opera cape with a red-velvet lining? Who has to out-deMille deMille by having deerskin puttees wrapped around the legs of a green Donegal tweed suit? Do you know what I heard from his assistant director? They were on location up at the Donner Pass for twenty-nine days, and in all that time Mitch Gardner never wore the same outfit twice."

"You're missing the point, you ass. That opera cloak got him a mention in every important column in town. Which, not incidentally, reminded people that a film named *Donner Pass* was being made."

"If you think so much of Mr. Gardner, why didn't you do the film with him?"

"Because, old sport, I wasn't asked. I wasn't even *here* to be asked."

"Well, *I* was," said Taylor. "And I turned him down. Cannibalism isn't one of my favorite subjects."

"You silly shit, didn't you read the script? *Donner Pass* isn't about cannibalism at all, not in the literal sense."

"Who says so?" asked a new voice.

"Mitch! Will you please inform this well-brushed cretin about your film. I've been trying to defend it, and—"

"That wasn't very wise of you, Errol," Mitch said. "Because Bob's absolutely right. The whole thrust of the film is a study of cannibalism. Rather like one of those 'how-to' films they're making for the Army."

"Come off it, Mitch. You're sending me up. Remember, old cock, I read the script."

"I know. But you see, Errol, I didn't shoot from that script. Its only purpose was to get me my financing. By the way, welcome back to town."

Errol Flynn stared at him incredulously.

"But what's Jack Warner going to say when he learns the truth?"

"By then I'll have my press, and we'll have a couple of sneak previews under our belts. If the film's a flop, I don't care what he says. And if it's a hit, he'll be so busy counting his money that he won't have time to say anything."

"Robert," said Flynn, "I withdraw everything I said about Mitch. He *is* a reckless bastard."

"Watch it. Watch who you call bastard."

"Sorry, Mitch. But of all people, why did you have to deceive *me?* I—"

"That's not enough."

"*What,* old cock?"

"You insulted my father. Sorry's not enough."

"Your father wasn't mentioned, my friend. Perhaps he's the one who should feel aggrieved. He's a fine gentleman and I'm only sorry I can't, at the moment, say the same for his son. Who, I might add—"

Mitch threw what remained of his scotch and water into Flynn's face.

The noisy room fell suddenly quiet.

Dave Chasen stepped up and handed Flynn a table napkin. Flynn wiped his face.

"Go home," Chasen told Mitch. "You know better than this."

"It's all right, Dave," said Flynn.

"Go home, Mitch!" Chasen repeated.

"Screw you, Dave," said Mitch.

Errol started for the door.

"Where are you going, yellow belly?" called Mitch.

"Outside," said Flynn. "You can join me if you insist."

Behind Chasen's, in a cul de sac formed by two high hedges and one wall of the restaurant, Mitch Gardner and Errol Flynn squared off in drunken combat.

"Call me a bastard, will you?"

Mitch, bringing a haymaker up from the ground, missed Flynn by a good three inches.

"You silly shit. I call *everybody* bastard!"

Flynn gave Mitch a push with both palms against the shoulders and sat him down on the concrete of the parking lot.

"Hey, no fair! We're fighting, not wrestling."

"I'd far rather we were drinking. Who knows, I might even catch up with you."

"Like hell."

Mitch jumped up and pummeled Flynn's shoulders and arms with wild punches. One connected on the actor's cheek.

"Watch it! Don't bruise the face. I'm shooting tomorrow."

"You'll be out cold tomorrow!" Mitch promised, renewing his attack.

Flynn held him off with outstretched arms.

"Don't make me hit you, Mitch!"

"*Hit* me? You kiwi fag, you couldn't hit the inside of a urinal if you squatted over it!"

Flynn's left fist flicked out and connected with Mitch Gardner's chin. Mitch promptly fell down.

Anxiously, Flynn bent over him. Mitch kicked him in the leg.

"Sucker punch!" Mitch complained. "I wasn't ready."

Flynn pulled him to an upright position and stepped back.

"Are you ready now?" he asked.

"Bet your ass, you sheep-fucker!"

Putting all his weight behind the punch, Flynn hit Mitch in the solar plexus with a straight right. Mitch fell down again. Flynn stepped back, lowered his arms, and looked around him.

"He made me do it."

"I know," said Spencer Tracy, bending over Mitch. "I saw it."

Mitch was gasping for breath.

"What the hell happened?" he said finally.

"You badmouthed Errol and he dumped you on your ass. You got up and badmouthed him again and he dumped you on your ass again."

"Get out of my way!" Mitch was struggling up.

Flynn retreated. "You've had enough."

"Like hell!"

Mitch threw a roundhouse swing. Flynn ducked under it easily and jabbed Mitch on the point of the jaw. For the third time, Mitch went down.

"Hold him back, Spence," Flynn said. "I don't want to hurt him."

Flat on his back, Mitch was shouting: "Got you on the run, haven't I?"

He staggered to his feet, much slower this time. Flynn looked around, trying to find an avenue of escape. But Mitch was relentless in his tottering pursuit.

"Stand still and fight!" he demanded.

Flynn put out his left hand. Mitch ran into it—and crumpled.

"Mitch," said Flynn. "*Don't* get up again. Please!"

On his hands and knees, Mitch groaned. "Do you give in?"

Flynn dropped his hands.

"Yes."

"I knew I had you the third time you knocked me down."

Mitch lurched to his feet and swayed into Flynn's arms.

"Come on, you kiwi bastard, let's go see my old man."

Charlie Gardner's bungalow door was closed and locked. Mitch pounded on the door and shouted.

"Dad!"

Flynn peered through the window.

"He's asleep, Mitch. I can see his feet on the bed."

"Dead drunk. Thanks a lot, Dad."

"I'll go get a pass key," said Flynn.

"Screw him. We'll both go and on the way we can have a drink in the Polo Lounge."

At Mitch's regular table, they sent the waitress for two martinis, straight up.

"How's your jaw, old cock?"

"Tender. How's your fist?"

Flynn laughed. "Skinned." The drinks came, and he lifted his. "I'm sorry I pissed you off."

"What the hell, it was a dull party anyway. I only wish the old man could have made it. It was all for him. I had to make out it was for the picture, so we could write it off. But it was really for Charlie."

"I know it was. You and he are very close, aren't you?"

Mitch laughed. "When we're not at each other's throats. I suppose you could call that close."

"But you're fortunate. You've spent a great deal of your life with him. As a child, on the road in the theatre. Then on Broadway, and finally out here. With me, it was just the opposite. When my father was working in Australia, I was packed off to school in England. And when I was ripping through New Zealand and points north, the pater had gone back to London. We have had what you might call rather a long distance relationship."

The night maitre d' paused at their table.

"How are you, Mr. Gardner? Did the party go nicely?"

"Nice enough," Mitch said, fingering his swollen jaw.

"Then your father felt well enough to attend after all?"

"What do you mean?"

"He was having a drink right here, at your table, around eight o'clock. I stopped by to say hello, and he complained of being in pain. I asked if he wanted to see the house doctor, but he said not to bother, he'd go back to the bungalow and take something for it. When his taxi arrived, we called the bungalow but there was no answer. I assumed he had driven on with someone else and had forgotten having asked for a taxi." He stared at Mitch, who had leaped up from his chair. "Is something wrong?"

"I'll get the key," said Flynn.

"Fuck the key!" Mitch said, running.

He had torn a gash in his ankle, kicking out the door panels. A few drops of blood dripped onto the expensive carpet as Mitch sat beside his father's bed, staring down at the still, quiet bundle of tuxedo-clad gray flesh and white hair that had been Charles Gardner.

The house doctor straightened up from his examination.

"He's been dead for some hours. From what you've told me, I would say it was heart failure."

"What caused it?"

"I couldn't say."

"Could exertion in a high altitude over a period of weeks have contributed?"

"Perhaps," said the doctor.

"Did it happen fast?"

"Probably. From appearance, I'd say that Mr. Gardner felt discomfort, severe enough to lead him to take a pain-killer. Then he stretched out. There is no sign of a struggle. He just slept away."

"What if someone'd been here to call you? Couldn't you have saved him?"

The doctor shrugged.

"Stop it, Mitch!" said Flynn. "Nobody in the world can answer a question like that!"

Mitch stared down at his trembling hands, still dirty from the fight in the parking lot.

"I should have been here. I was supposed to pick him up. But I ran out on him, to talk to those goddamned newspaper reporters."

Flynn gave the doctor a sharp look. The doctor nodded.

"Let me give you something for your nerves, Mr. Gardner—"

"Screw my nerves. Get the hell out of here. Both of you."

"Come with me, Mitch," said Flynn. "You don't want to stay here alone."

"Who says I'm alone? Move your ass, friend."

As Flynn and the doctor started toward the door, Mitch looked down at his father's motionless, composed face.

"You lying old bastard," he whispered. "You always said you were too mean to die!"

The door closed behind the two men.

"You couldn't wait, could you Charlie? Just when I was getting able to pay you back for all you've been to me, you had to go and do something stupid like this!"

He lifted his father's cold hand and stroked it.

"God damn it, Charlie, why the hell couldn't you have waited?"

"It was a nice funeral," said Dorothy Parker. "You really sent Charlie off in style."

"He wouldn't have settled for anything else. First class all the way. That was my old man."

Mitch and Dorothy were seated in the living room of her Garden of Allah cottage.

She touched his hand.

"When are you going to cry, Mitch?"

"I don't think I am."

"You ought to. Or commit suicide. That always brings relief."

"You should know, Dorothy. You've tried it enough times."

"I know," she said. "My wrists look like the underside of a washboard. I've had my head in the oven so often that the table waiter instinctively spreads it with butter when he brings the first course."

Mitch tried to smile.

"If you keep on committing suicide," he said, "you might permanently injure your health."

"You stole that! Bob Benchley said it first."

"Writers never steal. We call it 'research.'"

She gripped his hand.

"Please, Mitch. Cry!"

He stared down at her fingers, white-knuckled against his own.

"Well," he said softly, "at least now we know who was scheduled to be number three."

"Come on, Mitch. You shouldn't pay any attention to me when I start spouting that spirit nonsense. You and I, we're too beat up to believe in God and all that crap. It's blind chance, the whole poker game, and no power on or off earth can stack the deck."

"Lately I'm not so sure," he said. "I think I'm starting to believe in cause and effect."

"In other words, just because you acted like a shit, God punished you by killing your father? You know better than that."

"No, not God. But why was I so hard on Charlie? I drove him beyond his strength. I ridiculed him before the crew, to force him into dropping his broad stage mannerisms. I shamed him into playing the role without his false teeth."

"And you probably won him an Oscar. My God, Mitch, don't you realize what you've got on that strip of film? I'm sorry Charlie's dead—but because of what you put on film, he'll never be gone completely. Fifty years from now, people will be seeing Charlie's portrayal of George Donner." She smiled. "And while Marion Davies isn't exactly my favorite person, I think she'll be remembered for *Donner Pass* too. I've heard that you really dragged a tremendous acting job out of that pathetic woman. I hate to admit it, but after this they're going to have to accept the fact that you *are* a director."

"So what? Is that lousy gold statue worth my father's life? Does a scrapbook full of rave notices compensate for the fact that from now on there won't be any Charlie Gardner? No, Dottie, it's not a fair trade. If I had it to do over again, I'd never start the film. I mean that."

"And then Charlie would have dropped dead in a poker game and there wouldn't be anything left to remember him by. Face it, Mitch, his time had come. You didn't hurry things. They just happened."

"I don't believe that, Dorothy. I just don't."

"Try to believe it." She stroked his face. "You've got to believe it, don't you see? Or there's nothing left for you."

He buried his face against her breast.

"That's right," she said. "It's about time. Just let it go. Shhh, dear. It's all right. Let it all out."

22

The preview audience sat perfectly still in the theatre. There was no movement, no coughing, none of the smart comments that were standard from preview-sophisticated Los Angeles audiences.

Marion Davies, unrecognizable in her dirty, ragged costume, her hair wild and streaked with gray, was laying out the dead body of Tamsen's husband.

"Where are the children, George?" she cried. "Why aren't they here? Eliza, come at once!"

His false teeth out, his mouth gaping open, Charles Gardner made one of the most realistic dead men ever filmed. The audience gasped as Tamsen bound up his jaw with a strip of cloth.

"I won't leave you, George. They won't do to you what they've done to the others!"

Her mood changed and she began calling for the children again. The cabin door opened; Wallace Beery as the feeble-minded Keseberg stood there.

"Come away, Miz Donner. You don't want to see nothing."

She huddled over the body.

"Get out! You won't touch him!"

"We got to get his brains before they spoil," Keseberg mumbled, moving toward her. His huge chest filled the screen, which went black.

Time lapse dissolve.

The final party of rescuers reached the ravaged cabins. They moved silently from one abandoned shelter to the next, finding only grim scraps of flesh and clothing to testify to the existence of their former occupants. Finally they reached the cabin of Lewis Keseberg. He sat alone in the room, his clothing blood-spattered, huddled over a small fire. Heating near it were two kettles.

One of the men peered into them.

"That's *blood,*" he said.

"There's blood in dead bodies," Keseberg cackled.

"What happened to all the others?"

"They died. They up and died . . . All but me."

The men looked around the cabin, at hideous piles of human bones, still joined to tattered flesh.

"Let's get out of here," said one of the men.

Keseberg began tossing chucks of flesh and bones into a wooden box.

"We got to give what's left a decent burial," he said. As the camera moved in on his crazed face, he looked around and said, "I hope God gonna forgive me for what I done. I hope I gonna get to heaven yet."

The scene dissolved through, and once again the viewer found himself in the sky, skimming over the desolate landscape. Only now, instead of being empty snow and ice, ghostlike wagons moved through the long-buried pass, pushing on toward California.

The final title zoomed up:

THE END

"Look at those preview cards!" said Mitch. "Greats, sixty. Another forty Fines. Only two Lousys. Jack, they love it!"

"You mick bastard," Warner said. "So this is why you had it edited in secret! God knows that's not the script I okayed."

"You wouldn't have okayed this one."

"You bet your ass I wouldn't."

"But now?"

Warner shook his head.

"I don't know what the critics will do to us. But it's one ball-buster of a movie."

"Was I right?"

"All I can say is, Harry Cohn's ass wouldn't have itched once."

"How are you going to handle the release, Jack? You just can't send this out with a college fraternity musical."

"I know. We've got to have a sales meeting. Maybe we'll road-show it."

Secretly, Mitch had hoped for that decision.

"Make it a hard ticket?"

"Hell, yes. Two showings a day. Reserved seats. Keep it classy. This isn't just entertainment, let me tell you. This is art."

"Glad you think so."

Warner lit another cigar.

"It's too bad your old man couldn't have seen it. I bet he wins an Oscar. My God, that death scene. I had to look away. He's better than Charley Grapewin dying in *The Grapes of Wrath*. How did you ever get him to take out his false teeth? And Marion! She looks a thousand years old! She's never been this good. I don't want you to pass this any further, Mitch, but if it hadn't been for Hearst's money, she wouldn't have been in this film at all."

"She's an actress," Mitch said. "Now they'll have to give her real roles instead of all that fairy princess stuff."

"Yeah." Warner was quiet for a moment. "Except there's one problem, Mitch. Hearst *likes* that fairy princess stuff."

The call came at ten the next morning. By noon, Mitch was aboard William Randolph Hearst's private plane, en route to San Simeon.

"Can't you take it a little slower?" he complained to the pilot. The Fokker was trembling with speed.

"Sorry, Mr. Gardner. Mr. Hearst said to get you up there with no delay, and from him, that means you should have been there yesterday."

"Well, it won't do any of us good if the wings fall off this thing."

"We're almost there. Strap yourself in for landing."

"Strap myself in? Buddy, I haven't unstrapped since that rocket blast you call a takeoff."

A car was waiting at the field, and Mitch was on his way up to the Enchanted Hill before the plane's propellers stopped spinning. One of Hearst's executives was waiting at the foot of the marble steps. Without speaking, he led Mitch into La Casa Grande, right to Hearst's movie theatre. The lights went down as they entered, and Mitch could not see who was already there.

The main title of *Donner Pass* appeared, and the film began.

It was an eerie experience, sitting there, alone, watching the film with unknown viewers seated down front. There wasn't a sound in the room. This was the same rough cut that had been previewed the night before. The music track was ragged, and the projector change-overs were abrupt. But Mitch still was able, despite his familiarity with the material, to become involved in the story. He made notes to himself each time a bad cut or a mismatched reverse angle went by. He would correct those flaws before the studio went to release print.

Beery's face filled the screen, the ghosts of the Donner party moved slowly through the snowy landscape. The theatre lights came up.

In the first row there were several men and one woman. She got up and rushed toward Mitch.

It was Marion Davies, and she was crying.

"Oh, Mitch."

She held out her arms.

"I'm s-s-sorry."

Hearst's high-pitched voice said, "Leave us, Marion."

She stared directly into Mitch's eyes.

"Please don't blame me. I think it's a w-w-wonderful picture."

She pressed past him and was gone. Hearst stood, leaning against the stage. His executives flanked him like bodyguards.

"I presume you have an explanation, Mr. Gardner," Hearst said.

Mitch moved down toward the stage. The men around Hearst pressed in closer to their employer.

"I don't know what you mean," said Mitch.

"I mean for *that!*"

Hearst waved his hand toward the screen.

"For that garbage, that filth! Mr. Gardner, I gave you my hospitality. I lent you my name. I provided you with money. I thought we had a clear understanding of what it was I wanted. Then you have the arrogance to come back with . . . *this!*"

"*This,*" Mitch said, "is the film that will prove to the world that Marion Davies is one of the finest actresses of our time."

"Trash!" Hearst shouted. "Contemptible sensationalism, catering to the basest of human perversity and lust. How *dare* you?

Who, sir, do you think you are? You lowered Miss Davies to the level of a beast! She is shown slovenly, dirty, wrinkled. Ugly! This is not the film I agreed to help you make. And what is worse, you actually show her nude! How did you think you would ever get *that* scene past the Hays Office?"

"She's not nude. We see her breast once, in profile. And it's a beautiful sequence."

"It's pornography! If I were twenty years younger, I would horsewhip you, sir! As it is, I can only ruin you."

"I'm sorry you don't see the film as I do," Mitch said. "But that's your privilege. I think, after the sneak preview we had last night, Warners will be willing to return your guarantee. This picture will make money, but no one can force you to share the profits."

Hearst stared at him.

"Are you completely demented? You surely don't think this piece of garbage will ever be released."

Mitch stepped toward him.

"Go ahead. Put the pressure on. But I warn you, I'll fight back. You don't own every newspaper in the country yet."

"No," Hearst said softly. "But I own *Donner Pass*, every foot of film and sound track in existence."

"What the hell do you mean?"

"Just that I have already concluded an arrangement with Warner Bros. I paid a considerable sum of money over my original guarantee. At this very moment, they are burning the negatives and work prints of the picture. The print you just saw is the only one in the world, and I assure you, it will always be kept under careful guard in a vault."

"You can't do that, you—"

"I *have* done it, Mr. Gardner."

"You have no right! This isn't your film! It belongs to me. It belongs to those of us who created it."

"There would have been nothing to create without my money. You betrayed my trust. You own nothing. You are an employee. You were paid for your writing and you were paid for your direction. You will even be paid a percentage of the profit Warners will show by this sale. So you have no right to complain."

"I'll take you to court!"

"That is your privilege. But I would advise you to nusband your resources. You will find it very difficult to get work from this day forward."

"Why? Because I dared show her the way she *is* instead of the way you'd have her be? Mr. Hearst, Marion's an *actress!* She'd win an Oscar for this film. Ask her. Did you ever trouble to ask what *she* thinks?"

"What Miss Davies thinks is of no concern to you. I will have you driven down to the airfield. My pilot will take you back to Los Angeles."

"Screw your pilot! You can't just pronounce an edict from your goddamned magic mountain and then send me packing! *Donner Pass* is my film, Mr. Hearst! My father died making it! You aren't going to burn the negative and lock the only print up in your safe deposit box and figure that's the end of it. You don't own me, and you never will."

"Good day, Mr. Gardner."

Hearst turned away. Mitch stepped toward him. The other men blocked his path.

"You're old!" Mitch shouted. "You're going to die, and you're afraid! But you'll die anyway. Do you hear me, old man?"

"Show him out," Hearst's voice was muffled.

The men moved toward Mitch. He stiffened to meet them, then relaxed.

"Okay," he said. "You don't have to throw me out. I'll go. But this isn't the last you'll see of me. Do you hear that, Mr. Hearst? Times have changed. You can't just snap your fingers and start a war anymore. You can't stop me. You may have destroyed this film, but I'll make others."

"I wouldn't be too sure of that, Mr. Gardner."

William Randolph Hearst turned and left the theatre.

"I'll see you to the car," said one of the men.

Mitch backed away.

"Screw your car! I'll get off your enchanted mountain under my own power."

"No one is allowed in the road on foot," said the man.

Mitch laughed.

"So sue me."

He strode from the room, through the huge entrance hall, and down the marble steps. The road to the seacoast stretched five miles before him. He took a deep breath and set off. He heard excited voices behind him, but he did not turn. No one came after him.

The sun was still high. Far below, the Pacific was dark blue. The air was fresh and warm against his face.

Mitch Gardner took off his jacket and slung it over his shoulder. His stride lengthened.

The main highway was miles away, but he knew he would reach it before sundown.